ONE-BY-ONE THE SPIRIT-FILLED APARTMENTS AT BROUSSARD COURT CALL THOSE IN NEED OF SHELTERING COMFORT.

Madame Badeaux, the old woman they called *The Witch* was dead, but was she gone? Someone, or something, lingered on, guiding and protecting those who came to live at Broussard Court. An old man escaping his family's plan for a retirement home. A young woman fleeing her family's disapproval. A teen boy with no place to go. Solace and safety await them at Broussard Court, where secrets are revealed and lives mended. And when the circle finally closes, it brings home the person snatched away when she was small. Was her life a tragedy? Or did it serve a greater good?

Early Praise for True Memories

In Nancy Smith Gibson's long-awaited sequel to The New Witch, the spirit of Madame Badeaux lives on at Broussard Court as new tenants come to the Big Easy in search of change. While True Memories -- a warm family story -- stands on its own, those who enjoyed reading about Madame's heirs (Addie and Simon) in Gibson's 2017 book will not be disappointed. In New Orleans, every person has a story and Gibson's characters hold the reader's attention from start to finish.—*Diane Dove—social worker and avid reader.*

As Abner stood looking into the empty shop, he felt the tingling spread throughout his body. This was the third time he had come to stare into the big front windows, and the energy became stronger each time. It was as if electricity was running up and down his spine. Today it ran through his arms and reached his fingers where they grasped the door facing. The spirits were here, no doubt about it. He sensed them telling him there was something special about this place—something he should pay attention to.

TRUE MEMORIES

Nancy Smith Gibson

Moonshine Cove Publishing, LLC
Abbeville, South Carolina U.S.A.
First Moonshine Cove Edition May
2022

ISBN: 9781952439322

Library of Congress LCCN: 2022907975

About the Author

Nancy Smith Gibson has been a voracious reader from an early age, but didn't start writing until she had an empty nest--if you can call it empty when she shares it with a rescue dog and two rescue cats. She is the mother of four, grandmother of four, and great-grand of two.

Her professional years were spent as a "number please" and long distance telephone operator and supervisor, a census supervisor for various government surveys, and in real estate sales. For some years she also produced crafts for sales at arts and crafts fairs. The people she met and situations she encountered provide rich fodder for stories.

She is also active in genealogy research, tracing her family roots back several generations.

She writes contemporary and historical 'sweet' romances, often including

http://www.nancysmithgibson.com

TRUE MEMORIES

CHAPTER ONE

As Abner stood looking into the empty shop he felt the tingling spread throughout his body. This was the third time he had come to stare into the big front windows, and the energy became stronger each time. It was as if electricity was running up and down his spine. Today it ran through his arms and reached his fingers where they grasped the door facing. The spirits were here, no doubt about it. He sensed them telling him there was something special about this place—something he should pay attention to.

His old legs wouldn't hold him like they used to. He leaned on his cane as he made his way to the bench sitting in front of the empty shop and the one next to it—a jewelry shop, from the looks of it. The bench was painted the same azure blue as the trim around the windows of the structure calling to him. Bright and cheerful, the color gave off 'good vibes', as they used to say back in the days of hippies and flower power. A big Siamese cat came and jumped up on the bench beside him.

"Hello there, kitty," Abner said. The cat sat and stared at him intently.

They'd had cats throughout their marriage. The first had been a Siamese like this one. It had come to their door the first month they were married. They had named it Francois. Their last cat, a delicate black female, had died about a month after Latreece, as if it couldn't stand life without her. He knew that feeling. He didn't much like it, either. He would love to have a cat again, but his daughter-in-law couldn't stand them. Dirty creatures she called them. And ever since he sold the big house in the Garden District and moved in with his son and daughter-in-law, he had made every effort to be a good guest in their home. But he missed the place he and Latreece had lived for most of their lives, the house filled with love and laughter and the spirits of all those it had welcomed since it had been built.

"It's a lovely day, isn't it?" he said to his companion.

The cat looked at him raptly.

"Do you sit here often? I would, if I lived in this neighborhood."

Abner surveyed the shops on the other side of the street. A shoe repair, a beauty shop, a locksmith. Farther down in the other direction was a grocery. Baskets of tempting produce sat on benches under the plate glass windows.

A pleasant aroma reached his nose. He was seldom hungry any more, but suddenly he was ravenous. The bland food served in his son's home was nothing to look forward to, but his daughter-in-law insisted the spicy foods he craved weren't good for him. He thought because she didn't like it herself, she didn't want to be bothered with fixing it for him. That was all right. He didn't want to be a bother. Gradually, he had lost all joy in eating. Truth be told, he had lost all joy in living and sometimes wished death would come and take him to be with Latreece. A couple of times, the thought of suicide flickered, but he wouldn't ever do that. It was up to the spirits, he reckoned, to come fetch him when it was time to go.

Abner hauled himself to his feet and followed the delicious scent. With any luck, it would be coming from a nearby café. Sure enough, on the next corner sat a folding sign announcing *Simon's Place,* and the aroma of Cajun cooking floated out to greet him like an old friend. The open doors, diagonally placed at the corner of the building, were so welcoming they pulled him in as if by magic.

"Afternoon," the waitress said as she handed him a menu and placed a set of silverware by his elbow. It was wrapped in a white, cloth napkin. *Real cloth,* he thought. *Not paper like so many places use these days.* "It be plenty warm today. You be needin' somethin' to drink, I 'magine."

"Water, please," he said, and then changed his mind as she started to walk away. "No. Make that sweet tea." With no daughter-in-law to set down his dietary rules and no son around to back her up, he was darned well going to eat and drink what he pleased.

He savored a bowl of perfectly seasoned gumbo. How long had it been since he had eaten the cuisine for which New Orleans was famed? Too long. As he ate, he surveyed the neighborhood outside the window at his elbow. Across the street, next to the market, was an establishment that offered a variety of services. *Copying,* the sign said. *Notary. Packages mailed. Gift wrapping. You buy it—we'll wrap it.* Another white board next to it announced *Alterations and mending—reasonable prices.* A third sign proclaimed *Moving service. No job too large or too small. We are honest and dependable.* Under those words, in smaller print, *Don't strain your back—let us strain ours.*

When the waitress came back to refill his tea, he said, "It looks like this neighborhood has everything a person would need to live comfortably."

"You're right about that," she said. "Most of the folks around here, their families have been here forever, seems like. You don't have to go very far to get what you need."

"Do you get many tourists here?"

"More than you'd think, since we aren't in a main tourist district."

"What draws them?"

"That's hard to say. A few blocks over, there's bars and music places. I guess they just wander over from there. This is a quieter neighborhood. Nice for families, but enough businesses to keep us going. If Madame were still alive, she'd say the spirits send the people our way."

"Madame?"

"Madame Badeaux. You from N'Orleans?" He nodded his head. "Then you probably heard of her. She be a famous hoodoo woman. But she gone now."

"Yes, I've heard of her. She's . . . no longer living?"

"She passed two, almost three years now," she said, and walked away to help a couple, their clutched guidebooks and cameras hanging from straps around their necks marking them as tourists, who had entered and were looking around.

Two years. That's how long Latreece had been gone, too. Spirits, huh? So there were other people who felt the spirits. He and Latreece had talked about it—about how they were guided by something, or someone, unseen. *Take that road. Buy that. Talk to that person.* And perhaps even more importantly, *don't do that! There is danger—take care.* Latreece had thought anyone could be guided by spirits if they would just be still and listen.

He was sure that the spirits were around him now and urging him to—what? *What I'm thinking about is big. Too big for an old man like me?* He sighed. Maybe he ought to wait for a sign. If it was meant to be, the spirits would send him a sign. He was sure of that much, at least.

He ordered a fried pie, as much to linger a while longer as anything else. When the server brought it, he asked, "Do you know anything about the vacant shop in the next block?"

"Sure 'nough do. Miss Dani had a dress shop there until she and Simon got married."

"The Simon who owns this restaurant?"

"The same."

"Do you know if it's for rent?" *No harm in asking, was there? It's not like I'm making any commitment.*

"Probably is. You can ask in the shop next door to it."

"The jewelry shop?"

"That's the one. That's Miss Addie's shop, and her daddy owns the one what's vacant. I 'magine she's got a key. You interested in renting it?"

"Maybe." There, he had made a step. 'Maybe' was a tiny step, but a step, nevertheless.

"What you gonna sell there?"

He took a deep breath. Even saying it out loud took bravery, something he had been short of here lately. "Furniture. Antique furniture. Furniture my late wife and I collected from around the world. And knick-knacks." *Treasures,* he wanted to add. *Treasures of a lifetime, obtained from all over the world and valued beyond belief—at least to me. Reminders of a life now gone and never to be again.*

"That sounds good. Miss Addie is right particular about what goes in next door. That's why there's no sign about bein' for rent. She say the spirits will send her the right person. Maybe you be it."

"So Miss Addie believes in spirits, too?"

"Miss Addie be Madame's great-niece. She got the gift, too."

"I see," Abner said. And he did see, sort of. The gift of being able to hear what the spirits were trying to say. Maybe more gifts than that. It would be interesting to know what.

"She not there right now. Her an' her husband done gone to Dallas to see his folks. They comin' back this weekend. She be open Monday next, probably. If not, she be around the neighborhood somewhere."

* * *

Abner thought about it all weekend. "You're not getting sick, are you, Dad?" his son asked. "You sure are quiet."

But Abner was always quiet. There was little he could talk about with Bob or Janelle. Evenings he usually watched TV on the little set in his bedroom, or else he read. Bob usually worked in his office off the master bedroom, and Janelle watched The Housewives of Somewhere on the big TV in the den. Abner went to the library every week and checked out a stack of books to read.

This weekend, though, he spent his time thinking about his plan, staring unseeing at the flickering images on the TV. Sunday evening he found himself hungry and quietly went to the kitchen to get a late night snack. Bob and Janelle were sitting on the patio in the dark. He didn't mean to eavesdrop, but he couldn't help hearing what they were saying.

"I think it's time we seriously checked into nursing homes," Janelle was saying.

"I hate to do that," Bob replied.

"He just sits there, Bob, not doing anything. At least in a home he'd have the company of others his age."

"I know. I know."

"With both of us gone all day, he has no one to talk to. And he wanders around town. I'm worried about that. He might get lost, or hurt."

"I understand, Janelle. I see that. But I hate to think of him in one of those places."

"We'd visit whenever we could. And they have all kinds of activities for them. Bingo and movies . . ."

Abner stole away without even opening the refrigerator, snack forgotten. His mind was made up. All those treasures that had graced the rooms where he and Latreece placed them—oh so long ago. They needed to find new homes. The spirits would send him the new owners, send the sideboard and the curio cabinet and the armoire on to other adventures. Just the right person who needed the highboy or the prie-dieu would find him, would find his shop in that out-of-the-way spot.

And the spirits would guide him to where he was meant to be. Just because it was no longer in the home with the gracious rooms filled with memories didn't mean it wasn't the right place. And when the time came for him to join Latreece, then the spirits would be there as well.

The plan was on. Tomorrow he'd start.

CHAPTER TWO

First thing Monday morning, as soon as Bob left for work and Janelle left for whatever took up her days—shopping and meetings and luncheons with friends—he had called a taxi and gone to his attorney's office. Luckily, Rene DuBois was in that day and could see him immediately.

"Abner, *mon ami*," the elderly man said as he extended his hand. "It's been too long. How lucky I was present today. I only work about one day a week these days."

"You are lucky, my friend," Abner said as he shook hands. "to have that one day of work. I was looking forward to retirement. Now I look upon it as punishment for some unknown crime."

DuBois laughed, the sound coming out brittle, like a thin coat of ice on a window pane, soon gone and forgotten. "Sit. Sit. What can I do for you today?"

"You have some papers, something I asked you to do for me."

"*Oui.* Yes. I have them here somewhere." He moved papers around on the top of his desk. "They are in this muddle somewhere." He glanced up. "I used to be so neat with all my work. Now, I let it get scattered around. In this way I can fool myself into thinking I have a lot of important things to take care of. Ah, here it is." He pulled some sheets of paper from the confusion in front of him.

"I have come," Abner said, "to tell you to tear it up. Forget it."

"Oh?" DuBois looked over the top of his glasses. "Did I take too long?"

"Just long enough is more like it."

DuBois leaned back in his office chair, ignoring the squeak that demanded attention. His expression had become solemn as he studied his longtime friend. "What has changed? Have you had a falling out with your son?"

"No—no falling out."

"*Tres bien.* That is good. I have always looked upon you as having the perfect life. The perfect family. Until your wife's death, of course. You seemed to be blessed with good fortune—in business, in family, in health. Blessed."

"Ahh, good friend," Abner's words flowed out on his breath. "You do not know. You do not know."

"I know what I see. And I see good fortune and happiness all these years."

"You do not see all," Abner said, and he ran his hand over his eyes. "Latreece and I traveled the world. We were lucky that my business dealings afforded us the pleasure of going wherever we pleased. 'Life is short,' we said, 'we should enjoy it while we can,' and we did, although life has proved to be longer than we thought."

Sadness washed over him. His body seemed to shrivel into a ball, and his face reflected inexpressible sorrows held behind shadowed eyes. He paused in his account, gathering his thoughts. Dubois held his tongue. His old friend might have been telling Rene's own tale.

"We traveled the world, accumulating treasures to bring back home—bibelots at first, then larger pieces. Objects that would remind us of a pleasant day in Paris, a fascinating adventure in Turkey, a puzzling undertaking in Singapore or Malaysia or Istanbul." He smiled at the memories that came flooding back. "We bought special things. Things that imbued . . . well, I wouldn't want you to think my mind is . . ." He stopped speaking, caught as he was in the past.

"Some years had passed before Latreece became pregnant," he looked up and smiled, "We had determined that our world would have to be satisfactory without a child, but then everything changed and our world become perfect. Not that it wasn't perfect before that, because it was. But even more perfect."

He moved about in his chair. It was comfortable, but old bones can only stay still for so long before needing to stretch or readjust or rearranged into a new pattern.

"She was flawless," he said. "Curly black hair. Glowing blue eyes. A smile for everyone. We named her Lily."

DuBois' eyebrows raised, although he remained silent. He had never heard of a daughter, only the practical and businesslike son, Robert. He folded his hands together and brought them up to his mouth as he leaned forward to rest his elbows on the mahogany desk before him. He had a feeling that something bad was coming in his friend's story, and it might be necessary to hold in a sound of distress. He had heard many tales of sadness and grief in his years as an attorney, but this was one of his oldest friends sitting before him, and the story he was about to tell gave off waves of emotion in advance of the telling. DuBois pressed his knuckles tightly against his lips.

"She was five years old when we lost her."

It filled the room. Not silence, exactly. Non-speaking. The gentle ticking of a clock somewhere in the space sounded like the beating of a drum—loud and rhythmic.

"Later," Abner said, when he regained a bit of composure, "after some years had passed, we had Robert. A second miracle, we thought. And he was a joy, as a son ought to be. But he wasn't Lily. Wasn't a small girl with shining blue eyes and endless smiles."

He leaned back in his chair and offered a sad smile as he looked at DuBois. "Enough of this, my friend. Enough of sad memories. I have things I need you to do for me . . . important things."

CHAPTER THREE

When Abner told Rene DuBois about his plans, his friend flew into action, pleased that he could be of value to someone, especially someone he had known for the greater part of a century. DuBois, like Abner, had given up on doing anything significant at this stage of his life. There was nothing to be done in his office that could not be handled by some young lawyer just out of school. His son and his nephew handled anything important. They even saw to it that someone else took care of the unimportant tasks as well. The fact that DuBois came in to work one day a week was only a ruse, a ploy to convince himself that he was still needed in the firm.

The very next day, after his son and daughter-in-law had left the house, Abner visited first a physician, then a psychologist, both respected practitioners with ties to old New Orleans, with whom DuBois had spoken. Along with papers DuBois requested from Abner's own doctor, in days he had proof, in case Bob tried to have him declared incompetent, that he was healthy, in good state of mind, and perfectly capable of managing his own affairs.

Abner's next stop was his bank. As luck would have it—luck appearing to be firmly on his side—he had taken the first few steps into the august establishment when he ran into another old friend. There was something to be said about being from one of the premier families of old New Orleans.

"Ahh! Abner Crowbridge," the gray-headed gentleman said. "It is good to see you! I am on my way to lunch. Why don't you join me? You will know the people I'm dining with."

"I wish I could, *mon ami*, but I have business I must transact with your fine institution," Abner said as they shook hands.

"Then let me put you into the proper hands, my friend," and Abner was escorted to the office of a vice-president, who promptly obeyed his request to remove his son from any and all accounts that Abner's name appeared on—effective immediately. Bob's name was also removed from the authorized list of people who could access his lockbox, and his signature was no longer official on any check that Abner's name certified, business or personal.

* * *

When all assets were firmly back under his control, Abner proceeded to make an appointment to see the vacant shop he had been visiting recently.

"You can paint it any color you wish," the woman said, gesturing to the gaily decorated walls. "At your expense, of course. A clothing store occupied the space previously, and she liked these bright colors."

"And she went out of business?" Abner said, suddenly doubting his aim of opening a shop in this neighborhood. The air was escaping from the bubble of enthusiasm that he had been floating on the last few weeks.

"No. Actually, she outgrew the space. Besides selling to the public, Dani does costuming for period plays and movies. She needed more room for work space as well as the clothing on display."

Abner thought that might be a problem with him as well. It had been a while since he had visited any of the storage facilities he rented to hold the contents of the home in the Garden District when he had moved into his son's home. And besides those, he had other leased units filled to the brim with treasures gathered in the worldwide travels he and Latreece had enjoyed. Treasures that exceeded the space they had in their home. *Maybe I have let my excitement override my common sense in this matter,* he thought as he looked around at the space he had imagined as his new business.

His hostess saw his wrinkled brow. "There's more room in this next area," she said as she led him through a door in the back wall. Another space, not quite as large, greeted him. "This was her workroom, although it could be another sales space as well. Just take the door down and allow the customers to browse both rooms."

Abner opened an inconspicuous door in the back wall and found a washroom. Not large, but clean and sufficient. He went a few feet down the wall and opened another door. To the left was a staircase leading upwards, and in front of him was an exit to the back yard. A glance through the glass panes showed him a patch of grass surrounded by a tall wooden fence. Nice for some people, but unnecessary for him.

"There is an apartment upstairs. It has a living-kitchen arrangement, plus a fair-size bedroom and full bath."

Abner regarded the steep steps leading to the second floor. "I'm afraid I couldn't tackle the stairs." He had barely given any thought to where he would live. It wouldn't be comfortable at Bob and Janelle's after he told them what he was planning on doing. Their plans of taking over his life and his fortune had been firmly squashed, although they didn't know it yet. No longer would he be welcome to live with them, he was sure. Or if he was, they would pester him about his decision to change the course of his life.

The shop seemed small and inadequate for what he had in mind. The apartment was inaccessible for one such as himself. Nothing was what he had imagined it might be. His dreams were only that—dreams, not rooted in reality.

Perhaps I am just a foolish old man conjuring up what cannot be.

As they back-tracked through the shop, returning to the sidewalk, Abner berated himself for placing so much confidence in foolish thoughts. As the woman locked the front door, Abner noticed the cat that had sat with him previously was back on the blue bench.

"Does the cat come with the rental?" he asked in jest, trying to lighten the mood.

"Cat?" the woman said.

"Yes. That big Siamese cat," he said, nodding toward the blue bench. "It's been here each time I've come by, sitting there on that seat. We've had some fine conversations, he and I."

A smile lit the woman's face. "You saw the cat?"

"Yes." He looked around. "It was here just a moment ago. I don't know where it went."

"It comes and goes," she said. "It was my great-aunt's cat. It is a spirit cat, gone these several years. Not everyone can see it. Only certain people."

CHAPTER FOUR

"Let me show you another shop that might be more to your liking."

"I don't know, Miss . . .er . . .Mrs. . . ."

"It's Zappa. Adelaide Zappa. Well, my married name is Hyatt, but most people still say Zappa. Just call me Addie. Everyone in the neighborhood does." Her manner had suddenly changed from formal and businesslike to friendly. "This is my jewelry shop," she said as she took a few steps toward the storefront next door. "I have been thinking about moving to a new location. Thinking about a lot of changes, to be honest. My great-aunt always said, so I've been told, that the spirits would send the people who needed her, and I guess I believe the same thing. When you said you could see the cat, I knew you were the one."

I'm the one? Spirit cat?

Addie singled out another key on her ring and opened the door of the shop next to the empty one that he had just visited. When they entered, a wisp of breeze must have gone in with them. It set the crystals in the chandelier shimmering and tinkling, throwing out rainbow shards of light around the room and the sound of delicate chimes echoing throughout.

The room was wider and deeper by a couple of feet each way, otherwise it was much like the one next door. A plain room, awaiting whatever came.

"The glass showcases will be gone, of course, unless you could use any of them."

Addie strode around the room switching on lamps here and there. The various lampshades added more colorful shapes and shadows playing on the ceiling and walls. An imaginative person might see figures and forms moving among the more substantial contours in the room.

Images began to take shape in Abner's mind. An ornately carved cupboard or wardrobe there in the window to catch the eye of passers-by. The library table, the chairs, the . . . His thoughts tumbled as he recalled some of the pieces he had stored in various locations around the city. *Keep a couple of showcases to display the small and more fragile items.*

"Back here," Addie said as she went through an arched doorway, "like next door, is another room. It can be a workroom or more display space."

At least as large as the front room, it would be handy for cleaning or repairing or whatever Abner needed it for.

"And here," Addie said as she opened a door at the rear of the room, "are the living quarters."

The kitchen they entered could have come directly from some sort of decorating magazine. Or maybe a mix of two publications: one with the slick characteristics of the latest style, the other displaying vintage charm. The gloss of stainless steel covered the large refrigerator and range, while the plentiful cabinets were the style and color of the early nineteen hundreds. A large, round table and half-a-dozen chairs sat in front of a wall of many-paned doors that opened onto a courtyard.

"Charming," Abner said. He looked around the room, where a few dishes and pans added color and vivacity to the space. "Charming," he repeated to himself, and was surprised to find that he meant it.

"Through here is the living room," Addie said, leading the way through another door.

Again, the room was a mix of styles and colors. It was comfortable, meant for relaxing or entertaining friends, or just thinking. Abner could easily imagine himself in this room, settled into that comfy arm chair reading one of the books from those shelves.

"Does it come furnished?" he asked, taking a small step toward commitment.

"Yes. I think so."

"Could you check with the owner?"

She laughed. "I am the owner, so it looks like I ought to know, doesn't it? I inherited all this from my great-aunt, Madame Badeaux. There are four apartments in this compound, which is called Broussard Court. Plus the shop we just looked at." She tilted her head toward the front of the building.

"I live, or lived, in this apartment. My husband lives in the ground floor apartment across the courtyard." She walked toward the open French doors and gestured. "We got married a few months ago, and we live in both apartments. Sometimes in one, sometimes in the other. Foolish, I know." She chuckled at the thought, and shook her head.

"Before long we need to move to someplace that will accommodate both of us plus a baby." She looked up and smiled at him. "I am *enceinte*, you see, and neither this apartment or Parker's is large enough to be comfortable for long. The only unit in Broussard Court with two bedrooms is the one over this one." She pointed at the ceiling. "And I can't see doing steps with a baby carriage or stroller, not when there are other options.

"After I stayed the year specified in my aunt's will, not only did I become owner of Broussard Court, but of various properties all over the city. Parker and I are discussing the advantages and disadvantages of various places where we might live. We will be moving from here shortly," she said as turned and walked toward another door. "When we make up our minds.

"So both apartments will be available. I thought this one would be best for you because of the shop being connected. I will be moving my jewelry business someplace closer to whichever home we choose to live in. And I would prefer," she smiled at Abner, "to rent it furnished. I really don't want to get rid of anything in it." She looked around.

"Everything *belongs* here. You know?" She shook her head. "It sounds silly, I know, but there is such a feeling of . . ." She shook her head again.

"Rightness," Abner said. "As if everything—the furniture, the books, the pictures—this is their home."

"Yes, that's it," she said and smiled at him again. "You understand. I knew you would when you told me you saw the cat."

She showed him the bedroom. Generous in size, it held a bed canopied in the old style, accompanied by a set of steps to help one gain the high surface. An armoire, as large and more elegant as any Abner had ever seen, sat against the far wall, and a small velvet covered sofa offered a place to sit and enjoy the view of the courtyard through the French doors. Almost hidden among the larger pieces of furniture in the room was a rosewood prie-dieu, with ornate carving to draw the eye and padded blue velvet to cushion the knees.

The adjoining bathroom held a tub big enough for two plus a separate shower enclosure, ample in size. Through the glass doors of the cabinet setting beside the pedestal sink, Abner could see a stack of thick white towels. The nearby closet was large enough for anyone's wardrobe. The flat lacked nothing.

"I could have my personal property removed within a week," Addie said. "Sooner if you need the apartment before then. I'll move it across the courtyard into Parker's flat until we decide where we're going to settle."

When she quoted the rent, far more reasonable than Abner had thought he would have to spend, he looked out into the courtyard, more to give himself time to figure out what he truly thought about it, and saw the cat. It sat beside a chair the same blue as the bench the two of them had sat on together, and looked back at him.

"I'll take it," he said.

CHAPTER FIVE

Abner rose early, animated by the thought of the day to come. He was being a coward, he knew, by not mentioning anything about his plans to Bob. It wasn't like him. Usually a straightforward man who didn't shy away from unpleasantness that was sure to come, he had said nothing to his son about the plans he had been putting into action. Today, though, he could evade no longer. He had to stop explaining his reluctance with what were surely excuses.

His son might contact his own attorney and try to put some kind of barrier in his father's way. He might convince someone—a judge, a doctor, who?—that his father was senile and should be prevented from moving out on his own. Even armed with papers from doctors and officials swearing that Abner was perfectly capable of managing his own life, Bob would be able to delay what was inevitable, Abner's life on his own terms.

No, it would be safer to wait until the deed was done before informing him that his father was moving out. Abner thought about this as he packed a small suitcase with enough clothes to last a couple of days, his toiletries, and his medicines.

Don't forget the pills. That'd give Janelle evidence to say, "See, he can't even take care of his health. He needs to be in a home where they'll see to him."

Abner slipped the vial of blood pressure capsules into the luggage and some anti-acids into his pocket, just in case he decided on some of the gumbo at Simon's for lunch. He smiled at the thought of having fine Cajun food right down the block from his new home. Even if it caused a touch of heartburn, it was worth it.

He chuckled as he fastened the clasps on the leather bag holding his apparel and lifted it off his bed. He smoothed the coverlet over the pillows and patted the expensive spread Janelle had furnished him when he moved in with them. With his cane in one hand and the valise in the other, he went to meet the taxi waiting for him, as it had been every day for the last two weeks.

"The usual place, Mr. Crowbridge?"

"That's right, Pernell. The usual place."

* * *

T. Wayne stood eying the basket of apples on the bench in front of the market. His stomach growled, and the spasm it sent through his body made it harder to fight the temptation to snatch one and run. He knew stealing was wrong, but his hunger was powerful, almost powerful enough to make him disregard his grandmother's teachings.

"Stealin' is wrong, Thomas Wayne," she'd tell him. "Don't you never steal." And she'd tell him the story of the old woman, a witch or hoodoo woman or somethin', who'd put a hex on you if she caught you stealing. He didn't think the witch was around any longer, and Granny had passed three months ago, but her stories stayed with him.

He had rummaged through every garbage can for blocks around without finding so much as a scrap of food or the smallest item he could retrieve and sell to a second-hand shop for enough money to buy a meal. He had tried the areas where the fancy restaurants were, but they used big dumpsters to control their refuse, and he hesitated to climb into one in the daylight or the glare of bright lights of the parking lots. He thought he might find something to eat at a smaller establishment, like the one across the street. The smell of Cajun food drifted through the neighborhood, but there were no scraps or trimmings in their garbage he might eat. When he was searching through the paper and boxes that were the contents of the can, a worker came out into the alley to smoke.

"Hey, man. Don't you pull all that stuff out and make a mess for me to clean up. Ain't no food in there this early in the day. Go on, now. Get outta here."

So now T. Wayne was trying to make up his mind whether to steal an apple or not when two men came out of the building next to the market.

"I don't know what to tell you, Mr. Crowbridge," one of them said. "I apologize for everything running so late."

"But are you going to be able to move my things today?" said the old man leaning on his cane. "I had everything planned, you see."

"I don't know. My men just went to move a washer and dryer for Miz Robbins. It shouldn't have taken long, but they slipped coming down the stairs and the washer landed on Carl's foot. They're at the emergency clinic now. They'll be here as soon as they can."

"But will they be able to work?"

"That I don't know. It depends on what shape Carl's foot's in."

"Can't you call someone else to help?"

"Usually I call my cousin Ellis when I need someone else, but he's gone to Pascagoula with his wife. I'll have to think . . ."

"I can help move, Mr.," T. Wayne said, taking a few steps closer. "I'm strong . . . stronger than I look. I don't charge much—just whatever you want to pay me. I work cheap."

The old man looked him up and down. T. Wayne stood tall, trying to look tough and sturdy. "Stand up and look like a man," Granny used to say, and he tried. A job, however small, would mean money to buy food. He straightened to his full six foot potential and tightened his stringy muscles. He looked the moving man straight in the eye, to show he was sincere, and tried to look honest and hardworking.

"There's the solution," the old man said. "We'll hire this young man to help. Even if Carl is able to work, that would make three men working. We could make up for lost time."

"I don't know . . . ," the moving man said. "I don't know this boy."

T. Wayne shifted his gaze to the old man, and his eyes dropped to the ornately carved cane in his hand. A curving ribbon of scales twisted and turned around the dark wood, ending in a snake's head at the top. Beady eyes stared at T. Wayne, and the boy could have sworn the serpent was looking directly at him.

He shivered and his stomach growled again. Embarrassed, he dropped his eyes, but then, remembering how important it was, he raised his gaze and looked unswervingly at the old man.

"I'll work good, sir. I'll work hard. I'm honest. I won't do you wrong." He wondered if he sounded like he was begging. Which he was, but he didn't want it to sound that way.

The old man looked at him intently, and it felt like he was looking into T. Wayne's soul.

"Yes," the old man said. "That's the answer. "I'll hire this young man myself and I'll pay him. You won't have to, Mr. Tremont. If Carl is able to work, we'll have three strong men to help me move. Is that all right with you?" He looked first at T. Wayne, then at the moving truck man.

"Yessir. Thank you, sir," T. Wayne said.

"That'd be fine," Tremont agreed.

"And until your men get back here with the truck, this young man and I'll wait across the street at the restaurant. I need a mid-morning snack to pick me up." He turned back to T. Wayne. "If that's OK with you, young man?"

T. Wayne hesitated. He didn't have money to buy anything to eat, and sitting there with a growling stomach would be pure torture. He started to say that he'd sit on the curb and wait, but the old man spoke up. "I'll buy your breakfast. It'll be part of your pay. Got to have my moving man full and strong, don't I?" He offered his right hand. "Abner Crowbridge is my name. I'm moving into that empty shop across the street, where the jewelry store used to be. And your name?"

"Thomas Wayne," he stuttered as he took the offered hand. He wasn't used to shaking hands with people. "T. Wayne Johnson."

They crossed the street and went into Simon's Place. T. Wayne hoped the man who had stopped him from looking for food in the alley wouldn't see him. What if he did and said, "Hey, that's that kid who was pulling stuff out of the garbage can earlier." What would T. Wayne say? He dropped his head and tried to look small, instead of big and strong, as the old man led him to a table by the window.

"You sure in here early today," the waitress said as she brought them menus and silverware rolled up in napkins. "And looks like you got someone new with you." She looked T. Wayne over with a suspicious eye. "You know this boy, Mr. Crowbridge?" T. Wayne hung his head even lower.

"This fine young man is going to help move my things into the shop," the old man said. "Carl has injured his foot and may be unable to help. In any case, this lad is young and strong and will be a good helper."

"Who are you, boy?" the waitress asked. "You not from this neighborhood."

"Thomas Wayne Johnson." He tried to not sound belligerent at being questioned.

"You Ida Johnson's grandson?"

"No, ma'am."

"Who's your folks?"

T. Wayne didn't quite know how to answer. The question was a trap.

"Well?"

"My granny was Beulah Johnson."

"Was? She done passed?"

"Yes, ma'am."

"And you don't live close 'round here?"

"No ma'am. A few blocks away." More like a few miles. He hoped she wouldn't ask exactly where, or ask about his parents. He always hated to lie—another thing Granny used to lecture against—but he didn't want to tell anyone he didn't know who his father was, and his mother was in jail. Lucky for him, the waitress' questioning was over.

"What I be gettin' for you, Mr. Crowbridge?"

"I'd like a fried pie, Estelle, peach if you have it, and this young man needs a good feeding so he'll be able to help move my things into the shop."

"It bein' so early, the gumbo and jambalaya's not ready yet. How about a big ol' ham sandwich. That be OK, boy?"

"Yes, ma'am."

"I'll say this. He's got good manners, so far. Saying ma'am like that. Somebody done taught him right."

"It was my granny," T. Wayne volunteered.

"How about French fries to go with that sandwich, Estelle. Can we do that?"

"Yessir, Mr. Crowbridge, we can do that. What y'all want to drink?"

"I'll have sweet tea, but a growing boy needs milk to make strong bones."

With that, T. Wayne's stomach growled again.

"Before we eat, Thomas Wayne, perhaps you'd better go wash up. The restroom is that way," the old man said, pointing toward the back wall.

"Yessir." T. Wayne headed toward the restroom, grinning. He'd not only have a good meal, but could wash up and feel sort of clean for a change. Maybe he'd even get paid enough to eat tomorrow and the next day, too. This had turned out to be a lucky day.

* * *

Abner sat watching the boy wolf down the ham sandwich. He acted as if he hadn't eaten in days. *Was that possible?* It had been a long time since Bob was—what? Sixteen? Seventeen? But as Abner remembered, teenage boys were always hungry. This boy was the same.

Life, which had drug by in monotony the last two years, was moving rapidly these days. Only three weeks ago, Abner had been looking in the window of an empty shop building, and now, here he was, moving the treasures of a lifetime into it. And just when he had determined there was nothing more in life to be interested in, to look forward to, he was back in the middle of things, so to speak, with countless subjects to occupy his mind

CHAPTER SIX

It was late afternoon by the time one load of furniture and boxes had been moved from the storage facility across town to the new shop. It went smoothly. The addition of T. Wayne to the work crew helped immeasurably. Abner had thought he might ride in the moving van with the workers, but with the driver, Carl with a bandaged foot, and T. Wayne in the cab, there was no room for another person.

Abner called Pernell, who had been lingering not far away and came immediately.

"I'm finally getting it accomplished, Pernell," Abner said. "Sometimes I doubted it would happen."

"You seem like a person who gets done whatever he puts his mind to," the cab driver said.

"Yes. I am," the old man said. "or I used to be, but I had almost forgotten. Almost forgotten what it was like to be in charge of my own life." He was deep in thought as they crossed the city.

At the storage unit, Abner pointed out the pieces he wanted moved this trip. A variety of things to draw a diversity of customers. An ornate armoire, carved with oriental figures, dragons, and cherry blossoms. A large dining table with massive legs and the chairs that Latreece had always paired with it. Several smaller tables to be scattered around the home. A couple of velvet upholstered chairs with carved backs and arms. Glass fronted cabinets to hold the rare pieces of china and items that would come from the boxes that Abner pointed to with his cane. "Let's take that one . . . and that one . . ."

"You can stay here, can't you?" he asked Pernell when they arrived at the storage unit. "And perhaps take some of these boxes in your vehicle? Some things are too fragile to risk putting them in the truck with the rest of the load. The weight might shift. I'd hate to break anything."

He was glad he was there on the scene to call out. "Careful! Careful there!" when he thought Carl and the truck driver, Bennie, were handling things carelessly. It took several hours to load the truck to its full capacity, tie everything in place, and start back toward Broussard Court.

As they returned across town, Abner was tired—very tired. It had been a long time since he had spent a day like this. He leaned his head back and dozed, feeling safe in Pernell's care, only waking when the cabbie parked down the block from the new shop, leaving room for the furniture-laden truck directly in front of the business.

Abner supervised as the three workers unloaded the moving van, trying to envision where he wanted the merchandise placed. Most of it was much too heavy to be moved later, at least by an old man and a young boy. The armoire went by a front window, so passersby could admire the carving that covered the piece, but turned so customers could walk all the way around it if they entered the shop for a closer look. The dining table went close to a wall, surrounded by the chairs. As they were put in place, Abner ran his hand over each one, and in his head he greeted them. *So happy to see you again. Yes, it's been a while. I've missed you too. I'll find you a new home where you'll be admired once more.* His mind ran through the memories of the paintings that had once adorned his home. *I need to choose one—or even more—to hang on the wall behind the table. That will help people imagine the set in their own home.*

The boxes were put in the second room, the one that would be a workroom. He could deal with them later. Once the padded cover was removed, a velvet-covered chaise gleamed in the light from the chandelier, offering the elegance it was meant to represent. It had once sat in the room Latreece called the 'front parlor,' where it welcomed visitors to their home. *It, too, needs the painting that always hung over it,* Abner thought, *and the small table next to it, the one with dragon feet. I thought I brought it.* He looked around, and sure enough, there it was. He asked T. Wayne to move it, to set it beside its companion of several decades. It felt good, no, not good, *right,* to see them together again. If Latreece were here, she'd be smiling.

Who knows? She might be here. She might be *smiling.*

He and Latreece had shared many beliefs of the afterlife, of spirits and ghosts and apparitions that were frightening to most folks, but not to them. Abner had no qualms about the possibility of his late wife lingering nearby, watching what he was doing. She'd approve, he knew, of what he was up to. It was better than living in the stultifying atmosphere in Bob and Janelle's home.

When the furniture and boxes were unloaded, Abner removed the plastic that protected a particularly ornate chair, its back and arms carved into overelaborate designs. He sat down, his energy almost spent. He paid Bennie and Carl, and they departed. "I'll be calling on you again soon," Abner told them. "I have lots more to move." Where he'd put it was another question, since the room was almost full.

"Yessir, Mr. Crowbridge. We'll be here, awright! You jest call!" A good tip always insured eager service, and it was important to have reliable help, especially when you lived alone.

T. Wayne remained, moving boxes that were scattered around the room into the workroom. "I'm stacking them by what's in them," he told Abner. "They're all labeled, so's I can tell."

"That's good, T. Wayne. That's good."

The boy was a marvel. Quick and efficient, Abner never had to repeat an instruction, and T. Wayne intuited much of what needed to be done and how to do it.

"T. Wayne, I'm tired. I think our day is about over."

"Yessir." He set the box he was holding back on the floor.

"And I don't know about you, but I'm hungry again."

33

"Yessir." T. Wayne grinned. It looked like he was going to get to eat a second time today.

"Why don't I give you some money and you hustle down to Simon's Place—you know, where we ate breakfast—and bring back something for both of us."

"Yessir! I can do that."

Abner pulled out his wallet and remove a couple of bills. "You wash up first," he gestured toward the small washroom off the workroom, "You don't want to go into Simon's Place dirty, and then bring us some dinner. A sandwich for me. The one you ate this morning looked especially bodacious, and I don't think I need to eat anything spicy this late in the day. It might keep me up tonight. You get whatever you want to eat."

"Yessir!" T. Wayne said as he headed toward the washroom.

"And a big glass of iced tea for me," Abner added

As T. Wayne was leaving for his chore, a muffled chime came from Abner's pocket. He withdrew his cellphone and checked to see who was calling. His face scrunched in a frown and he closed his eyes for a couple of seconds, the phone gripped tightly in his hands. If anyone was watching, they might have thought he was praying. Finally, after resting his head on his hands and taking a deep breath, he opened his eyes and touched the phone's surface.

"Hello, son," he answered, his voice artificially cheerful.

"Dad! Where are you?" A worried voice sounded on the phone.

"Good evening, Roe-bare." Abner pronounced his son's name in the French fashion, something he hadn't done in many years—ever since the boy, then in his teens, had announced that he was an American and wished to be called by the American version of his name. In fact, he preferred the shortened version—Bob.

"Where are you?" his son repeated. "It's late. You're usually at home when I get here."

Abner smiled at the thought of an adult child treating his father as if their roles were reversed. "I should have talked to you before, Robert, but I've been busy. I apologize for springing it on you like this, but I have moved out."

"Moved out?" Bob's voice rose. "You can't move out!"

"Obviously, I can and have."

"Why? Why did you move out? And where did you go?" Bob was so upset his voice sputtered. "Are you in a home somewhere? A retirement home?"

"I thought it was time," Abner calmly replied. "I've lived with you and Janelle long enough. And as to where, I found a lovely apartment where I think I'm going to be very happy."

"But . . .but . . ." Bob was still floundering about, unsure what to say next.

"You don't have to worry about me. I'm perfectly safe and comfortable. I really don't want to talk about it right now. I'll get in touch with you in a few days. Don't worry about me," Abner repeated. "Goodnight."

And with that, Abner did something he had never done before. He closed his phone. Hung up on his son.

CHAPTER SEVEN

Abner hadn't been back to the Broussard Court apartment since the day he rented it. Now, waiting for T. Wayne to return with their supper, it seemed like a good opportunity to look around. Part of him was slightly apprehensive about what he had done so impulsively a week earlier.

During his working years, Abner Crowbridge was known for his snap judgements, his knowing decisions that were, to others, based on nothing but intuition and hunches. His competitors were agog when he bought or sold based on nothing more than instinct. Truth be told, although gut feelings and a sixth sense often led him, Abner had done more research than other people realized, and his business moves were based on knowledge of the market combined with his awareness of what the world was signaling it wanted, along with the much mentioned insight and premonitions. Others, judging his actions of the last few weeks, would wonder about his mental alertness, but to Abner, it all made perfect sense.

He had been falling into a pit of despondency. Bob and Janelle were kind. He had a lovely room in their home, and he was offered well-prepared meals, but he felt more dejected each day that passed. He had a television set in his room, or he could watch the large one in the family room. He had the daily newspapers and several magazines that were delivered to him, and a library card provided books to read. Comfortable luxury surrounded him. Nothing troublesome marred his days. Anything he needed, he had. And that was the problem.

Abner was bored. There was nothing to worry his mind, tickle his imagination, or demand his attention. There were no problems to solve. He was slowly dying. Not of any disease or condition, but because there was nothing to live for. No job to go to. No new people to meet. No puzzle to decipher. Nothing to organize or fix or plan. Ennui filled his days. It was time . . . past time . . . to change his life.

When Abner had walked into this dwelling—was it only a couple of weeks ago?—the atmosphere had wrapped itself around him. If spirits could speak, the ones inhabiting this space would be saying, *We've been waiting for you. Come sit and let us tell you things. We'll whisper secrets in your ear. That girl who lives here—that Addie—she's nice, but she can't hear us. She has some gifts, but not like you do. We're so happy you have finally arrived. It seems like we have been waiting for you forever.*

As he walked through his new abode, he could feel the stamp of all those who had inhabited these rooms over the past hundred years or more. He felt peace, and more than that he felt respect, love, welcome, esteem, approval. All were there, as were mystery and intrigue. Abner felt at home as if he had lived there all his life. He was returning to where he belonged.

As he made his way through the living room, the plush sofa and comfy easy-chairs called him to come sit awhile. One of the decorative pillows came sailing across the room and hit him on the leg as it fell to the floor. Abner smiled as he picked it up and returned it to the sofa, stroking its silky fabric on the way. *Don't worry. I'll come back and sit with you, but not tonight.* Joy filled him as he realized how attuned to him this place really was. *I'm going to live here now,* he thought happily as he looked around the room. *In this place where everything is alive in its own way, I will be too. Alive once again, as I used to be.*

The books and curios begged him to come explore. *Come look!* they called out. *We have all kinds of interesting things to tell you.* Abner had to force himself to leave the room, or else he would have snuggled into the comfortable seating and fallen asleep there, a book in his lap.

Later, he told himself. *Tomorrow, or the next day. I have all the time in the world, and now I have a new life to explore. Here where I live, there are things I never thought about before. Who knows what I may learn? Mysteries I've never considered before are waiting.*

For the first time in a long while he had something to look forward to. Something to live for.

In the bathroom adjacent to the bedroom, he washed his hands, using the oval of scented soap that smelled familiar. He couldn't come up with the association, but he knew he had encountered that fragrance in the past. He splashed cold water on his face and dried it with the fluffy white towel that hung on a brass hook beside the pedestal sink.

Refreshed, he stopped to look around the bedroom where he would return in an hour or so. The canopied bed sat tall and imposing, and a set of steps led up to the pristine whiteness of the sleeping surface—crisp sheets, puffy pillows, an old-fashioned coverlet. Two layers of draperies were gathered around the ornate posts that marked the corners. Shear white fabric could be pulled to enclose the area in order to keep the plague of the swampy city, mosquitoes, at bay. In the style of a century ago, the heavier cloth could be drawn tight to hold the body heat of the sleepers, necessary in the damp chill of winter nights.

I'm lucky everything is furnished, Abner said to himself. *I didn't give a moment's thought to accoutrements such as towels and sheets and dishes. Miss Zappo . . . Addie . . .left me well prepared to move right in. Somebody is taking care of me.* He smiled as he looked around the room. His idea about who it might be would probably differ a great deal from that of most people with more mundane beliefs.

The large armoire setting against the far wall was of the size and quality equaling the furniture he would be offering for sale in his new shop. Whether it had come from France with the furnishings of the immigrants who settled in the new town of Orleans, or had been made on one of the plantations somewhere up the mighty Mississippi and brought downriver for a town home, it had the prominence required for the home of an important citizen. When Abner swung open one of the doors, he found the inside bare of clothing, and a mirror reflected the image of a distinguished gentleman. It took a few seconds to recognize himself. The patina of the glass pictured him as he might have appeared half a century ago or more, younger and exceedingly dignified. He blinked and the image morphed into the self he was used to seeing in the mirror.

On the wall beside the armoire hung a portrait, an oil painting framed in ornate gold molding, a picture of a beautiful woman. Her skin was a creamy tan, and her cheeks held a hint of rose, as if she had been sitting outside in the courtyard letting the sunlight burnish her. Black curls fell over one shoulder, and her eyes . . . her deep brown eyes . . . were looking through him, as if she could see his thoughts, his intentions, his self. After staring into what seemed to be the eyes of a living person, Abner closed his own and dipped his head in acknowledgement of the importance of this woman. "Madame," he whispered, and when he looked at her again, he thought he caught a suggestion of a smile on her face.

CHAPTER EIGHT

T. Wayne felt like singing—like shouting somethin.' Maybe *halleluiah*, *or praise the Lord,* like the old folks did in Granny's church when they got all excited. He didn't know exactly what he wanted to do except to let that good feeling spill out. *You pretty bad up, boy, when you feel like jumpin' jest 'cause you gonna eat two meals today like you used to. 'Cause you worked doin' somethin,' 'stead of wanderin' 'round town lookin' in garbage cans for food and checkin' the ground for coins folks's dropped.*

He had money in his pocket, plenty of money. 'Course, that was Mr. Crowbridge's money, and it was to buy supper for the two of them, but still, it was a good feeling, made him feel like somebody, to have foldin' money, even for a few minutes. And Mr. Crowbridge would pay him for working, T. Wayne was sure he would. Even if it was only the change coming back from the meal he was going to buy, it would be something. And anything was better than nothing. Life had been handing T. Wayne nothin' here lately. It was about time things changed.

The sun was lowering in the sky, and the air was cooler. The sticky heat of earlier in the day was fading, and the merest hint told that autumn was on its way. T. Wayne shivered. Before long, he'd have to figure out a way to get a jacket. He wished he had thought of that when he put clothes into his backpack. But he hadn't thought ahead that far. His only plan had been to get out, get away before the lady came back to take him to a foster home.

Three months ago life had been different. Safe. Then everything changed. His rock, the only person in the world he could count on, had died. He came home from school one day to find an ambulance technician pushing a gurney out of the front door to the apartment house where he and Granny lived.

"Granny!" he called out and tried to get to her side.

"Here, boy," the medic said. "We need to get her to the hospital. Get out of the way!"

So he did, but the ambulance driver stopped beside him and kindly told him what hospital she'd be in. Then they drove away, carrying the slight form of the only person in the world who cared if T. Wayne lived or died, if he had something to eat or a place to sleep, or if he did right and was a good person.

He made his way to the hospital on foot, and he kept asking until he found his grandmother. A heavy canvas curtain separated her bed from the one occupied by another woman, who was watching a rerun of an old I Love Lucy show on the TV that was mounted high up on the wall. He laid his hands on his grandmother's, and she grasped him, stroking and patting as if she were the one doing the comforting.

"Thomas Wayne," she said, her voice so low he had to lean down close in order to hear what she was saying. "You do what I tell you, now." She looked at his face, studying to determine if he was listening.

"Yessum."

"When you go home tonight, you do what I tell you," she repeated. He knew that when she repeated something, it was important.

"Yessum."

"First off, there's a picture of Jesus hanging on the wall over my bed."

"Yessum, I know it."

"Take it down and look at the back of it."

T. Wayne frowned.

"You look close, Thomas Wayne. There's brown paper covering the back—I cut up a grocery sack and put it on there with tape."

He didn't know how to answer her crazy talk. He looked down and played with the edge of the coverlet, smoothing it with his fingers.

41

"But in one corner, it's loose. That's how I put money inside, hid away."

"Money?" He looked up and studied her face.

"Yes, money. I puts some every month, just in case I needs it. Nobody'd think to look there—steal it. You get it. You get it quick, understand? Before anybody knows I'm gone and comes seein' what all they can find."

"Yes, ma'am. I understand." *No! She can't mean what it sounds like. She doesn't mean that she's dying. She just means before people know she's in the hospital. She can't die. Not my Granny.*

"Next, you find my Bible. It'll be by my chair." She raised and lowered his hand. Up and down. Up and down. "You take it and keep it. You hear?"

"Yessum. I hear."

"It has things in it, papers and . . ." She stopped and closed her eyes.

"Granny?" T. Wayne was scared. Real scared.

"I'm still here," she said. "Still here on this earth." She opened her eyes. "On the cards and papers and all, there's information you'll want. Your mother's address is on a slip of paper in that Bible. I write to her from time to time. Maybe you'll take it in your heart to do the same. And your father's name, and what little I know about him. It's all there. You'll need that, Thomas Wayne. You'll need it, someday."

"Yessum," he said, but he didn't believe it. He had never even met his father, and he could barely remember his mother. As far as he was concerned, she was in prison, and T. Wayne figured she would be there forever. He didn't *want* to remember her. The only person that mattered in his life was here in this hospital bed, and he was terrible afraid that she was dying.

"And my purse, Thomas Wayne," his granny said as she struggled to turn slightly toward the metal stand beside the bed. "Open that door there. My handbag is in there."

He did as he was told.

"Open it and get my little coin purse."

He pulled out the worn leather pouch.

"Take it, Thomas Wayne, it and the money what's in it. All of it."

"All of it, Granny?"

"All of it, Thomas Wayne. Where I'm going' I won't need no money. I'll be walkin' the streets of gold with Jesus."

A nurse came and ran him off. "She needs her rest," she said. "You come back tomorrow."

He didn't want to leave Granny here alone. He wanted to stay with her, but the nurse stood in the doorway, waiting for him to leave, so he stood up, shoved the little leather pouch into his pocket and took a couple of steps.

"Thomas Wayne," his granny called to him.

"Ma'am?"

"Always remember to be a good boy. A good man. Remember what I taught you."

"Yessum."

"And remember that I love you. When I gets to the other side, I'll come be with you, iffn I can."

He couldn't speak. His throat had done swole up. He nodded, then turned and left.

* * *

It was almost dark and beginning to rain by the time T. Wayne got back to the apartment he shared with his grandmother. As he entered the building the old man who lived on the ground floor stuck his head out of his door and stared. He kept standing there as T. Wayne went up the stairs.

He was using his key when the woman in the next apartment came into the hall. "I locked that door," she told him. "When the ambulance came and took her away, I figured some folks in this building would rob you blind, so I locked it for you. I hope you don't mind."

"I don't mind," T. Wayne said. "Thank you."

43

"She die?" another voice chimed in. He turned and saw the neighbor on the other side, looking through the narrow opening of her door.

"No ma'am. She didn't die. "She's in the hospital. She be home in a few days."

"Huh!" the old woman snorted and slammed her door shut.

"I hope she gets better," the first woman said. "She's always been nice to me, and she took care of my kids when I needed her." She closed her door gently.

He went right to work, as if speed was important. One never knew what was going to happen the next minute, the next hour, the next day. When he went to school that morning, he didn't have a clue that today would end like this. He took his backpack, so old it was coming apart, and went into Granny's bedroom. He emptied it of all the school supplies he had carried that day, piling the books and papers on the bed. He took the picture of Jesus, arms extended, light shining from his white face, and placed it on her bed. Once, when he was little, he had asked Granny if Jesus really cared about him, since in every picture he saw of Jesus the Son of God was white. "White folks don't care, Granny," he had told her. "Why does Jesus?"

"He do care, Thomas Wayne," she told him. "Jesus care about ever'body."

"Even bad people?"

"Even them too, but he wants them to stop being bad. He wants them to straighten up and be good. Jesus loves everyone, even when they bad."

But T. Wayne was dubious about that claim. He couldn't reconcile the idea of anybody, much less Jesus, loving bad people. That's what they said in Sunday School too, but he wasn't swallowing that story whole. And he wasn't too sure about white people caring even a little bit about black people, especially a skinny, no-account black boy. But he never argued with his grandmother.

44

He put Granny's Bible into the backpack. The black cover was worn, and the edges of the pages showed which passages she turned to most often. It was stuffed with all sorts of things: cards and photos and yellowed clippings from the newspaper. Granny had always kept it close. When she sat in her favorite chair and watched TV, during commercials, or when a show was on that she didn't care much about, she would look at the bits and pieces she had been accumulating all her life. A couple of heavy-duty rubber bands kept it semi-closed and held most of the memories in place. T. Wayne knew she would count the Bible as the most precious possession she had. He put it as deep into the bag as he could get it.

He turned the picture face down and saw the loose paper on the top right corner. Carefully, he tore it a little bit at a time, until he could see inside, and sure enough, it was filled with money. Bills. Mostly fives, but lots of ones as well. Some tens, and one twenty. He made a stack, smoothing the rumpled cash as he sorted it into piles. When he had it all neat, he counted it. He had one hundred fifty three dollars. He sat staring at it as he studied what to do.

It was important to Granny to keep it safe. *She will get better,* he kept telling himself. *She's not going to die. She's not! And when she comes home, I'll give all this money back to her.*

T. Wayne went to the kitchen and found a bread wrapper. Granny kept them, all clean and neatly folded, ready to use. "No need to spend money on that fancy stuff when you get perfectly good plastic for free with a loaf of bread," she said. "Use what you got and save your money."

He put the stack of bills into the tube and folded the excess around and around. Taking a rubber band from the stash in the kitchen drawer, he secured the packet. Placing it on the kitchen table, he kept it in his sight as he made himself a peanut butter and jelly sandwich for supper.

I'll keep everything safe, he kept telling himself. *When Granny comes home, everything will be just like she left it.*

He slept with the money safe under his pillow, not that he slept much for all the tossing and turning he did. And when he got up at the first crack of dawn, he didn't feel much rested, but he couldn't stand to stay in bed any longer.

He was eating a bowl of cereal and milk when someone knocked on the front door. He left the chain connected as he opened it just wide enough to see who was there. A woman smiled at him. It wasn't anybody from the neighborhood. He could tell from the way she was dressed and the notebook in her hands that she was from some agency or another. Agency people all had the same look about them.

"Thomas Wayne Johnson?"

"Yes ma'am."

"My name is Althea Simpson. I'm from Children's Protective Services. May I come in?"

T. Wayne would have loved to say, "No. No you can't come in," but his grandmother had taught him a long time ago that it was best to get along with anybody who came calling from any agency, assistance group, or city or state authority, else they could make your life worse than it already was in many ways. "Listen to what they have to say, Thomas Wayne, and tell them what they want to hear. Then, when they're gone, you decide what's best for you to do," she used to tell him.

"Yes ma'am," he said, and slid the chain out of its holder. He opened the door wide and admitted her to the small apartment. He thought about what Granny would say if she were there.

"Won't you have a seat?" He gestured to the lumpy brown sofa with the brightly colored pillows adorning it. A picture of Martin Luther King hung on the wall behind it.

"What good manners you have. Your grandmother has taught you well," Miss Simpson said as she sat down. "Thomas, I have some bad news." Her smile disappeared. "Your grandmother has died."

T. Wayne couldn't speak. Try as he might, nothing would come out of his throat. He closed his eyes and attempted to hold in the tears, but a few of them escaped and trickled down his cheeks. He felt her hand on his knee as she made an effort to comfort him.

"I don't want you to worry, Thomas. You'll be taken care of. You won't be left to fend for yourself." She removed her hand and thumbed through the folder she held. "I see that your mother is . . ." she cleared her throat, " . . . is incarcerated, and your father is . . . not in the community."

T. Wayne thought that must be a polite way of saying nobody knew who or where he was.

"But you don't have to worry. Children's Protective Services will find a place for you. A nice home." She looked around the neat apartment. Granny always kept everything in its place, and the floor swept and the tables dusted. A bouquet of plastic flowers sat on top of the television set, and doilies topped every surface. The recliner where Granny spent most days had some magazines beside it, and the blanket she covered her arthritic knees had slid to the floor, but otherwise everything was in its place.

"Yes ma'am," T. Wayne said. *Yeah, right! Like I believe that. I know kids in my class who are in foster homes. No way! No way am I going to someplace like that.*

"Will you be OK here by yourself for just a little while? You're old enough to stay by yourself for a few hours, right? You're what? Thirteen?" She studied him with sympathetic eyes.

"Fifteen," T. Wayne corrected her. "I'm fifteen." He drew himself up, trying to look older.

47

"My goodness, yes," she said, looking at the papers in the folder. "Fifteen. So if I go to make some arrangements, you'll be all right here alone?"

"Yes ma'am. I'll be OK."

"You could spend some time getting your clothing together to take with you. When I come back maybe the funeral home will have your grandmother's . . . have your grandmother ready for viewing, if you'd like to go see her."

"Yes ma'am." He'd have liked that. To see Granny one more time. But that wasn't going to happen. He'd already seen his beloved grandmother for the last time.

"And after that, I'll take you to your new home."

"Yes ma'am."

She smiled and patted him on the arm as she went out the door. "I'll see you in a couple of hours, Thomas."

He hurried to do what had to be done. In the backpack, he put the money, a change of clothes, extra shoes, and his toothbrush on top of the Bible that was already there. Going into his grandmother's bedroom, he rummaged through her old jewelry box until he found the pin she always wore to church on Sundays—an ornate spray of glass jewels in the shape of a peacock's tail. For just a few seconds, he held it to his heart, then put it in the bag with the rest of his treasures.

He stopped before going out the door for the last time and looked around. "Bye, Granny," he murmured and slipped out into the hall.

CHAPTER NINE

Memories of his grandmother still slipped into T. Wayne's thoughts from time to time, but not as often as they once did. Seemed like when he was happy, like he was this evening, he wanted to tell her—share his good feelings with her. Back when he was small, he'd put his arms around her and bury his head in her apron.

"What's got you to feelin' so good, Thomas Wayne?" she'd ask.

"I got an A on my math test today, Granny," he'd say.

"I'm so proud of you," she'd say as she hugged him. "You so smart! You gonna be somebody someday. You somebody *today.* You Thomas Wayne Johnson!"

And even when he was happy just because it was a good day, like today, he'd hug her and feel safe just because she loved him. It had been a while since that had happened, but today T. Wayne got those same kind of vibes because he had worked hard, helped somebody, done good, and was going to have an excellent meal for the second time in one day.

"Two ham sandwiches, two glasses of iced tea, two peach fried pies, to go. That right?" the woman behind the counter asked. She looked over the top of her glasses. "You got the money to pay for all this?" she asked T. Wayne.

"Yes ma'am. I do," he answered, nodding his head for emphasis.

"You don't look like you got no money."

"I do!" he reached toward the bills stuck in his pants pocket.

The waitress turned toward another server who was walking by, order pad in hand. "You think this boy gonna have money to pay for what he order?"

The second woman looked him over. "He was in here this morning with Mr. Crowbridge—was gonna work for the man. You know," she said to the first waitress, "Mr. Crowbridge be the man what's movin' into Miss Addie's old shop." She looked back at T. Wayne. "He pay you for workin'? You got money?"

"I got money," T. Wayne said, pulling the bills from his pocket, "He sent money to pay for our supper." He thought he'd add a little persuasion. "We been working hard, moving furniture and boxes from across town into his new place. We both hungry. He sent me after food."

"What's this?" a big black man asked as he came through the swinging door from the kitchen.

T. Wayne looked up and down at the new arrival. He was tall—taller than T. Wayne's six feet—muscled, and he looked serious. Nobody'd lie to him if they knew what was good for them.

"I was just makin' sure this boy could pay for what he's ordering."

"I can pay," T. Wayne said.

"I vouched for him. He's helpin' Mr. Crowbridge move into Miss Addie's place."

"That right?" the big man asked. "That's a good thing, helpin' somebody. Addie was tellin' me she had rented the shop and her apartment to someone. His name Crowbridge?"

T. Wayne nodded.

"He gonna sell furniture and what-all in the shop? And live in the apartment?"

"Yessir."

"An' you be helpin' him?"

"Yessir. We got a truckload of stuff moved today. He says he's got a lot more, but it don't look like he has room for anything else."

The big man stuck out his hand. "I'm Simon. I own this place. I reckon I need to make acquaintance with the new person on the block." He shook hands with T. Wayne. "You be . . .?"

"Thomas Wayne Johnson, sir." He drew himself up to the tallest he could be. "Folks call me T. Wayne."

"You not from the neighborhood. You live with Mr. Crowbridge?"

"No sir." He couldn't say anything else because he couldn't confess that he didn't have any place to live. He found shelter wherever he could, sleeping behind dumpsters or tucked away in any nook or niche he could find. Anywhere far away from his old neighborhood, where the lady from Children's Services might find him and take him away to juvy or some foster home. He had known some foster home kids at school. No, not for him.

"Let me have that order," Simon said, taking the order slip. "I'll fix up a nice welcome supper for the man." He headed toward the kitchen. "And his helper," he added, winking at T. Wayne.

When he returned a few minutes later, Simon had his arm around a big sack. "Let's go," he said to T. Wayne, who held out the bills Mr. Crowbridge had given him to pay for supper. "Nah. No charge this time. This is to say welcome to the neighborhood."

Together they walked the half-block back to the quadrangle of apartments. Simon stopped at the wrought-iron gate that secured the courtyard, but T. Wayne continued to the shop front and opened the door. "Come through this way," he told Simon. To tell the truth, he hadn't looked around enough to know that the fancy iron gate was another way to get to where they were going.

They proceeded through the maze of furniture into the back room, then made their way among the stacks of boxes to the door that led into the kitchen, where they found Abner Crowbridge, eyes closed and nodding.

"Good evening," Simon announced himself in a loud voice.

Abner woke with a start. He looked around as if to familiarize himself with his surroundings, then replied, "Good evening." He struggled trying to stand up.

"Don't stand! Don't stand!" Simon said, setting the sack on the round table in front of the doors leading out onto the courtyard. He turned and offered his hand to the elderly man. "I'm Simon Bondurant, and I own the café on the corner. I just came along with T. Wayne here to introduce myself and say welcome to the neighborhood."

He started removing cups and bowls and packages from the brown paper bag. "The boy here ordered ham sandwiches and fried pies, but I thought I'd bring you some samples of what we serve down at Simon's Place." He winked at T. Wayne. "So you'd know what you might want to order next time."

The table top was half-full by the time Simon finished unloading the food he had brought. "What you don't eat tonight will be handy for your lunch tomorrow."

"It certainly smells good," Abner Crowbridge said. "Sit down and join us, Mr. Bondurant."

"Just call me Simon, like everyone in the neighborhood. Thanks, but I ate earlier, Mr. Crowbridge. All this is for you two." He pushed a cup toward T. Wayne. "Try this with your sandwich, T. Wayne. It's gumbo. Or this," he pulled the lid off a small carton. "Shrimp etouffe."

He continued suggesting the contents of various dishes he had brought in small containers. "T. Wayne ordered a couple of fried pies and they're in here," he said as he placed a small brown bag liberally stained with grease between the man and the boy, "but I also brought some bread pudding. Simon's Place is famous for its bread pudding.

"You'll have plenty to eat tomorrow, I reckon," he said, looking around. "I 'magine Addie has a microwave 'round here somewheres." He chuckled. "That's Addie's type of cooking—warming up left-overs." He opened a cabinet and brought two glasses to the table.

"You know my landlady then?" Abner asked as he unwrapped a ham sandwich.

"I'd say I do," Simon said as he poured tea from a jug into the glasses. "We be . . ." His brow furrowed as he looked off into space, "cousins, I reckon. Yeah, we be cousins."

Abner stopped eating and stared at the man. "I'd never have guessed," he finally said.

"No, I guess you wouldn't, what with me bein' black and her bein' white and all."

"See . . ." Simon started the story as he pulled out a chair and sat down. "Her grandmother and my grandfather were brother and sister. Her grandmother was light-skinned, what people used to call 'high-yellow' back in the day, and she ran away—left—and married a white fellow. Never told a soul about her family back here in New Orleans.

"This place," he looked all around and motioned with his hand, "belonged to her sister, Madame Badeaux, and when Madame died, she left everything to Addie, who was, understand, her niece, even though Addie didn't know it. And they didn't know about me at all. Me, my daddy was their brother, and he joined the army and got hisself killed in the war before he knew I was on the way. So I was a surprise, you might say, that Addie puzzled out after she moved here from back east."

"I imagine there's an interesting story behind all that," Abner said.

"There is. Sometime when you have a day or two," he paused and stood up, "or three, I'll tell it to you.

"I better be getting back to my place. Welcome to the neighborhood, Mr. Crowbridge. I hope you enjoy living here. If you need anything, just send T. Wayne here to get me."

Abner stood and shook hands again with the restaurateur. "I can tell that I'm going to very comfortable here. It already feels like home." They strolled toward the door that led into the shop.

"A question, if I may," Abner said. "The portrait in the bedroom," he gestured toward the rear of the building. "Is that Madame Badeaux?"

"Yes. Yes it is," Simon answered.

"A formidable woman, no doubt."

"She was that. And very powerful."

"Powerful in her influence, or . . ." Abner couldn't pick a work to use.

"Yes. Powerful in her influence because anybody who knew anything about New Orleans knew of her other powers. Blessings or hexes or anything in between, Madame could get it for you."

Abner was quiet, mulling over the message Simon was conveying with those words. The power that had once inhabited these rooms still lingered, he could feel it.

A slight movement behind him brought his attention back to the present. "Thomas . . . T. Wayne, I imagine your family is worried about you by now. Hadn't you better get home?"

"Nobody's worried 'bout me," T. Wayne answered. "It's OK." He didn't want to add that he was safer here, in the former home of a witch, than he usually was, sleeping behind a garbage can in an alley.

CHAPTER TEN

"Make no mistake, the Lord God's wrath is mighty—mighty indeed against those who sin against Him. And there are many who today are ignoring His word and living a sinful, immoral life. Hellfire and damnation await all those who do not turn their back to sin and return to live moral lives."

Lexi stared at her lap, willing her fingers to be still and not twist the fold of her skirt. Whenever she looked up, it seemed as if Reverend Phillips was staring right at her, so she kept her head down.

"This world has become a terrible pit of sin, we all know that. There are sinners all around us and they practice their perversions, their lewd and immoral behaviors daily. If you have a television in your home, you know, you see, this is going on everywhere, and people say it is their right to act in this manner. They try to lure our young people, even those who are old enough to know better, into their world of depravity.

"This might be the day—the day the Lord calls you home. Where will you go? To heaven or hell? This might be your last chance to repudiate the sin that is filling your mind, body and soul. Oh, friends! Do not delay. Call on us! We will pray you through it! We will pray you through your sin."

'Amen' rang throughout the congregation, and the choir began to softly sing.

"Just as I am and waiting not . . ."

"Stand! Stand my friends, and raise your hand if you want me to come pray with you—pray that you be relieved of your sin."

"To rid my soul of that dark blot . . ."

Lexi stood with the rest of the congregation, but if he thought she was going to raise her hand, he had another think coming. The portly preacher came down from the raised dais, his clip-on microphone keeping his voice booming above the music. He stopped in front of old Mrs. Whithers, who raised her hand for prayer every Sunday. He placed his right hand on her head and raised his left to the heavens. She didn't have to tell him what she needed prayer for, he was well rehearsed in her ailments.

"Oh, Lord, we ask You to visit your healing upon this child of God..."

Lexi tuned it out. He was going to come to her—she knew he was. Her sin was supposed to be a secret; her stepmother had promised not to tell, although why Lexi ever thought it would be kept from her father she didn't know. And if her father knew, it went without saying that the minister did, too.

Her father had exploded in anguish and rage. "It's working with those two queers! They've brain-washed you!" he had yelled. "That's what homosexuals do—try to recruit more people to be like them. You'll quit that job immediately."

Lexi had tried to tell him it wasn't so. She had known for years she was attracted to girls, not boys, but he wouldn't listen.

"Nonsense. You liked that boy who lived next door—what was his name? Jason? He was always over here with you."

"We watched TV together, Daddy. We did homework together. I didn't like him like a boyfriend."

"And you went to the prom with Alan Jessup's son, Brad." Pleading, he added, "This is just a phase." His voice grew belligerent again. "You've been around those fags and it's rubbed off."

"Daddy!" She'd never heard him use that word before. Her father had always been kind and soft spoken. Lexi had never seen this prejudiced side of him. "I went to the prom with Brad Jessup because I was trying to fit in. I knew then what I was, but I was trying to deny it. When I fell in love with Shannon, I knew. I knew for sure." Tears came to her eyes as she thought about that betrayal. She and Shannon had planned to move in together, until a week ago when Shannon had announced she no longer loved Lexi, and that she and Roberta were moving to Dallas together. That was what had brought on the tears and despondency that caused Lexi to confide in her stepmother. And, of course, her stepmother told her father.

Once her father knew, he'd run straight to Reverend Phillips for advice. Truth be told, her father wanted to make sure no one thought it was *his* fault. *He* had raised her right, and if his daughter had gone astray, *he* wasn't to blame.

Reverend Phillips stopped by Joe Barrow, who fought the temptation of the bottle and regularly lost. He was a Sunday morning regular, too, asking for forgiveness and living a sanctimonious life that lasted until Friday afternoon when he got off work.

When the pastor took his hand from Joe and continued up the aisle, Lexi could tell his eye was on her, and before he took two steps, she snatched up her purse from the pew and ran. She could not—would not—endure his attention on her.

Her first impulse as she pulled out of the church parking lot was to drive as fast as she could, as far as she could, but in the next block she pulled to the curb and put the car in parking gear. She had to calm herself or she'd end up having a wreck.

Covering her face with her hands, she prayed. *Can I still pray? Will God still listen to me? Maybe not.* Dropping her hands back to the steering wheel, she took a deep breath. "Please, God." Just that. She didn't know please, what. Just, "Please, God."

She didn't want to go home. Her parents and younger stepsister would be back there shortly, and another lecture would be forthcoming, Lexi was sure. More than a lecture. A tirade. Her heedless rush from the church was the least of her shortcomings, and her father would have plenty to say about it. Plenty of condemnation. Plenty of hate—not toward Lexi, perhaps, but toward others. And she wasn't about to hear any more about the sins of her friends.

She started driving. She'd go to the shop. Creative Catering wasn't open on Sunday, but it was the place she felt most at home. The happiness and peace she found there soothed her, and when she lost herself in the work it eased the pains of life. Maybe she'd bake something. Yes, that was it. She'd check the calendar for the upcoming week and see if there was something she could start preparing. That would make her feel better.

When she pulled into the parking lot, she noticed Chad's car parked there and wondered if he had come in to work also, or if he had left it there last night and rode home with Barry. Sometimes, when they left work, they took only one car and stopped somewhere for dinner and drinks. That was another sin in her father's eyes. Chad and Barry were not only gay, open about it, living together in sin, but they sometimes ate at places that served cocktails. Yes, they drank. Liquor. Not Drank with a capital D, like Joe Barrow, but drank with a little d, cocktails before dinner, wine with, and luscious looking dessert drinks after. That was another black mark against them.

When Lexi unlocked the door and went in, she found the pair standing in front of the huge bulletin board, rearranging notes on various colored papers. It was their version of what they called a 'flow-chart'. It told them what events they were catering when, what they would be serving, and as near as they could determine, who would attend the 'happenings'. They did their best to see that people weren't served the same dish at any successive three events.

"Lexi, sweetie, what are you doing here on a Sunday?" Chad asked. Then he got a good look at her face. He immediately went to her and gathered her to him. His long, thin arms held her close to him, and the minute she put her face on his shoulder the tears she had been holding in burst out of her.

Barry awkwardly patted her back. "That cheating Shannon, she was no good for you. No good at all. I could tell from the first time I met her. You'll find a better girlfriend than that—you'll see. Be glad she's gone."

When Lexi could speak, she lifted her head and said, "Shannon wasn't the straw that broke the camel's back. That was my family. Oh, Barry, Chad! Was it hard when you came out to your families?"

Chad pushed her back from him and held her at arm's length. "You mean they didn't know? Not until now?"

Lexi shook her head. "No, they didn't. But I was crying over Shannon, and my stepmother was sympathetic until she found out it wasn't a man I was crying over. She told my father and he hit the roof." The memory of that conversation came rushing back, and the tears started again.

"I assume they didn't take it well?" Barry said.

"No. Not at all. My stepmother didn't say anything. She just got up and left my room. She's scarcely spoken to me since then, and she's keeping my little stepsister away, like she might turn gay if she talks to me. It's my father who is so upset. He's said the most hateful things."

"Some of them about us, I imagine," Chad said.

Lexi was silent. She wouldn't hurt her friends for anything in the world.

"That's OK, sweetie," he said.

"We're big boys. We can take it," Barry chimed in. "I'll bet he said it was our fault."

Lexi avoided his eyes.

"Some people think homosexuality can be caught, like the flu," Chad said. "Just ignore them."

"I can't ignore my family," Lexi cried.

"Mary Alexandra, you are twenty-three years old. It is high time you were out on your own and living your own life—not the life your father thinks you ought to live."

In theory, Lexi agreed with that, but it was harder than she had imagined it would be.

"I'm glad your mother is dead," her father had said, and Lexi gasped. "I wouldn't want to see the pain you would be causing her if she were still alive."

But the final thing was when her ten-year old stepsister, Jenny, sneaked into Lexi's room after bedtime that night. "They're going to have a prayer intervention for you Friday night. Everyone's coming to our house and they're going to pray over you until you aren't gay anymore."

Lexi spent the next week making plans with Chad and Barry, and Thursday, when her parents were at work, she packed her car and left.

CHAPTER ELEVEN

"I can't believe I'm doing this," Lexi said as a single tear rolled down her cheek."

"You'll be fine," Barry said as he put his arm around her shoulders. "Just keep saying to yourself, 'I'm a strong independent woman. I can take care of myself.'"

Lexi repeated the phrases to herself, but it didn't help. This was a big step. She had never done anything like it before.

"I'm running away from home," she said sheepishly.

"Don't make it sound like you're ten years old," Chad said. "You are plenty old enough to be on your own."

"I know . . . I know."

"Let's go over everything one more time before you leave." Barry held up his left hand with the fingers spread apart. He used his right pointer finger to tick off as he talked.

"You withdrew almost everything in your bank account and opened a new one in another bank, one *without* your father's name on it."

"Yes, I did that. It's in a bank that has branches all over the south."

"Good. Next, you bought a new cellphone."

"Right here," Lexi said and patted her jeans pocket. "I have both your phone numbers in it, and the shop number, and the phone numbers of your friends in New Orleans."

"And where is your old phone?" Chad asked. "You know they could use it to find out where you are."

Lexi reached into a different pocket and withdrew the phone she had been using for over a year. "I'm going to leave it here with you. Right?"

"Yes," Barry said as he reached for it. "When he comes looking for you, and he will, we'll tell him you left it here on the counter last night when we closed."

"You don't have the number in it of anybody who knows what you're doing, do you?"

"No, I don't. There's nobody who's in on this anyway. They can call every number on the phone and won't learn a thing."

"And you packed everything you should ever need?" Chad asked. "At least for a long, long time." When he saw tears forming again in Lexi's eyes, he reached and pulled her into an embrace. "Someday this will be better. "Someday your father will be so happy to have you back as his daughter, it won't matter that you're gay." He set her back and looked at her face. "These bad times won't last, you'll see. And you won't be alone there in New Orleans. Our friends will see to it."

"Yes," Lexi said, nodding her head. "I know it. I've just got to do what needs to be done. Establish life on my terms."

She slid into the driver's seat of her Toyota and pulled the door shut beside her.

"Here," Barry said as he thrust a paper bag at her. "You'll be on the other side of Texas by lunchtime, and you might not see any place you want to eat. This is a sandwich and chips and some other snacks. That way you can drive until you're ready to find a motel to spend the night."

"Now, you pick a nice motel, you hear? Nice and clean. Upscale," Chad said. "Don't try to save money by staying at some cheap place."

"And I put a card in there," Barry said, pointing at the sack. "Something to cheer you up and remind you of us. Tonight, if you feel blue, open it and feel better."

"Oh, guys, I miss you already."

"You better leave now," Barry said.

"Before you drown us all in tears," Chad added, as he wiped his eyes with his hand.

At first Lexi drove as if a posse made up of her father's friends and fellow church members were hot on her trail. Somehow it became an urgent matter, getting away from the town where she had lived her entire life.

Hurry, hurry! Get away while you can! Before they catch you and bring you back to tell you what a horrible, sinful person you are. Hurry, before those people who ought to love you tell you they can't possibly love the person you are, that they can't possibly love you until you change into the person they want you to be. Finally, anxious and panicky, she pulled off to the side of the road. Leaning her head on the steering wheel, she closed her eyes and commanded herself to get a grip.

I'll never make it this way. I'll have a wreck, or at the very least get a speeding ticket. And that would only back up what my father has been telling me, that I'm young, immature, don't know what I'm doing, and need him to guide me through life.

After taking several deep breaths she remembered some meditation methods she had once practiced before tests at school. Breathing slow and easy, she reassured herself that she was smart and capable and could do anything she put her mind to. *The future is what I make it. I choose to make it calm and happy. I will find a new place for myself that will be exactly what I need at this time in my life. My future holds new experiences, happy ones, and new friends. A new home awaits me. I only have to go claim it.*

After a few minutes, she felt like resuming the journey to her new life. She slipped the car into drive and started out once more. *No more fears. No more tears.* The mantra played over in her mind. "No more fears. No more tears," she said aloud.

At the next small town she got a soda. "Cold, wet, and plenty of caffeine," she said aloud. She began to notice the land around her. On her few previous trips around the state she had been more interested in her companions, or the conversation, or the songs on the radio than she had been in the surroundings. Now, leaving West Texas, perhaps for the last time, she became aware of the vast fields of sunflowers and cotton for which the area was known. Farther along they gave way to cattle grazing on rolling pastures before changing yet again to acres of corn. Ranches, their entrances marked by arches over the drive spelling out the name or brand in iron, marked their territory with barns, silos, and large houses sitting away from the highway in lonesome splendor.

She veered to the south, missing the complex that was Dallas and Fort Worth, not wanting to get caught up in the traffic that pulled everyone and everything into the activity of doing business in the metroplex.

Lexi was well into the center of the state when her stomach told her it was past lunchtime. Buying another soda, she found a small park in the town she was going through and pulled in under a spreading oak tree.

She needed to walk around first, she decided. To limber up. She locked the car and went to the restroom located close to where she had parked. When she returned to her vehicle, she first stretched, touching her toes, running in place, and doing a few jumping-jacks before unlocking the car and resuming her place.

The sack lunch her employers had provided was delicious, the ingredients gathered from the lunches they had catered during the week. A sandwich, canapes, vegetable sticks, olives stuffed with cheese, several kinds of cookies: the best of the best. When she came to the bright blue envelope at the bottom of the paper bag, she almost opened it. She held it to her cheek and smiled as she thought about her two bosses. They thought more about her welfare and the state of her emotions than anyone else in the world. *I'll save opening this until I'm blue and need a pick-me-up,* she thought as she started the car and pulled back out onto the highway.

The sun was showing its last hour of daylight when Lexi was stopped at a traffic light in East Texas and saw the motel ahead. A major chain, nicer than any she had ever stayed in on family or school trips, was just ahead. She determined it would be her stop for the night. It fit the description of what Barry and Chad had told her to look for, quality and safety. To add to its appeal, her favorite fast food place was right next door.

After a hot shower and dressed in cuddly pajamas, Lexi ate her hamburger at the small table provided, then climbed into bed to watch a true crime story. She drifted off to sleep before finding out who did it, and the television timed out sometime in the night, turning itself off.

When she awoke, slivers of light were sneaking in around the black-out drapes. She hurriedly dressed, anxious to get back on the road. There was a free breakfast buffet laid out in the lobby. When she went to check out, she fixed herself a cup of coffee and picked up a wrapped sweet roll to eat on the road. *I can be well into Louisiana before I need to eat more than this, and I'll be in New Orleans by tonight.* A thrill of excitement raced through her as she pulled onto the highway once more.

CHAPTER TWELVE

Thin slices of daylight were making their way into the bedroom when Abner awoke. In the courtyard birds were awakening as well, tweeting their greetings to the day. He stretched, appreciating the feel of crisp sheets against his skin. The air was cool, signaling the arrival of autumn, and he burrowed a bit deeper into the warmth of the bed. Although by the time the sun was fully up one would swear it was still the midst of summer, early risers could tell the year was ambling toward shorter days and longer nights.

Waking here in Broussard Court was quite a contrast to his son's home. At Bob's, there was nothing to cause Abner to rise in anticipation of what the day would bring. He already knew it would bring boredom. He would watch TV. Read the books he brought home from the library every week or two. Read the same news reported by the same people in the same words. One newspaper reported what a wonderful job the president was doing. Pick up the opposing paper and read that the president ought to be impeached. Abner wasn't much into politics. It didn't matter to him. Nothing much did. What motive was there to even get out of bed?

The reason, Abner knew, was to keep his daughter-in-law from insisting that he ought to be in a retirement home. Some days the only thing that stirred him, got him up and dressed, was to show Janelle that he could care for himself. That he was not bed-bound and beyond caring where he was.

This last month had been different. Now there was every reason to get up and get going. Who knew what was going to happen today? The people who wandered into his shop were entertainment enough, better than any program Abner might find on the television set or in any book he might read. Local residents came in to see exactly who this new person in the neighborhood was and what he was about. To ask questions about the unique and obviously foreign merchandise displayed around the rooms and in the curio cabinets. To tell stories about their youth, and remanence about these premises when Madame Badeaux ruled over the neighborhood. To wonder over the ornately carved cabinets and chairs and how Abner came to bring them to America, and marvel at the prices displayed on the attached tags.

"Somebody would really pay that much for that cabinet?" he was asked daily. When anyone commented that they had an item of furniture much like it, Abner would say, "If you ever want to sell it, let me make you an offer," and they would go home talking among themselves about how rich they would be if they sold the family heirlooms, or else how foolish some people were for paying that much for an old table, or chair, or prie-dieu.

Abner slid off the bed, leaning against it as he gained his balance. At each corner the massive posts that held the bed-curtains made excellent supports for an old man first thing of a morning. He stood there until he was sure he could navigate, then started toward the bathroom. He had bought a walker to help keep his stability maneuvering around the flat, but it wasn't necessary every morning. Sometimes, like today, his legs were stronger, ready to bear him for whatever the day might hold. Other times, it was expedient to use additional support when he first began walking. The bench in the large shower stall was handy and prudent. As he shaved, he admired himself in the mirror. *I wonder if I might grow a goatee? Latreece didn't approve of one, but now . . .* He chided himself for finding anything positive about not having his beloved wife at his side any longer, but still . . . He turned this way and that, looking at his reflection.

Dressed, he made his way to the kitchen, assisted as he was most days by the cane ornamented by an all-too-real looking snake. He had bought it in a small hole-in-the-wall shop in Bangkok, and was told that it possessed uncanny properties. Once he had learned what the mysterious item could do, he was never without it, crediting much of his success to the wisdom of the serpent beneath his hand.

Oatmeal this morning? That was a 'healthy' breakfast, although with all the add-ons he favored, it probably lost the healthy label. After starting his coffee brewing, he stood looking into the refrigerator and noticed the bread pudding from Simon's Place. "An admirable substitute for oats," he said aloud. The microwave would have his breakfast warm in no time at all.

He pushed the double French-doors open with the rolling tray he kept in the kitchen for just such a need. The morning was ideal for eating outside, almost cool enough to be labeled 'chilly,' but when the sun's rays gained strength, the heat of the day wouldn't be far behind.

The bougainvillea had ceased blooming for the time being, but fall leaves on the small trees added color to the confines of the cobbled courtyard. Abner could have sat there for hours, drinking in the beauty and ambiance of his new residence, but today he had things to do and decisions to make. At some point in the future he would dawdle the morning away—it was his choice to make—but not today.

With a sigh of contentment he took the last sip of his coffee, stood, and guided the rolling tray that had served as his breakfast table back through the French doors and into the kitchen. With a quick rinse of the empty bread pudding bowl and the pouring of a second cup of fragrant coffee to carry with him, Abner was ready for whatever the day might bring.

He was surprised to hear a faint murmur of voices through the door to the workroom. As he entered the sales area, already filled with treasures recently retrieved from storage units all over New Orleans, he saw where the voices came from.

Two women stood in front of the newly constructed opening between Abner's shop and the one next door—the one he had considered in the first place.

"This is perfect," a young black woman was saying. "Just perfect. And I love those doors."

"It is," Addie said. "And I love them as well." She reached out and touched one of a pair of wooden doors—massive structures with impressive brass hinges. They were show pieces on their own, capable of holding interest among the notable objects filling the room.

"They look like they might have come from some castle in Europe," the other person said.

"They are fitted with heavy-duty locks, as well as a stout bar that can be put in place," Addie said. "So that if we wanted to separate the shops again, we could do it easily by shutting, barricading and locking them."

"I guess if you didn't want to rent the two places together any longer, that would be the thing to do."

"Yes. Easy-peasy."

"It worked out well, what with you owning this side and your father owning the other."

"Indeed, and it would never have worked if we hadn't gotten along as well as we do."

"Yes," Abner spoke up, making his presence known. "I agree. It was fortuitous. This will work wonderfully." He took a few more steps toward the two women, and the snake carved around his cane seemed to refocus its vision. "I will hire some help to rearrange what I have already moved into the space. I'll put the large items here," he said as he walked into the far room, "and smaller items in there." With the tip of his cane he pointed back to the room he had just exited. "Not that I'm really concerned about shop-lifting." He smiled toward the visitors. "I think that won't be a worry with these items. There is a certain . . . power . . . or atmosphere, if you will, about them that would discourage thievery."

"Mr. Crowbridge," Addie said, "I'd like you to meet Danielle Bondurant—Dani. She had her shop in this location before she outgrew

69

it. I hope you don't mind that I used my key to let us in. I didn't know if you were up and I didn't want to disturb you."

"That was before Simon and I married," the African-American woman said, extending her hand in greeting. "I'm happy to meet you, Mr. Crowbridge. You are a welcome addition to the neighborhood. Everyone is talking about the interesting things you are bringing into the space."

"Mrs. Bondurant," Abner said, "I am pleased to meet you as well. Your husband has been keeping me well-fed."

"Just call me Dani," she said. "We aren't that formal here."

"When Dani first moved here she excelled in remaking vintage clothing, giving it new style. Then the movie people found her, and they keep her busy finding and making what they're looking for. When she's not doing costumes for films, the public can't get enough of her designs."

"That sounds interesting, Dani," Abner said. "I'd like to hear more about it sometime."

"What you have here is fascinating," Dani said. "Simon tells me that you collected all this yourself on your travels all over the world?"

"Yes. That's right. My late wife, Latreece, and I traveled extensively, and we liked to buy the unusual, the mysterious, the arcane items we came across. What we didn't use in our home, we stored away to use 'someday.' When we filled all the storage units we could rent close to our residence, we went farther and farther away, until we had possessions stored all over the city."

"You certainly collected some interesting pieces." Addie said.

"Perhaps someday you'll tell us the stories behind the things we see here," Dani added.

"Yes, I would be happy to do that. Those doors," Abner said as he pointed with his cane, "came from Great Britain. Times have changed, and it has long since become financially difficult, if not impossible, to maintain a castle. Giving tours of the place doesn't bring in enough

70

money to support such structures, much less make them livable for modern folk, with running water and central heat and air. In many small towns across England, in order to preserve the local castle in the manner it deserves, the remaining family, or else the town itself, divides it into several separate households. To call them flats would be an injustice. Apartments is not a grand enough word. Condominiums come nearer. A small castle can make three or four households, if not more."

"My goodness," Addie said. "I never thought about anything like that, although I had heard that taxes make it difficult for large estates."

"Indeed it does. And in dividing the local stronghold into more living units, some things are sacrificed. Like these," he said, running his hand over the set of doors separating the two rooms. "I happened to be lucky enough to be present when these were brought into the shop where the artifacts from the castle were offered for sale. I bought them at first sight, not knowing what I was going to do with them. I only knew I had to have them—that I would have need of them someday." He turned to his audience. "And I was right. I needed them here, to join these spaces."

"You have collected the most interesting things, Mr. Crowbridge," Addie said. "I could stay here looking all day."

"You are welcome to do so. I don't mind at all." His cane gave support as he made his way back into the part of the shop that connected with his new home. "I know what you mean. I like looking at everything as well. Much of this was in our home." He paused and looked around. "I've missed living with it—seeing it every day." He took a seat behind a massive desk that served as the sales counter. "It feels good to be around these belongings once more." He looked around at the reminders of a life spent in foreign travels. "It feels like home once again."

"This is a piece that fascinates me," Addie said, stopping next to the large cabinet displayed in the window. "I could study all the carving on it for hours and not see everything." She put her fingers on a swirl of leaves and flowers, tracing the pattern.

"It is called a 'Story Cabinet,'" Abner said. "Supposedly, if you look closely enough you can find your own story in the designs—past, present, and future." He readjusted his glasses as he studied the swirling patterns, intersecting and morphing as they covered the wooden surface.

"Really?" Dani questioned as she moved closer to the side nearest to her. "How could it do that?"

"Magic. Many of the items we collected were reputed to be magical."

"The story of the person who owns it?" Addie questioned as she ran her hand over a particularly busy part of the design that crisscrossed one of the doors.

"The story of whoever puts the essence of themselves on it by touching it. Some say it will tell the tale of your life even if you only stand nearby."

"Look, Addie," Dani said, running her fingers over a figure. "It's a woman holding a baby. Maybe it's me."

"Could be," Addie replied, her finger tracing the spreading branches of a tree.

"And that figure next to your hand! Look, Addie, that woman is pregnant!"

Addie took one finger and placed it on the image Dani pointed out. She smiled.

"Addie! Are you?"

Addie just grinned. "Maybe. I hope so. But . . ."

"But what?"

"I haven't done a test yet, or been to the doctor."

"But the Story Cabinet says you are. It must be true" Dani wiggled in excitement. "I can't wait. We'll have children less than a year apart in age."

Addie took her hand away from the ornate wooden enigma. "A person sure couldn't lie about anything with this around. It would out you for sure."

"If I were around it much, I'd wear it out touching it. It can't be good, people rubbing it all the time to find out things." Dani looked ruefully at the intricate designs. "Before long the beautiful carvings would wear off."

"Actually," Abner said, it's supposed to be a good thing for people to touch it. It primes it, gets it to working more, telling more stories. Sort of the more you use it the better it works."

Turning away from the fascination of enchanted furniture, Dani said, "I'd better get back home. Simon's taking care of Ramona, but he needs to start the day's cooking so he'll be ready to open."

"Is Morgan enjoying school?" Addie asked.

"Yes, he is. He loves it, but he hates to leave his little sister. He could stand and look at her for hours. He is her protector, he thinks."

"Protector from what?" Addie asked.

"I don't know. Anything. Everything. He likes being a big brother."

They chatted as they walked toward the front door to the shop.

"I'll be back soon, Mr. Crowbridge. I'll want to hear more stories about the things you are going to sell in your shop," Dani said as she exited.

"Come back any time you want. I'll be unpacking more things, so there'll be plenty of stories to tell. And I'll start moving things around, putting them in just the right spot to catch a buyer's eye."

"I can help you move things, Mr. Crow . . . Crowbridge." T. Wayne stepped out of the shadows. "Just tell me what you want moved and I'll move it."

"Ah, Thomas Wayne. I wondered when you'd make your appearance," Abner said.

"I just came by to see if the workmen got those doors installed," Addie said. "And to give you this key to the other half of your shop."

She laid a key on the desk that was now positioned near the front door. "I hope you don't mind that I used it to come in. I'll be going."

"Use it anytime you wish, Addie. Anytime you wish," Abner said as he turned toward T. Wayne.

CHAPTER THIRTEEN

It was the safest T. Wayne had felt since his grandmother died. It wouldn't last, he knew, but it sure felt good for now, and he wasn't going to spend any time worrying about the future. Why should he? He had plenty to eat, thanks to working for Old Crow, and a place to sleep out of the weather, dry and warm. Nobody had discovered him yet, his hiding place, which meant that if he was careful and stayed out of sight, he could stay there for a while. Sooner or later, though, people would probably rent all these vacant apartments, and he'd have to leave. If it turned rainy and cold and he had to clear out, well, he'd worry about that problem when it happened. He'd just enjoy the good while it lasted. Granny used to have an expression for that. *Don't look a gift horse in the mouth,* she'd say. T. Wayne couldn't figure out what a horse had to do with anything, but he knew she meant to enjoy things and not worry about where they came from or when they'd go away.

He worked for Old Crow just about every day now and got paid pretty good for it, too. Not like he had a real job, but enough that he could eat even when he didn't go to Simon's Place to buy meals for both of them with Old Crow's money. He folded the bills he had saved into two small bundles. One of them he put in his shoe, the other in the bottom of the old backpack he still carried around. He kept a couple of dollars and some change in his pocket.

T. Wayne had left his grandmother's apartment in a hurry. When the Children's Protective Services lady came back from making arrangements, she was going to put him in a foster home somewhere. If he was still there, that is. And he didn't intend to be.

A foster home was where people got paid to keep kids like him who didn't have any other place to live. Not for him. He knew some kids at school that didn't have a regular home, kids that Children's Protective Services had placed either in the big building on the other side of town—Juvenile Detention, otherwise known as Juvy—or in homes where the people got paid for keeping kids. The horror stories they told convinced him it wasn't something he wanted any part of. No sir. T. Wayne Johnson could take care of himself.

So he had filled the backpack with Granny's Bible, an extra pair of shoes, jeans, underwear, and a couple of tee shirts and got as far away from where he and Granny had lived as he could. At first it was kind of an adventure, almost fun, even. But as the days went by, it wasn't nearly as easy as he thought it was going to be, living on the street.

Wandering around New Orleans was entertaining, he'd give you that. He listened to music, watched street performers, admired the artists that drew and painted for the tourists. When he got hungry he'd buy what he felt like eating. He used the restrooms at the various places that welcomed the crowds of people who came from all over the country to watch what went on in The Big Easy. Using his backpack as a pillow, he slept wherever he could find a spot where he couldn't be seen, like behind a dumpster. If it was raining he'd find a doorway that offered some shelter and spend the night there. He tried to sleep on park benches, but the police always ran him off.

But after a while, he began to feel . . . lots of things. Bored, for one thing. There's just so much singing and dancing and drawing a person can stay interested in. If he could do one of those things, it'd be different, but none of that was T. Wayne's talent, if he even had a talent.

T. Wayne missed home—a place to go to that was his, where he belonged, and where his grandmother was waiting for him and always asked about his day. The apartment they had shared wasn't fancy, but it was his—his and Granny's,—and the sense of belonging that it gave him was gone now.

He missed school. He never thought that would happen. It was a surprise to find out that he liked learning things. He had been looking forward to the World Geography lessons that were coming up. And he enjoyed—really enjoyed—mathematics. Liked seeing the numbers coming together to form an answer, and it felt good to be able to come up with the *right* answer. T. Wayne was looking forward to taking algebra next year. Now, he didn't know if he would be going back to school anywhere or not. He guessed there wasn't any way somebody who had no home could attend school. He spent one afternoon puzzling over a way to show up at a school and convince them that he had just moved to the area and he should go that school for classes. He finally gave up on that problem. He just didn't think it would work. For sure they'd call Children's Protective Services to check him out, and they'd come take him away and put him in a foster home.

Days went by. Little by little the money got spent. What would he do when he ran out? He tried to find a job, anything a fifteen-year-old boy could do, which wasn't much, people thought. He swept the sidewalk in front of a market and got paid two dollars. A man sitting on a park bench, tried to instruct T. Wayne on how to lift a wallet out of a tourist's back pocket. "I'll distract him while you act like you stumble. You fall against him and slip the wallet out and run away." Or T. Wayne could do the distracting while the man snatched the wallet. "We'll split the take," he had said. T. Wayne just looked at him with disgust. He wasn't about to become a thief, what Granny would have called 'a juvenile delinquent,' just because she wasn't around any longer to tell him to 'be a good boy.' Because she was gone didn't mean he forgot what she taught. He knew what was right and what was wrong without her there to tell him every day.

The worst—the very worst—was being dirty. He hated to feel grimy and gritty. At home he took a bath every night. He was always clean when he went to school, and extra clean when he went to church on Sunday morning. Wandering around the city he saw several churches, but he felt too dirty to go in. Granny had taught him that if you went into the house of God, you needed to be clean, both in body and in mind. He knew he wasn't clean of body, and he suspected that staying hidden from Children's Protective Services wasn't exactly being clean of spirit, either. It was sort of living a lie.

The money finally ran out. The day he didn't have any cash to buy food, he had been standing in front of the basket of apples, contemplating what to do, when he overheard the conversation between Old Crow and the moving company man. What happened next brought change in T. Wayne's life, and he credited it to the prayer he had said that morning when he woke up. *Please, God. Show me some way to earn money to eat and take care of myself. Something honest. Something Granny would approve of. Thank you.*

That was when T. Wayne had misunderstood the man's name. He thought people were calling him Mr. Crow. It wasn't until later that he realized the man's name was Crowbridge, not Crow, but by then he had firmly planted in his brain that the old man's name was Crow. He'd have to be cautious and not use the wrong appellation for his employer. He liked the man, and didn't want to make him mad by calling him the wrong name. The jobs T. Wayne did for Abner Crowbridge were interesting, and he was paid more than enough. Sometimes Old Crow . . . Mr. Crowbridge, explained what some of the unusual items were and where he had bought them.

"I've never heard of that place," T. Wayne had said. "Where is Bangkok?" Or Swaziland or Timbuctoo? To him they all sounded like made-up names in books for little kids.

"Someday," Old Crow said, "when we come to the box with a geography book in it, or a globe, I'll show you where that country is."

T. Wayne was looking forward to it. He was always happy to help Mr. Crowbridge with whatever he needed. He liked unpacking the boxes and crates and admiring the oddities that had come from a foreign country. Old Crow usually was all too happy to take the time to explain what the item was, what it was used for, and where it came from.

"Just tell me what you want moved and I'll move it," he said from the back of the room, where he had been listening to Mr. Crowbridge tell about the magic cabinet. He hoped nobody wondered how he got to where he was standing. If he had come in by way of the front door, they would all have seen him enter. There were other ways to get in, the iron gate that opened into the courtyard for one, but it was kept locked and T. Wayne didn't have a key to it. There was a wooden door at the back of the center court that led onto the alley, but he didn't have a key to that, either, so he couldn't have come that way. *Maybe I ought to figure out some way of getting in and out without people knowing, else I might get caught out with no place to stay.*

"I'm glad you're here, Thomas Wayne," his employer said. "I've called Pernell and he'll be here shortly. I'd like for you two to go finish clearing out one of the storage units. It's about empty—nothing but smaller boxes left in it. I'll stay here this time and let you two go. It's full of things I bought in Ireland." T. Wayne put aside his worries about being found out, ready to hear more stories about where Old Crow had bought the souvenirs and the magic they were said to possess.

"But first," Mr. Crowbridge said, "I think we need to talk about where you have been spending your nights."

CHAPTER FOURTEEN

Pernell guided the van in and out of the traffic. Not for the first time he wondered how Abner Crowbridge had found all these storage places scattered around town. It seemed like the man had merchandise in every nook and cranny offered for rent in New Orleans. He must have a good memory to keep up with where he had things stored, or else he kept good records in that little notebook he pulled from his pocket when they started planning where to pick up from next.

"What did he say we're getting this time?" he asked the sullen teenager in the passenger seat. A grunt was the only response. "Oh, yeah," he said, glancing in T. Wayne's direction. "I remember now. A box of bananas and a partridge in a pear tree." Still no reaction.

"So are you going to carry the elephant or am I?"

They were several blocks down the thoroughfare before T. Wayne stirred. "Were you talking to me?"

"No, I was just talking to myself. You got something on your mind this morning?"

"Yeah," the teen mumbled then lapsed into silence once more.

"Anything I can help you with?"

There was a long pause before he answered. "Everything was going good. I mean, I had plenty to eat, a good place to sleep—inside in the dry—and I could even wash up and be sorta clean." He shook his head. "I probably could have even taken a bath, but . . ." His voice trailed off.

"And you can't anymore?"

"Old Crow . . . Mr. Crowbridge caught me."

"Caught you?" Pernell couldn't imagine what that might be about. It couldn't be anything too bad or Crowbridge wouldn't have sent T. Wayne with him to get the boxes. "Doing what?"

"Sleeping in the empty apartment."

"An empty apartment where he lives? Where the shop is?"

"Yeah."

"Why were you sleeping there? Why don't you sleep at home?"

T. Wayne didn't answer.

"There something going on at your place so you can't stay there?"

After a pause T. Wayne said, "I don't have a place. Not anymore."

"No home?" Pernell was shocked. He knew there were homeless people around the city. You saw them sometimes, sleeping in doorways or in camps under bridges, hidden away where they hoped the police wouldn't see them. But this young boy? This obviously smart and hard-working young boy? "How did you get that way?"

"My granny died, and I didn't have any place to go."

"Is . . . was she all you had?"

"Yessir."

"What about your parents?"

"My mother—she's in prison." T. Wayne was ashamed to say that to anybody, but in another way it felt good to get it out in the open at last. To say out loud the things he used to be able to talk to Granny about. She would tell him everything was going to work out, that God was going to take care of him, and he believed her. He wasn't so sure any more. Things didn't seem to be like God would want them to be, if God really could do all that Granny said He could. To begin with, why would God let Granny die? And why would God leave T. Wayne hungry and with no place to live? Of course, he hadn't been hungry in a couple of weeks now, ever since he met Old Crow, and he had a safe, comfortable place to sleep. But it looked like he was about to lose that. Why would God do that?

"What did Mr. Crowbridge say?"

"He said it wasn't right for me to be using that apartment without Miss Addie saying it was OK."

"Uh-huh."

"And he said he'd think about what to do."

"And you're worried about . . ."

"He'll call those people . . . Children's Services . . . and they'll put me in a foster home. Or in juvy."

"Would that be a bad thing?"

T. Wayne looked toward Pernell with a look that said 'you've got to be kidding.' "I know kids from foster homes," he said at last. "I guess sometimes it's a good thing, but . . ."

"Not for you?"

"No. Not for me. Sometimes there's lots of kids in one home, and they take your stuff . ." Not that he had much stuff, but what was his was his. "And sometimes the people who take you, they aren't . . ." Again his words trailed off. "They . . . do things. Bad things." He gave up trying to explain and just shook his head.

They arrived at the U-Store-It and the conversation ended, but Pernell kept thinking about T. Wayne's problem. He didn't have a home. It was as simple as that. He seemed like a good kid, a hard worker who was always helpful and polite to Abner Crowbridge, who trusted him in many ways. It was something Pernell hadn't given much thought to, having been raised in a loving home, with parents and sisters who were always there. In his youth there had been grandparents as well. The idea of having no family at all was hard to imagine. Even now, if he needed anything, even just cheering up, all he had to do was take out his cell-phone and call. Although his parents were gone now, there were numerous sisters and brothers-in-law, nieces and nephews, even cousins, who would be there if he called. To be without anyone in the world was unimaginable. And sad.

CHAPTER FIFTEEN

"Trudy, I'm so sorry," the blonde leaning against the door frame frowned as she spoke.

"It's just the way it goes." Trudy pulled a sweater from the bottom drawer of her desk and put it in the bag she was holding. "We've known for ages that the company was downsizing and wondered who would be let go. Now we know." She shut the drawer with a bang. "It's me."

"You've had it rough lately, what with your grandmother dying and now this, losing your job. It sucks."

"I'm trying to think positively about it," Trudy said, picking up her handbag before boosting the paper bag full of odds and ends onto the crook of her arm. "Something better will come along."

"I've always said that you see the bright side of everything, but I can't think of anything positive about losing your job."

"Grandmother was into so much doom and gloom, I had to be positive to survive. I made it a habit to think of something optimistic no matter what happened. If I had believed her prophesying about all the bad things that were going to come to pass, I would have been worried all the time. Losing this job leaves me open to something new. *Something more interesting than what I have been doing,* she thought, but she didn't want to say that aloud.

"Well, she died, didn't she? That's pretty bad."

Trudy grimaced. "Yes, but she was old. We can't live forever." She had another thought that she couldn't voice. *And now I am free. Free to explore the world!* Immediately she felt guilty for having such unloving thoughts about the woman who had taken her in when her parents were killed. If not for her grandmother, there's no telling where

83

she would have ended up. Adopted, likely, by some family who wanted a little girl, instead of taken in by her natural born relative. As irrational as her grandmother was at times, she loved and protected her granddaughter the best she could, and for that Trudy was grateful.

"I guess my break time is over," the blonde said, looking at her watch. "I'd better get back to my desk or I might be the next person without a job. Call me next week and we'll do lunch."

"The week after that, maybe. I have my trip to New Orleans coming up." Just the thought of it put happiness into her day, even with losing her job.

"I had forgotten about your trip. Are you still going?" She asked as they walked down the hall together.

"I am. It's all paid for, and they won't refund my money. I might as well go enjoy myself and look for a new job when I get back," Trudy said as she headed toward the door. *Grandmother said so many hateful things about New Orleans that I wouldn't back out now. It would be like saying she was right.*

"Call me when you get back and tell me all the exciting things you did."

Trudy stopped beside her friend and they hugged. "I will. I promise." She said her goodbyes to everyone along her way to the parking lot, promising several people that she'd stay in touch, although she knew she wouldn't.

As she climbed into her car, she thought about the upcoming trip. It was about all she had on her mind lately. Just because she was no longer employed didn't mean she was going to forgo the venture she had been looking forward to for years.

New Orleans was like a magnet and she was metal. It kept pulling at her, and at last she was going to visit the city that had fascinated her as long as she could remember. Grandmother had always discouraged any conversation about the quirky metropolis, so unlike any other place in the country. "It's a sinful place," she told her granddaughter. "People doing all sorts of evil things. Showing their bodies. Showing what ought to be covered up." Trudy read about the differentness—the strong French influence, the food, the music. Although Grandmother had not allowed anything having to do with NOLA, as it was called, into her house, it hadn't stopped Trudy from reading books set in south Louisiana and listening to jazz music when she was away from home, out of her grandmother's hearing. Now she punched a button, and her car was filled with the sounds of trumpets backed by tubas and saxophones, playing with the unique sound and syncopation that identified it as Dixieland jazz. She couldn't perceive anything sinful in what she heard.

Trudy wondered, not for the first time, why her grandmother thought so poorly of the famous city. There were family secrets involved, she was sure. The family that she refused to talk about when she was alive. Secrets that would never be revealed now that Ruby Miller was dead and gone.

Trudy had a vague memory of life before she came to live with her grandmother. Elusive recollections of a man and woman she had loved dearly floated in and out. Even today, all these years later, a sense of sorrow and longing overcame her when she tried to recall her parents. She was so young when they died that she had no definitive memories to fall back on, only a sense of love. All her guardian would tell her was that her mother ran away with someone Ruby didn't approve of, and when Trudy was quite small they were killed in an automobile accident. She, Trudy, was at the babysitter's, and so she was saved and came to live with her grandmother in St. Louis. All the memories Trudy had were brief riffs of the music she loved and glimpses of gaiety and celebration that research told her was Mardi Gras. Only those fleeting clues hinted that she and her parents may have lived in New Orleans.

Grandmother, having lost her only child, was over-protective of her young granddaughter, keeping her nearby by at all times and allowing no close friendships for either of them. It was as if death or something or someone could sneak up and snatch her away if she took her eyes off the child for even a moment.

As Trudy grew older and tried to gain some independence, it angered her grandmother, and when that happened, the story of how she had taken in her only grandchild changed. "They didn't die," she would say. "They just didn't want you anymore. They were tired of you. Tired of trying to make you mind. You were such a bad child they gave you away to me. I took you because nobody else would have you. If you don't behave, I'll give you away too. Maybe no one will take you, and you won't have any place to live."

"No! No!" Trudy would cry. Ruby thought she was pleading to be allowed to stay, but what the child was saying no to were the things her grandmother was saying. Her parents would never have given her away. Never. They loved her. She couldn't remember them, but she knew that they loved her, and she loved them. Once, when she reached her teen years, Grandmother was yelling over some misdeed and Trudy had threatened to go and find them, her mother and father, and ask them to take her back.

"Oh, I was lying," Grandmother said, once more reversing the story of how Trudy came to live with her. "They're dead. Dead and buried in that big cemetery in New Orleans. They couldn't take you back even if they'd wanted to. There's nobody to take care of you but me. Nobody loves you but me. Nobody."

At least, Trudy thought, now I know that I'm from New Orleans. Unless Grandmother is lying about that as well.

Other times Ruby was loving and caring and all her threats were forgotten. She played dolls with her granddaughter as if she, too, were a child. They visited the library, bringing home books that Ruby read aloud, making up funny voices for all the characters. They had pretend tea parties and played dress-up with fancy hats on their heads and silky shawls around their shoulders.

Then, like somebody had flipped a switch, the good days would be over, and Ruby would revert to being a threatening shrew. Trudy would take refuge in the makeshift tent she made with a quilt pulled over a couple of chairs and pretend she was in another country until her grandmother's 'spell' was over.

They attended a small church whose members all seemed to isolate themselves from the rest of the world much as Ruby did. It was because of their influence that Ruby was convinced that Trudy must attend school, if not public school, then a private one, which is why Trudy attended the church-based "Bible academy," where she learned the basics of math, reading, writing, and some selected history. Most of their class time was spent on studying the Bible, especially what a person should and should not do. When Trudy had questions about the hows and whys of the Bible, she learned to keep them inside, unspoken. According to Ruby the Good Book was resolute, unquestionable, unyielding. It didn't matter if you understood it or not.

Trudy excelled in everything, and as she grew and advanced in those subjects she thought surely there must be more. More to learn. More to study. More of the world than this little circle of knowledge, but Grandmother told her she would learn enough in the church school. "Reading and writing and mathematics are all you need. Anything else is just foolishness."

To those people in church and in school, she was Gertrude. Grandmother was quick to correct her if she tried to shorten it to the name she found in a book. "Trudy is *not* your name," she said. "Gertrude is a perfectly good name, the name of my mother. You are named after her. You will please remember that and not call yourself by that vulgar nickname. It is an insult to her memory." So Trudy remembered, as long as she was at home or at school, that her name was Gertrude, but privately she thought of herself as Trudy, and when she completed school, such as it was, and went looking for a job, she told everyone her name was Trudy Miller.

Trudy was a pretty girl. With no help from any artificial means, her black hair formed curls around her face and ringlets that cascaded down her back. She had sparkling eyes and a smile that coaxed one back. Boys paid attention to her, giving her small treats and flowers they picked in the park. She talked to them at school, but Ruby allowed no socializing if she were nearby. When she was sixteen, Trudy came to her grandmother and asked, "Tom Byers asked if he may take me to the movies Saturday. Can I go?"

"No! Absolutely not!" Ruby cried. "Boys, they're all no good. They're just after one thing, and then you'll have a baby, and you'll be a slut." The longer she talked, the more upset she became. "No! No boys!" She walked from room to room in their small home. Her voice becoming quieter as she mumbled and walked, but Trudy heard snatches and phrases which told her that Ruby's mind was still on the imaginary baby. "You'll have to give it away! Away! No baby! No more baby. No room, no room for a baby. People will talk."

Trudy tiptoed away and tried to keep out of sight until Ruby went to bed, which she often did when one of her spells came upon her. It might be several days before she arose, dressed, and rejoined the world once more. Then she frequently had her days and nights reversed, sleeping all day and roaming the house by night. When her grandmother was like that, it was difficult for Trudy to get to school and do her homework each day. Her mind was filled with worry for the old woman, and she tried to think only positive thoughts instead of worries about what was wrong with Ruby.

When Trudy completed her studies, she hoped that she might attend college, even if it was one there in St. Louis. Her intellect called out for more. More answers to questions that brewed in her mind. Friends with ideas different than her own. More learning. She loved the library, and when she could get away from Ruby for a few hours, she spent them at the magnificent place, reading books about countries around the world—studying the customs of the people in faraway places.

Looking at picture books of the people and ways of life of other civilizations, far away in either distance or years.

Ruby swept all thoughts of college out of Trudy's hopeful mind. "Get that out of your head! You've had all the studying you need. It's all foolishness." Trudy thought she might defy her grandmother. Sneak away and enroll in some classes. But even the merest hint of that sent Ruby into a panic, one of her 'spells' took over, and Trudy finally gave up the idea.

Trudy, even with her limited view of the world, realized that there must be some source of income to sustain them. The house they lived in was small and in an old but well-kept neighborhood. The furnishings were unfashionable, but must have been expensive in their time. There was always plenty to eat, purchased by Ruby on her trips to a nearby market. If not in school, Trudy accompanied her, making herself useful by searching for items and putting them in the buggy. If her guardian was in a good mood, the child could request something she wanted to eat and Ruby would comply. At other times their meals would be weird combinations of foods chosen at random for reasons known only to the old woman.

Once a month a cleaning lady came and when she left the house was if not spotless, at least sanitary and neat. Over the years, several women had the job, none of them very friendly or talkative. A nod of the head was the most communication that Trudy ever had with them. Sometimes, when Trudy wasn't in school, she overheard arguments between the adults, and when that happened it wouldn't be long before they had a new cleaning lady. Whether the old one was fired or quit, Trudy never knew.

By the time she reached her teen years Trudy wondered how they paid their bills and bought food. She was tempted to ask, but bringing up a subject like that might throw Ruby into one of her spells, and that was something Trudy didn't want. Life was much more peaceful without her grandmother pacing the house, mumbling angry monologues about anything and everything, but especially about giving babies away. Any information Trudy might have gained on their situation was kept in a small, locked room that Ruby referred to as her 'office.' "It's a secret," she would respond when asked. "You don't need to know. My secret. Mine."

When Trudy completed what the church school deemed sufficient for an education, they had a celebration, including a small ceremony with speeches by the pastor and teachers, punch and cookies, and a diploma. She said a prayer that Ruby would be well enough, calm enough, that they both could attend the simple ceremony. And later she whispered 'thank you' to the supreme being that was said to control all such things. *Thank you God, for letting us get through this evening without embarrassment.*

Trudy had given a lot of thought to what she would do at this point in her life, especially since her grandmother had squelched the idea of college. Although she wanted more freedom than what life with Ruby Miller gave her, she was reluctant to just leave the household. For one thing, she had no other place to go nor, as far as she knew, other relatives to go to. No way to support herself or home to live in. No way to earn a living. She spent weeks playing dress up with Ruby, who seemed to still regard her as a small child. "Gertrude, come play with me," she'd beg. "Let's put on all my jewelry and pretend we are princesses." And they would spend the day in this bizarre manner, reminding Trudy of a scene from Alice in Wonderland.

Finally, she came to a conclusion. "Grandmother, today I am going to go look for a job," she told Ruby one day.

"A job? Why do you want to do that?"

"To earn money." She could have added, *To feel free. To have my own money. To see what it feels like to be able to buy whatever I want.* But she held her tongue.

"You don't need money. I buy you everything you need."

Trudy was ready for that argument. "But I want to buy *you* things, like you buy me things."

Ruby was flummoxed by this answer. It had been so long ago that anyone had given her a gift she was unable to reject the idea. Turn away a present? Unheard of. "What will you buy me?" she asked with a coy smile.

"You'll have to wait and see. It's a surprise."

Ruby clamped her hands to her mouth, eyes alight. The idea of a surprise pleased her no end, so she became in favor of Trudy's plan. "A surprise," she repeated, over and over. "A surprise for me."

Until she took a stand to gain some sort of existence outside the little house on the quiet street, Trudy lived a life that almost entirely ignored the rest of the world. It revolved around her grandmother and what they would do for amusement each day. Now that her schooling was complete, such as it was, there was no amusement, no challenge, nothing to keep her interest. Ruby offered no encouragement, no praise for things she did well, no reassurance that life would offer her anything but the empty days she endured week after week. Television, books, occasionally getting away from her grandmother for a few hours at the library, those things were all she had to fill her time. She read about the world and what it contained but that was all she could do—read about it. Until she decided to push away from the nest, like a baby bird, she was bound to Ruby by invisible chains. Now she had taken those first, brave steps into that world that she had only seen on television or in the newspapers and books.

It only took Trudy three days to find a job. When you have no talents, even when you are looking for a job that takes minimal expertise, it presents a problem, especially for someone who doesn't know how to go about looking. What she did have—a pleasing appearance, pleasant personality, and adequate language skills—might not be enough to get her hired. This thought was starting to eat away at her usual positive attitude. She just might need to know more, be able to actually do something. Living with an acerbic old woman and attending a small church school that primarily studied the Bible might not be enough to help her find a job.

She spent two days walking around the neighborhood, looking for signs in the windows of various establishments. She recalled seeing such signs from time to time, squares of poster board stating 'Help Wanted,' but she had never thought much about them. The day when their meaning became apparent to her, there were none. She went inside some places where she and Grandmother had shopped and asked if they had need of a new employee. They didn't. It was beginning to occur to Trudy that not only did she not know how to do anything, she didn't even know how to ask for a job.

Trudy not only had no idea how a person asked for a job, she no clue about how to find out which stores or shops needed help unless they placed a sign in the front window. Then she recalled the few times she had the chance to read a newspaper. *Isn't there a place in the paper where people who want to hire someone put an ad?*

She stopped at the corner newsstand only a few blocks from home. There were several stacks of newspapers, not only from St. Louis, but from other large cities around the country, plus others that specialized in various interests.

"Excuse me," she said politely to the man taking money from people walking up to the open-sided shop. "Which one of these newspaper has ads for jobs?"

"You lookin' for a job?" the gruff man asked, then turned away to make change for a customer.

She pulled herself up to her full five feet and three inches before responding, "Yes. Yes I am."

He looked at her, studied her face, in between helping customers buy things from the racks and displays that surrounded him.

"Whatcha done before?"

"Nothing."

"Nothin'?" His eyebrows went up.

"No sir. Nothing."

"Why? Why ain't you worked?"

"I was in school. I didn't need to work."

"And now you do?"

"Yes sir."

Trudy just stood there while he waited on one customer after another. Small change. Small amounts of money. In between exchanges, he glanced at her, seeming to study her, trying to gauge some unknown quality. Finally there was a break in the stream of customers, and he spoke.

"Bud came to work drunk this morning. I fired him. You drink?"

"Spirits? Liquor?"

"Yeah," he answered sarcastically. "Spirits, liquor, beer. Anything that gets you soused. You drink?"

"No, sir."

"Reckon I could give you a try. Reckon if you ain't worked before, you don't have any bad habits to break."

Trudy's smile lit up her face. "Yes, sir. I mean . . . no, sir." She felt like bouncing up and down like a child with a new toy.

"Come around to the door," he said, pointing toward a door Trudy hadn't noticed. He stepped into the area behind where he usually stood and waved her through the opening. "I'll see what you can do," he said. "Put this on if you want to keep your clothes clean," he said as he handed her an apron. His tone indicated he didn't know why anyone would want to remain clean, but if you did . . .

He pointed toward another door on the back wall at the end of a wall of magazines in wire holders. "That's the toilet," he said. "Here's the prices." He pointed toward the large sign above them. "No tax, it's included in the price. Makes things easier." He pulled out an open drawer under the counter. "There's a change drawer on each side, so when it's busy we don't run over each other." He pointed to the other one. "If anyone pulls a gun on ya, give 'em the cash. They need it more than you need a bullet in ya."

A man in a business suit walked up and threw a dollar bill on the papers spread over the counter, picked up a paper and left. Trudy looked questioningly at her boss.

"That was Joseph Bellini. He's a big-wig. Don't never speak. Most papers are a dollar."

"Thank you!" she called after Bellini.

"My name is Scarfino. Joe Scarfino. What's yours?"

"Trudy Miller," she replied.

"How old are you, Trudy Miller?"

"Seventeen. Almost eighteen."

"Jesus Christ! A baby." He shook his head. "Just don't cry, Trudy Miller. Whatever anybody says, don't cry."

Trudy wondered what he thought she might cry about, but she didn't ask. She hadn't cried in many years now, since she stopped crying over the fuzzy memory of the man and woman she loved.

The afternoon went smoothly. She made change for candy bars and gum, newspapers and magazines, and Joe Scarfino gave a running comment on the customers who tossed their bills or change on top of the stacks of papers. "Magazines we keep on the back wall," he explained. "They have to ask if they want one, and they have to pay for it before you hand it to them. Else they would stand around and read it for free. We'd have a crinkled, dirty magazine that we didn't get paid for, understand?"

Sometimes a man would approach the booth, catch Joe's eye and motion toward the door with his head. Joe would move to the back of the booth and allow the stranger entrance to the narrow back space between the magazine rack and the restroom. There, Trudy noticed, they transacted some kind of business. Joe Scarfino would pull a small notebook and the stub of a pencil from his pocket and makes notes. Often, money changed hands, although Trudy didn't see anything the person might have bought. Other times Joe gave the visitor money. When that happened, the man would leave smiling and when Joe returned to stand behind the newspapers he would have a frown on his face,

In the late afternoon, the flow of customers slowed, and her boss said, "Well, Trudy Miller, you did OK." He pulled a wad of money from his pocket and peeled off some bills, handing them to her.

"Be here in the morning by seven. You get off when the customers stop buying. Wear comfortable shoes and dress for the weather. You think you can do that?"

"Yes sir. I can do that! Thank you!" She threw her arms around his chubby frame and hugged him. "Thank you Mr. Scarfino! Thank you!"

Embarrassed, he took a step back. "Just call me Joe." He cleared his throat. "And just some advice, Trudy . . . ."

"Yes, sir?"

"Don't go huggin' people. Not men, anyways. They's liable to get the wrong idea, if you get my drift."

"Oh, OK," she said. She retrieved her purse from under the counter. "See you in the morning." She left dancing, even with her feet sore from standing all day.

CHAPTER SIXTEEN

Trudy went to work the next day with stars in her eyes and wings on her feet. The fact that she had a job—a real, honest-to-goodness job—gave her self-confidence that she had never had before. She offered her smile to everyone who came to the newsstand, even those with a frown on their face or a surly attitude. "Good morning, Mr. Bellini," she said to the one customer whose name she knew. Startled, he looked up and responded "Good morning," in a surprised voice.

"You have a good day, now," she said to several customers, some of whom sidled away as if they expected her to demand something from them. Conversation, perhaps. As for her side of the business dealings, the dollar or fifty-cent exchange, the chance to speak to people she didn't know and likely never see again, was exciting—thrilling even. She'd never done anything remotely like it in her life. This was a new world for this unworldly young woman. The only people she had ever spoken to before this were the people at church and at school, a few folks at the grocery store, and the ever changing cleaning woman who came to the little house on the quiet street. The stream of customers who stopped by the newspaper stand were varied and quite different from anyone she had ever met personally before. It was like the people on the television screen had come to life to parade in front of her eyes every day, and she got to speak to them. Sometimes they spoke back.

The line of customers slowed in the late morning. Joe reached into the back of the stall and pulled a tall stool from behind a stack of boxes. "Here," he said. "Take a load off. It takes some getting used to, being on your feet all day." Gratefully, Trudy accepted.

"Did I tell you to bring a sandwich or somethin' for lunch?" he asked her.

"No. You didn't."

"Well, I shoulda. Tomorrow, you bring somethin.' And somethin' to drink. You need to keep your energy up to do this job."

She nodded her head, wishing she had thought of that herself. *I need to learn to think of things for myself. That's what people do. They don't have somebody like Grandmother or Mr. Scarfino to tell them what to do next. They have to figure it out for themselves.*

"Here," he waved his chubby hand toward the rack of candy behind them. "You get you one of these. Any kind. On the house. You want a Hershey bar? A Baby Ruth? Anything you want."

Trudy chose a Hershey Bar with almonds. She had eaten few candy bars in her lifetime, but she remembered this one. When Ruby was in a good mood while they were shopping, she bought a treat for each of them. Sometimes a chocolate bar, or a roll of Lifesavers. Ruby favored the different colored circles of candy. "You can choose a different color every time," she explained to Trudy. "And you can eat some now and save the rest for later."

That afternoon, when they had few customers, Joe said, "You done OK, kid. Better than OK for your first day." Like the day before, he pulled the wad of bills from his pocket, where he had been sticking the contents of the cash drawer every hour or so, and counted out her pay. "Tomorrow, same time," he said. "And bring your lunch, and somethin' to wet your whistle."

Trudy took one of the dollar bills and handed it back to him. "I'm going to buy a candy bar for my grandmother," she told him. "She's . . ." she searched her brain for an appropriate word to describe the old lady. "She's old, and she's special. She doesn't always understand things. I promised I'd bring her a surprise, and yesterday I forgot. I can't forget today."

Joe pressed the bill back into her hand. "You take one, no charge. It'll be part of your pay. You take one to her every day. Not many kids today thinkin' of their grandma, or thinkin' of anybody but themselves.

Yessir. It's part of your pay." He turned away, and Trudy didn't notice when he took his handkerchief from a pocket and wiped his eyes. "Getting soft," he muttered. "See you tomorrow," he said gruffly.

As days went by, Trudy's greetings to her customers began to be noted. To Joe's amazement, he heard responses, at first almost undetected, then louder and more cheerful. "Good morning, Trudy. Fine day, isn't it?" "Good morning Mr. Connelly. You're looking well today. You must be getting over your cold." "Yes, I'm feeling much better." "Miss Pointer, that dress is very flattering on you." "Why, thank you, Trudy, for noticing." "Mr. Coldwell, what a fine tie you're wearing," "My wife gave it to me." "She has good taste."

Scarfino thought the increase in business must be due to his new employee. Who would pass up a pretty girl who made your day begin with a smile? Nobody, that's who. He had something special that the newsstand three blocks farther along the thoroughfare didn't have.

One day he brought a clear glass fishbowl to work. On the side he had taped a sign that said, "Trudy's Tips". He put it at her end of the counter and put a couple of dollar bills in it, to indicate paper money, not change, was expected.

"Oh my," Trudy exclaimed when she got to work. "I don't know . . ." She put her hands to her cheeks, which had blushed a pretty rose color.

"Well, I do," Joe responded. "In all these places," he motioned around the block with his hand, "they got tip jars. Now you got one. You're as good as them."

The fish bowl was full almost to the top every day. The businessmen who picked up their morning paper were all too happy to put in a bill or two, in exchange for a cheery greeting from someone who not only remembered their name, but whatever bit of information they had shared the last time they were a customer of Scarfino's newsstand. "Good morning, Mr. Townley. Did your team win last night?" "Mr. Davis, did you get that contract signed?"

Of course, as the way things go with a pretty girl, she got offers. Offers that she didn't know how to respond to, or at least politely and firmly turn them aside. "What time do you get off work? What say I come by and take you to dinner?" "I can show you the town. A pretty girl like you doesn't need to stay home in the evening." "Do you dance? I'd like to show you some new steps."

When Joe was sure that Trudy wasn't interested in the older men who daily offered dinners and more to the young innocent who worked for him, he talked to her about them. "Be firm, Trudy. Say no right up front and let them know you mean it."

"I don't want to be snooty or seem stuck-up."

"You won't. You'll seem like a nice girl."

In her school, the female teachers had a couple of classes that touched, briefly, on those things Ruby only muttered about. The least they could say about the matter, the better they liked it. What went on between men and women was best left unspoken, and Trudy being the inquisitive person she was, had to turn elsewhere for information. She did enough reading at the library to learn the implied meaning of the term 'nice girl.' The more she read, the more she understood the tacit meanings behind Ruby's gibbering statements, made when her spells came upon her. Trudy had no one to explain sex, or pregnancy, or 'nice' girls, or being 'easy,' so the library was her go-to place when she had questions. Obviously, someone in Ruby's world had gotten pregnant and had a baby that was given away. Or perhaps, even worse, the baby was aborted—never born. Maybe it was even Ruby's daughter, Trudy's mother that she tried so hard to remember. Maybe there was more to the story than her parents being killed in an automobile accident. Now that Trudy was older, she realized that many of the things her grandmother muttered and mumbled about had to do with men and sex and pregnancy, but Trudy would never ask questions about all the things Ruby left half said.

And what Joe Scarfino was saying, without saying it, was that these men who were asking to take her to dinner or dancing or wherever wanted more from her than her company. They wanted what she was not willing to give. She had to make it plain to them so they would stop asking.

So she tried. "No, thank you." She said, "I'm not interested." Finally "Please stop asking. I'm not going to go out with you," she said firmly to those who wouldn't take a simple rejection.

One day a younger man, flashier than the businessmen who usually bought the morning paper on their way to work, started the usual come-on with a suggestion that he come by and take her to dinner. "We'll have a little fun, sugar," he said as he reached for her hand, pulling her forward where he could grasp her arm. His fingers started working their way toward her shoulder. "I can show you a really good time, sweetheart and . . ." That's as far as he got in his spiel. Joe grabbed him by the lapel of his coat and pulled him over the counter. Leaning close to the man's ear, he lowered his voice to a low growl.

"Listen here, you low-life. I don't never want to see you anywhere around here again. *Capiche?* Not around here or anyplace else where this lady might happen to be. I got friends, understand? I got friends I can call on to take care of any problems I might have, and any friend of mine takes care of this young lady as well. You lay one hand on her again, and they'll find your body in that big river that runs near here. The Mississippi gets rid of all kinds of problems we don't wanna see again. You understand what I'm sayin'?" The man nodded as vigorously as possible while being held stretched out over stacks of newspapers. "You find yourself another place to buy your newspaper." Joe shoved as he let go and the man stumbled backward, almost falling.

"Now get outta here! I see you around here again and I call my cousin to come do a job for me." The man started running and disappeared around the next corner.

Trudy didn't know what to say. She looked at Joe through a different lens. The man that had appeared to be a wise old uncle took on a completely different personae, more like some of the characters she watched on TV. The incident was never mentioned again.

Trudy enjoyed the job. She enjoyed getting out of the house, enjoyed even the simple job of making change. She started helping Joe with the scribbled records he kept of how many of which papers were sold. In slow times she straightened the magazines and refilled the candy and gum rack behind them, and generally kept the stand as neat as possible.

Her tip jar was filled every day, but after the set-to with the man in the brown suit, word got around and she no longer had unwanted invitations. Men still smiled and greeted her, but were careful to be polite and say nothing untoward. One day a nicely dressed man approached the kiosk and spoke directly to Joe. In his hand he held a business card. "Joe, I want you to know that I mean nothing uh . . . nothing bad . . .uh. This is on the up and up." Joe frowned at him. "Here is my business card." He handed it to Joe. "Our receptionist quit unexpectedly yesterday, and we really need to fill that spot. I can't think of anyone any better to take her place than Trudy. I've seen her working here for several months now, and she's just what we need. Friendly, attractive, speaks well. If she'd come to our offices—just in the next block there," he gestured, "and go to the personnel office and tell them I sent her, I'll give her a reference. It's a good place to work, opportunity for advancement. Probably better salary."

Joe looked at the card, then back up and the man, and nodded. "Thanks." He nodded again. "You're right. She's too good for this dump."

CHAPTER SEVENTEEN

Another new beginning. That's the way Trudy thought of it. The beginning of a new adventure, just as the job at the newsstand had been. She had been saving her pay and tips since she began work—hiding her money away where neither Ruby nor the sporadic cleaning lady would find it. *What could I spend it for?* There was nothing to buy that Ruby might not do away with. She admired treasures in shop windows, but it would be useless to buy a trinket or bauble only to take it home and have Ruby confiscate it, and she could think of nothing they needed for the house that they didn't already have.

Now, with the prospect for a new work environment presenting itself, she took a few bills from her stash and went shopping for clothing suitable for working in an office building. On one of her visits to the library she had read a book titled "Dress For Success" and filed away the information in the recesses of her memory, just in case she ever needed it, unlikely as the opportunity for success might be to a girl like her. Now she reckoned that was what she needed, advice on what to wear, and Ruby would be useless on such a matter. Buying herself a gray skirt, a matching gray jacket, four blouses and a sweater, along with accompanying underclothing and shoes, she felt she could blend in with the other women working in the company, at least until she could look around and get the lay of the land, so to speak.

Getting hired was the easy part. "Ken Maddox told me he was sending someone to apply for the job," said the woman in the personnel office, whose name tag identified her as Patty Watkins. "And if Ken Maddox recommends you, then you've got the job." After a few questions about her former employment, Patty said. "Come in at eight Monday morning. Report here. I have forms for you to fill out and sign, and I don't have time to do that today. Welcome to the company," she said and smiled.

Monday, the first problem to present itself had nothing to do with clothing. "What is your Social Security number?" Patty asked her as she typed in answers on a form.

Social Security number? What in the world is that? Trudy had heard the term Social Security on television, but she had no idea what it was or how it applied to her. *Where would I find that?*

"I . . uh . . ."

"Don't know it by memory?" Patty asked. "Don't worry. I don't know mine either. Do you have your card with you? No? That's OK. Bring it in tomorrow." She continued typing. The other questions were easy. Name. Address. Phone number. Age. Next of kin. Who to contact in case of emergency.

"We'll have a name tag for you in a couple of days. I'll order it today. Now, let me show you around."

Patty led her on a tour of the company, with its sets of offices leading off this way and that. "This is Norma," she said when they circled back to the front desk. "She's been filling in since the last person quit, but she has her own job to get back to when you get the hang of the place."

The cheery red-head took over showing Trudy the jobs she would be expected to do, which were simple: taking messages, whether by phone or in person. Directing people to the right department or person, answering questions or else transferring the call or visitor to someone who could help them. "You'll catch on in no-time," she told Trudy. "It's easy, really, which is the reason most people don't stay here very long. They move on up to a better job."

When Trudy went home for the day she had one important task on her mind: to see if she had a Social Security number. *If I don't, what then? How do I get one? Will it mean I can't have the job?* She worried about it on her walk home, and it was the first thing she confronted Ruby about when she got in the door.

"Grandmother, I'm supposed to have a number, a Social Security number. Everyone has one. What's mine?"

"Hmm. A number?"

"Yes. I need mine for work. I have to have one."

"Did you bring me a candy bar?"

"No, Grandmother. Remember? I don't work at the newspaper stand any more. I work at a new place. I don't have any surprises for you yet, I'll have to get some. But I need my Social Security number to get the job." Ruby looked around the room as if the card would come floating by at any minute. "I have to have the card to get the job, I can't get you any presents if I don't get the job, and I need the card to do that. Do I have one?"

"Yes," Ruby said after some thought. "I think so. Maybe it's in my office."

"Can we look for it?"

"Yes, we can do that. I want surprises," Ruby added and started toward the door that was always kept locked. Drawing a ribbon from where it was tucked into the front of her dress, she pulled out a key and unlocked the door to a room Trudy had never been inside before. As she turned the knob she paused and looked back. "You are a good child. A good granddaughter. You always remember what I like. I'm so glad I found you."

"I'm glad you did too, Grandmother, and I like to buy you treats. I'll buy you more if we find the card I need," she said, offering a little bribe to keep her grandmother on track.

They entered the tiny room, almost full with a desk, chair, and a couple of small tables nearly hidden under piles of paper. Ruby walked around to the back of the desk and sat down. She started moving papers from one pile to another without any noticeable goal in mind. She straightened and patted and lined up edges, pulling first one document then another and laying them aside. Finally, with a puzzled look on her face, she said, "What is it I'm looking for?"

"My Social Security card, Grandmother." Trudy wondered if this was going to be a fruitless search, and what she would do if it turned out she didn't have what she needed so badly.

"Oh," Ruby said. "Yes, of course." She promptly opened the top drawer of the desk and moved more papers this way and that. As Trudy was about to despair ever finding what she needed, Ruby pulled a card from the debris and Trudy got a glimpse of it. Ruby turned it this way and that. Red, white, and blue trimmed the edges. Some symbol that looked slightly like an eagle gave the impression it was government issued. Ruby studied it carefully, her forehead wrinkled in thought.

"Is that it, Grandmother?"

"I think so. I think it is."

"May I see it?"

Ruby was silent, studying the document. She placed her hands carefully around the edges, fingers just so. It took her some time to position the card just the way she wanted to before turning it toward Trudy.

Grandmother is getting odder as time goes on, Trudy thought as she watched *More particular about things being just so. The napkins folded and refolded until she is satisfied. The newspaper folded numerous times until each page is even with the next. The dishes stacked in a particular way. At least that's better than when she wanders around the house talking to herself.*

"Yes, you may," Ruby said politely and leaned forward, holding the document at arm's length. "You may see it."

Trudy wished she could hold the Social Security card, proof of her very existence. She wanted to feel the texture, run her fingers over it as Ruby had done. Even smell it, maybe. This would have to do, though. It was important that she have the number to put on her paperwork, and she didn't want to risk upsetting her grandmother, who might pull back and lock the needed number back in her desk drawer.

Taking a slip of paper from a small pad on the desk, she carefully copied the number. Reaching one finger to touch the name printed there. Gertrude Ann Miller, it said. Followed on the next line with the long set of numbers. *There I am. Real.* Somehow, in the back of her mind, Trudy had always felt that she wasn't genuine. That she was only a figment of her grandmother's imagination. How silly. Of course she was real. The United States government said she was. How much more real could she be?

CHAPTER EIGHTEEN

Trudy took to her new job as easily as she had the one at the newspaper stand. She quickly learned everybody's name and department, what to do with the minor problems presented to her, and who could solve the major ones. She offered smiles and friendly greetings to everyone and in received theirs in return.

Within a few months she had decided that the only way to advance to an occupation that was more challenging and paid more was to take classes and add further skills and knowledge to her limited talents. It took more than smiles and friendliness to get a job that paid well, although those helped.

The new thing at the office was computers. Many of the workers, both male and female, were complaining about learning the new technology that everyone was talking about, using Trudy as a sounding board as they came and went. They saw technology as something they shouldn't be expected to master. "There weren't such things as computers when I was hired," many of them said, "and I'm too old to learn to use them now," Trudy heard daily, along with "that's not in my job description." They left the impression that in truth they were afraid—afraid of not being able to learn and afraid of being left behind. Trudy wasn't afraid. She saw it as being on a level playing field with those who had worked many years in areas where she had no familiarity. Now everyone had new things to learn, not just her. She saw it as a way to get ahead.

She had been saving her money from her first days working for Joe Scarfino, and she did the same thing at her new job. Other than a cautious amount spent on improving her wardrobe, she had substantial savings in the bank account she had established as soon as she realized that the Social Security number opened more doors to things she hadn't even thought about as being possible. She could afford to attend night school or Saturday classes at the local business college and learn the new skill that everyone was either discussing or complaining about. Her problem was transportation.

It took some negotiations with Ruby to be able to spend the next several Saturdays taking driving lessons followed by car shopping, and after that computer classes at the business school. It was hard enough keeping her grandmother happy so she could go to work each day. Adding more hours or another day to be away from home was not easy. Trudy herself had made the monster by setting the standard of bribes. How much to pay to go to work each day? What to bring home to make Ruby content? A candy bar, perhaps, or a small bag of chips. A box of animal crackers was a special treat. Now that Trudy was an adult, her grandmother seemed to be growing more childlike as the years passed and the 'gifts' for Ruby's cooperation grew in size and cost. As Trudy's absence from the home was necessary for her to work her way into a better position in the company, she kept a stock of negotiable items in the trunk of her car. Small items, such as candy or a simple toy, bought an extra hour after work or a quick trip by herself on Saturday. A puzzle or doll would excuse her for a longer period.

As Ruby grew older, however, Trudy worried that the problem wasn't only that her grandmother would be angry and have a tantrum when her granddaughter wasn't present when Ruby thought she ought to be, but that Ruby was becoming unable to be left by herself all day. She no longer could be trusted to use the range. Trudy left sandwich makings and fruit for lunch, and plenty of snacks, and Ruby was easily entertained by television. Although she seldom read books any longer, she would stay enthralled by a jigsaw puzzle for hours. The time was near, however, that she would need near constant companionship.

Where Ruby had always kept to herself, seldom speaking to other people unless necessary, Trudy was the opposite. She was naturally friendly, and although Ruby had discouraged this trait, when she reached adulthood Trudy's true nature emerged. So it seemed normal to make acquaintance with the new neighbors who moved into the little white house next door.

The McClain's were a typical family. Bill McClain was a traveling salesman, away from home several nights a week as he traveled Missouri, Arkansas, and southern Illinois selling office supplies. Marsha McClain had worked in a retirement home, she told Trudy, until their daughter was born. Now she stayed home, a full-time mother to four-year-old Bella. The adorable child was the key to Ruby's cooperation.

"She's just the size Gertrude Ann was when I found her," Ruby said. "And I brought her home and she's lived with me ever since."

Trudy explained the meaning of that peculiar statement to Marsha. "My parents were killed in an accident when I was that age. Grandmother adopted me, and I've lived with her ever since."

"She loves you, I can tell," Marsha said, watching Ruby sitting on the floor playing dolls with Bella. "And she's lucky to have you, otherwise she'd be in a nursing home somewhere."

"She didn't abandon me when I needed her, and I won't abandon her now," Trudy said. "But it is becoming difficult to work and leave her alone."

With a lot of trial and error, Marsha became a life-saver. Or job-saver, more like. Trudy would see that Ruby had breakfast and was settled happily working a puzzle or watching television before she left for work. Marsha and Bella would drop in later in the morning and throughout the day.

"I'm so glad I found you," Ruby told Bella, using the same words she had years before when Trudy was small. Bella didn't know how to respond and looked to her mother for assurance.

"We're glad *we* found you, *too*," Marsha answered, watching the old woman and the small girl play dress-up or tea party or color the simple images in the coloring books Trudy kept Ruby supplied with.

Years went by quickly, and as Bella grew in stature and learning, Ruby became more childlike. It was soon obvious that she needed an adult, a caretaker of sorts, with her, or at least nearby, at all times. Trudy insisted on paying Marsha for her almost constant presence in Ruby's life. "It's like you're working at an old-age facility," Trudy said, "with only one patient."

"Yes, but I can run back home and change the laundry over from the washer to the dryer, or check on what I have cooking in the slow-cooker. It's not like I have to get in the car and drive half an hour to get to work and then drive home again in the afternoon. The hours are perfect for me, and if Bella doesn't have school, she can come over here with me. If this is a job, it's the ideal one."

So they agreed on a salary and Trudy was able to work without worrying about her grandmother. She agreed with Marsha's description of the job. It was ideal for her as well.

"Why should I call her Grandmother?" Bella said when she was approaching her teen years and challenging everything. "She's not my grandmother."

"Because she is an old lady," Marsha replied. "And now that Trudy is grown up Ruby misses having a granddaughter she can play with. You can pretend she is your grandmother, can't you? We pretend that is so because we are kind,"

They finally agreed on the term Granny Ruby as a proper term of address that satisfied both Bella and Ruby, although it soon got shortened to Granny R, which sounded cool enough to the pre-teen and slid by Ruby unnoticed.

* * *

"You ought to go," Marsha told Trudy. "You never go anywhere or do anything. Now's your chance."

"I don't know," Trudy used her finger to trace a pattern on the brochure she held in her hand. "That's a big responsibility. What if she gets one of her spells and talks crazy and paces the floor? If I'm gone . . ."

"What do you mean "what if"? She already talks crazy and wanders around the house talking about a lost baby and telling Bella she's glad she found her. She won't be any more trouble than she is right now. The dates of the trip," Marsha reached over and plucked the folded form from Trudy's fingers, "are the same time when Bill is going on a long sales trip. He's going to hit more towns and businesses than he usually does. He'll be gone all week. Bella and I will simply move over here while you're gone. Your room will be comfy for the two of us."

"You're sure?" Trudy said. "You're sure you don't mind?"

"Not a bit," her friend replied. "You've talked about going to New Orleans for years now, ever since I met you. This is a sign, getting this advertisement from the travel agency," Marsha said, waving the brightly colored leaflet. "Now go pay the money and book the tour."

When she paid for the bus tour, a large amount that left Trudy astounded that she could bring herself to spend that much, thoughts and plans concerning NOLA occupied much of her time. She had learned years ago that mentioning anything concerning the Cajun metropolis brought quick a reproach from Ruby, so now she made sure her grandmother was fully occupied with something else before discussing the upcoming trip with Marsha.

"I hope I'm able to visit the cemetery," she said. "I want to look for my parents' graves."

"Maybe there is a record of everyone buried there. That would save time."

"Yes, it would. And I'm assuming there is only one "big cemetery" as Grandmother calls it, in New Orleans. But that might not be the main problem."

"What else?"

"The names. Have you noticed that my last name is Miller and so is Grandmother's?"

111

"I hadn't thought about it."

"And my mother was Ruby's daughter who ran off with a man and had me," Trudy stated.

"OK," Marsha puzzled over the importance of this fact. "So they didn't get married. Or if they did, your mother kept her maiden name. A lot of women do that these days, especially if they have made a name for themselves in business."

"I'm guessing that, or my last name would be different. So maybe I can find my mother's grave with the last name Miller, but I wouldn't have a clue what my father's last name is."

"Hmm. You're right." They studied on this problem. "If they died together in the car wreck, they'll most likely be buried side-by-side. And they'll have the same death date, or at least be within a day or so of each other."

"Yes!" Trudy smiled. "I may have to look at a lot of graves to find them, but I do have some sort of clue. The common death date."

As the bus tour grew closer, Trudy's enthusiasm for the adventure grew. At last she would visit the city of her birth, the place she had lived with her parents for the first few years of her life. Maybe, just maybe, seeing the places she had not visited in over thirty years would bring back more memories— not only memories of the city like the ones that lingered in the recesses of her mind, but memories of her parents, the two people she had loved so much. She might have forgotten their appearance over the years, or their names, but she hadn't forgotten how she felt. She hadn't forgotten how safe she felt with them, and she had blurry memories of bedtime stories being read from a colorful book and the scent of the woman who sat beside her and read aloud about a rabbit and his friends.

She spent the last couple of weeks before the scheduled departure working as diligently at her job as ever, making calls, correcting records, transferring information to other departments. Ruby was quieter than usual, and Trudy wondered if she had gotten wind, somehow, that her granddaughter was planning an escape, if only briefly, from the house they shared. But Trudy wasn't going to mention it. Let Ruby live in ignorant bliss as long as possible.

Ruby dozed off in front of the television regularly, awaking with a jerk and commenting on the program playing out on the screen.

"Does she ever go to the doctor?" Marsha asked.

"She used to," Trudy answered. "I'd come home from school and she'd say things like 'I saw the doctor today. He says I'm in good shape." Sometimes she'd say, "The doctor says I'm normal and everyone else is crazy."

"What's your doctor's name?" Trudy would ask Ruby. "How do you get to his office?"

"His name . . . it's . . ." I forget, Ruby would say. An hour or so later she would say, "Doctor Pine. That's his name. I remembered. I take a taxi when I go see him." And Trudy would plan to get an appointment with Dr. Pine to talk about Ruby's mental condition, but time would pass and Trudy, busy with her own life, would drop the idea of meeting him.

From time to time the phone would ring and Ruby would have a strange-sounding conversation with somebody she obviously knew. "I'm doing fine," she say. "Yes, I have plenty to eat. I went to the market and bought lots of groceries. No, I don't need anything, thank you for calling. Thank you for checking on me."

When Trudy asked, "Who were you talking to?" Ruby would challenge her.

"That's rude," she'd say. "That was my phone call. It was private. You don't need to know. It's not any of your business." But she would bring the conversation back up later. "That was my attorney on the phone. He takes care of me. He pays my bills." If Trudy tried to push for more information Ruby returned to her standard answer: "That was my phone call. It was private. It's none of your business."

From those hints and others like them, Trudy surmised that Ruby's livelihood was managed by some kind of trust, by an attorney who furnished enough money so that she and Ruby could live well but not extravagantly. The housecleaner that came monthly must be managed from the same trust. Both she and Ruby were safe, dry, clean, and fed, so whatever the legal arrangement was, it was working. Where did the trust come from? It could have been established by Ruby's parents, or perhaps it was insurance money from the wreck that killed Ruby's daughter. Maybe it was even in Trudy's name—insurance on her mother that was supporting them.

Time grew closer for the trip. Several weeks earlier Trudy had requested vacation time off from work. She wanted everything to be in good shape there as well as at home. Ruby was unusually easy to manage, never demanding something to eat they didn't have nor arguing about whether it was indeed time to eat or go to bed. "Age," Marsha said, "She is growing older and calmer. She remembers the way we did things yesterday or last week and goes along with whatever I suggest."

Trudy had taken to seeing Ruby to bed each night, pulling the sheet up over her grandmother and saying goodnight to her, as the older woman once did for her. "Goodnight, Grandmother," she said as she reached to turn off the bedside lamp.

"Goodnight, Gertrude Ann. I love you." She grasped Trudy's hand as she said it and gave it a squeeze.

"I love you too, Grandmother," Trudy replied, squeezing back, and was surprised to realize that tears had formed in her eyes as she admitted to herself how lucky she was to have had Ruby in her life when her parents died. Without Ruby she would have been alone.

The next morning, Trudy was dressed for work and had breakfast on the table. When she opened Ruby's bedroom door she expected to see the old woman struggling with her clothing, as was typical, but the motionless figure in the bed warned her.

"Grandmother?" she said as she entered the room, but there was no response. "Oh, Grandmother," she sighed and sat down beside the still body, tears filling her eyes.

CHAPTER NINETEEN

Lexi was happy she had come to New Orleans. Things weren't exactly working out as she had hoped, but then she hadn't had any specific idea of what the city, so different from her hometown in west Texas, would be like that she couldn't say she was disappointed. It's just that neither was NOLA offering her a spot that was hers, or a career, or . . . anything.

She was still sleeping on the pull-out bed in Jon and Carlton's guest room slash office. They had welcomed her just as Barry and Chad said they would, telling her she could stay as long as she needed, but Lexi felt like she was intruding on their peaceful lifestyle. It couldn't be easy to accommodate another person in their small but fashionable apartment.

She tried to be a good guest, staying out of the way as they scurried each morning to get off to work. Carlton was an attorney with a large law firm, working mostly, he explained, on contract law. Jon was a photographer. He was gone on various 'shoots' all day, and when he had time to spare he worked on building his collection of photos he hoped to turn into a book someday.

Lexi kept quiet until they left, running the vacuum and unloading the dishwasher while her hosts were at work. After a couple of days, they came home to a cooked meal served on a lovely imaginative 'tablescape,' as Lexi called it.

"Lexi, honey, this is delicious," Jon said. "You ought to be able to find a job doing just this," he said as he took another bite.

"But there are lots of good cooks here in New Orleans. Many much better than I am."

"True that," Carlton replied, using the peculiar phrasing common to New Orleans. "You are good, don't get me wrong, but you hit the nail on the head. There are lots of good cooks in The Big Easy. It will be hard to find a job in that field."

"And I don't cook Cajun," Lexi said, pushing her salad around with her fork.

"Maybe not, but everything you do make is delicious. This salad dressing is special."

"Thanks. I made it any time we provided green salad on one of our setups. I was kind of known for that dressing."

A week went by. She went to every café and restaurant she could find. Even looking for a job was harder than she thought it would be. Her first thought was to search the local newspaper for job openings. She soon found that the major paper, the *Times-Picayune,* was not published every day, and when she finally caught on and started searching on the appropriate days, there were no listings for anything suitable. There were plenty of ads for people to deliver food, but she didn't think those would be profitable, since she didn't know her way around town and would spend more on gas than she would make. Besides, that wasn't what she was looking for at all.

"Tonight, we're taking you out to eat," Carlton said one morning as he left for work. "You've been cooking for us. Now we're going to feed you."

Jon juggled a camera bag and a notebook. "We'll take you to one of our favorite places."

"Do I need to dress up?" Lexi asked.

"Nah," Carlton said as he slipped out the door. "It's like eating with family."

Lexi didn't know what to expect, perhaps something like the brightly lit, noisy, establishments, full of music and laughter, that were so plentiful in New Orleans. When they arrived at Simon's Place, she was surprised at the low-key atmosphere. There were no bright neon lights, no crowds wandering in and out among the businesses in the neighborhood. It was nothing like what she had seen of the famous tourist district so far. But neither was it formal and reserved. It was just like Carlton had described it: "Like eating with family."

The aroma of Cajun spices wafted through the air as they walked from the parking spot to the restaurant. "I'm glad I called for reservations," Jon said as they waited to be seated. "Simon is beginning to bring in the crowds."

"He deserves it," Carlton replied. "The food is excellent and the prices are much more reasonable than most of the spots everyone has heard of."

They were seated quickly and served with such speed Lexi was surprised. Her hosts ordered for her. "Honey, you've got to try everything," Jon said. "How do you know what you like if you've never tried it? She'll have the New Orleans Sampler," he told the waitress.

Lexi looked around the large room. It wasn't elegant, but she hadn't been expecting glamour in a place described as 'like home.' It reminded her of a west Texas country diner, but larger and dressed up with antiques. It had wide wooden plank flooring softly gleaming in the lamplight, antique sideboards, mirrors, and paintings that all looked to be older than the building itself. The bus-boys hustled to keep tables cleared for the next set of diners who stood by the door waiting for a place to sit.

"This was delicious," Lexi said as she leaned back in her chair. "I'd be fat in no time if I had this to eat every day."

"We make up for it by eating salads for a couple of days after a meal like this," Jon told her.

"Maybe you can make your special salad dressing for us," Carlton added. "I'd love to try it."

Lexi noticed a tall African-American man making his way across the dining room, stopping at every table to greet the diners. He looked more like a football player than a restaurateur. When he reached their table his broad grin widened. "Jon! Carlton! How did you gentleman like your meal tonight? And Miss Lady, welcome to Simon's Place. I hope you enjoyed everything."

"Simon, I always enjoy a meal at your establishment," Carlton answered. "It was delicious, as usual."

"Simon," Jon said, "We'd like you to meet our adopted niece—Lexi Hobart. She has just moved here from west Texas and is staying with us while she looks for a job."

"Very pleased to meet you, Lexi. What kind of job are you looking for?"

"In Texas I worked for a catering company. We prepared meals for groups of people, and decorated the room where the event would be held. Or at least the tables."

"Ah. . .This is something I have an interest in. I'd like to know more," Simon said. "Gentlemen," he looked at Jon and Carlton, "may I sit with you for a while and ask your houseguest some questions?"

"Certainly, Simon," the men said. "Of course."

Simon pulled out the fourth chair at the table and sat down next to Lexi. "Now, tell me more."

For the next half hour, Simon listened and asked questions about every issue included in the subject of catering. Did they provide the venue? How many choices did the guests have for the entrée? How much decorating, if any, did they do? Did she know how they figured cost?

"I'm so sorry, *mon ami*, for taking over your party," Simon said. "Forgive me, please." He signaled to the waitress who was watching from nearby. "Estelle, desert for these good people. On the house!" He turned back to Lexi. "I need to talk to you more." He stood up and pushed his chair back under the table.

Lexi hardly knew what to say. "Of course, Mr. . . . ."

"Simon. Just Simon. Would it be possible for you come back tomorrow and visit with me? I'm sure I'll think of a hundred things I should have asked you."

Lexi was stunned. "I . . . I . . . certainly. I can do that if somebody will draw me a map of how to get here, that is."

"I have this big room," Simon gestured toward the double doors at the back of the room, "that I thought I needed for when business is busy and this room is full. I planned and worried about it, and when I finally got the space, I find that I don't use it like I thought I would. When I open it for customers, it takes more wait-staff to service it, and then if it doesn't fill up, if only one or two tables are used, it's hard to juggle. The waiter or waitress has to run back and forth between the rooms. I'm thinking I ought to offer it for groups. People having a party of some kind."

"Exactly!" Lexi said. "We didn't have a place of our own to host the events, although we wished that we did. We just catered to other venues."

"You carried food into other places?" Simon frowned. "And served it there?"

"Sometimes. If it was at a place that served food already, but the customer wanted more than was offered there, wanted it more special than they provided, we didn't do the meal, but did something more, like the decorations and a fancy cake, sometimes party favors if it was a really special affair. Usually we did events at places like meeting halls or churches. Then we provided everything."

"Yes, I really want to talk to you. Would nine o'clock be too early for you?"

"No, not at all," Lexi answered. "Unless I get lost trying to find my way. I don't have GPS in my car."

"I'll give you my phone number and if you get lost you can call me and I'll come find you." Simon grinned. "If you're a little late, don't worry. These days we're busy at home first thing, getting our son off to school and with the new baby and all."

"That's right," Jon said. "I had forgotten about the expected addition to your family. Do you have a daughter or another son?"

"A daughter," Simon said. "Ramona. She's as pretty as her mother." He accepted their congratulations with a broad smile. "See you in the morning," he told Lexi as he went back into the kitchen.

* * *

Lexi was bubbling with enthusiasm the next day as she drove across the city. Traffic was heavy with throngs of tourists exploring the city and New Orleans residents making their way to work. Not for the first time since she had moved to this larger town, she wished she had GPS in her vehicle, but at the time she bought her car she had thought it an unnecessary expense in the Texas town where she knew her way around. NOLA was a different thing altogether.

Maybe this will lead to a job. If not with Simon, then perhaps he can tell me places to look. I can't stay with Jon and Carlton forever. I have stayed too long as it is.

It was ten minutes after nine when she reached Simon's Place. Parking was relatively easy to find this early in the day. She rushed into the empty dining room, full of apologies.

"I'm so sorry I'm late," she said to the Simon, who was standing by the door, drinking a cup of coffee. "Traffic was worse than I thought it would be. I should have left earlier."

"That's OK," Simon replied. "I didn't realize you had to come from across town. I thought you lived around here somewhere."

"I'm staying with Jon and Carlton until I get a job." she answered. "I'll have to find my own place then."

"They're good folks," Simon said. "They've been eating with me ever since I opened this place. I met them when I worked at another restaurant—a popular spot with tourists. When it became obvious that I'd never be anything but an assistant chef there, I saved my money and rented something I could afford." He gestured around the quiet room. "I've been building a following ever since. It may not be in the most popular tourist area in town, but it's doing well for me. Everything always turns out for the best if you have faith. As least that's what my mother has told me since I was a kid." He turned and poured himself more black brew from a pot sitting behind the counter. "Can I get you something to drink? Coffee? Tea?"

"No, thank you. Maybe later."

"Then let me show you the space I'm wanting to utilize," Simon said as he walked toward the back of the room. Large double doors led into another area. He opened them wide and went to a panel where he began turning on lights. "Plenty of room, as you can see," he said, walking around the space. "Outside entry." He waved his hand toward street side. "Back room for storage, small office, restrooms." He gestured toward the back of the building. "I thought I just had to have this space, and now that I do . . ." He shook his head. "I'm not using it. The potential is there, I know it is, but I just can't seem to . . ." His words trailed off.

He pulled a chair from a table for four. "Have a seat." He claimed a chair across from her and sat down. "Tell me again what you did where you lived in Texas. Tell me about catering. Tell me about banquets and parties."

Lexi talked and answered questions for the next hour. Simon halted her and went to get himself more coffee. "You must be dry by now," he said. "What do you want to drink?"

When he came back he was bearing a tray with not only her cola and his steaming cup, but two enormous cinnamon rolls, forks, and large white linen napkins. He set it on their table, then went back to shut the doors between the area they were in and the main part of Simon's Place, which was beginning to fill with customers, most of whom were straining trying to see who was with Simon in the room they seldom saw into. "Nosy people," Simon muttered as he closed the doors.

"You've given me a lot to think about," he said as he cut into the steaming twist of sugary pastry in front of him. "A lot." He took a bite and stared off into space. "First," he said, and paused, "is to figure out who my customers will be. I thought that would be an easy question to answer, but it's not."

"Who do you *want* them to be?" Lexi asked. "Do you want to carry food to other venues, or do you want to bring them in to eat here, or both?"

"I want them to eat here. I don't want to serve people at other locations."

"OK. That's a start. But would you prepare food in large quantities for pick-up?"

"Yes. That's fine. We already do that. It's what led my thinking along these lines. But I don't want to do what your employers did." He shook his head and took a sip of coffee. "I don't want to go set up somewhere. I want to keep it all here." He cut another bite of cinnamon roll. "And . . ." he chewed and swallowed, "I have to figure out how to get those customers here."

"And who they will be," Lexi said. "Who would want to have a big dinner and need a place to do it?"

"People who want to have a party . . . a celebration of some sort . . . and they don't have room at home."

"Or don't want to cook at home," Lexi continued, "or don't have another place, like their church or another hall of some sort, or . . .." She trailed off, taking another forkful of the sugary roll, her mind gathering possibilities.

"Yes. Lots of people fit that description," Simon added. He pushed back in his chair and stared into space. "Birthday parties, anniversaries . . ."

"Baby showers, retirement parties," Lexi added.

Simon brought himself back to the present. "So how do I find these people?"

"Well," Lexi was the one to stare into space. "There's lots of ways. It depends on how much you want to spend and how hard you want to work."

"Name some."

"Most expensive, television ads. Newspaper and radio ads. Billboards."

"Too big," Simon said. "Smaller. This is just one place. One room. All that sounds like overkill."

"I agree," Lexi said. "I'd say start with flyers. You can have different ones printed with different messages depending on where you are going to distribute them. We had good results with flyers," she said. "Back in Texas that is."

"Uh-huh. More personal, maybe."

"Yes. Meet people. Introduce yourself. Hand them out." Lexi's mind was turning over with possibilities. "And with flyers, they're cheap enough that you can change them depending on what group you are trying to reach. Even have several different kinds. You could mail them out. I imagine there are mailing lists to be had."

They spent the next hour discussing possibilities when Simon came back to the present with a start. "I've got to go see that the kitchen is running smoothly. Lunch is always busy." He studied the young woman sitting across from him. "And that's another problem. I don't have the time to spend doing what will have to be done to get this underway. And without working with it, doing something, I'll still be sitting here with this unused space next month and next year and . . ." He stopped talking and studied Lexi. "You've got the job, if you want it."

"The job?" Lexi's voice squeaked.

"The job of hostess, or party manager or . . . we'll have to think of a title," Simon said. "You come up with the ideas. Run them by me. When I say OK, you do them. Let me run Simon's Place. You run this new business." When he told her what her salary would be, she almost squeaked again. It was more than she had made in her previous employment. Plenty enough to rent her own place and pay the bills.

"Let me get this straight," she said. "I get paid for coming up with advertising, getting people in here—groups of people—and managing the events or parties or whatever?"

"That's right. But I want to OK everything, at least to begin with. I want to be involved—part of whatever is happening."

"And you take care of the food and the service."

"Yes. I take care of the food. You take care of décor, finding customers, all that stuff."

"Back in Texas, I cooked some of what we served. Will I do that here?"

"No. I have cooks for that. No cooking for you. In fact . . ." he looked off into space again. "I'll sweeten the deal. In addition to your salary, you eat here free. Every day. Whatever you want to eat. Just as long as it's something already on the menu. That will save you some time and money."

"Yes. Time will be a factor," Lexi said. "I'll have to leave earlier, or else find a quicker way across town. I don't like to be late to work."

"Are you going to continue living with Carlton and Jon?"

"Well, no. Now that you mention it. I always intended to find a place of my own as soon as I got a job." With a start, she realized that was exactly what had happened. She had a job, one that offered an interesting new twist on what she had been doing for several years. Now she had a new challenge, not only starting a new business for Simon, but also finding place to live. "Now I need to take some time to find an apartment to rent. I don't know where to even look for a place I can afford."

Simon stood up. "I think I can help you with that," he said. "My cousin Addie has a couple of apartments for rent just down the street.

You can walk to work." He gathered up the dishes they had used and put them back on the tray. "And I'll guarantee that you can afford it."

CHAPTER TWENTY

Abner let the book slip from his fingers and lay in his lap. It wasn't that he was uninterested in the subject matter—spells and rituals for everyday use—but it was a lazy day and he kept drifting off to sleep. The rain had let up a bit, but there were still no customers on the street. The weather that had swept in when the hurricane veered to the east left New Orleans gray and stormy. *I should have left the closed sign up,* Abner thought. *Nobody is going to be out and about today.*

But it was just as pleasant, sitting here in the shop in this big leather chair that used to be in the den of his home in the Garden District, as it would have been in the living room of this new abode. Abner ran his hand over the soft texture. *I just might have Pernell or T. Wayne move this chair into the living room here. It's the most comfortable seat I've ever had. Maybe I don't want to sell it.* He watched the water form beads and run down the big plate glass windows of his shop. *A sure-fire way to put someone to sleep, Mesmerizing. Not that I've had any problem sleeping since I moved here.*

Suddenly a figure dashed to the door and opened it, causing the bells hanging from a loop of ribbon to jingle, adding the sound of gaiety to the room.

"Good morning. I'm surprised to see you open."

"Pernell. What are you doing out in this weather? Keeping busy? I imagine lots of folks take a taxi when it rains."

"Probably, but I'm not a taxi driver anymore."

"You aren't? I saw you were driving a van instead of the cab, but I thought that was just to have room to carry boxes for me."

"No sir. I just got tired of being a taxi driver." He used his hands to brush the droplets of water from his hair. He removed the tan coat he was wearing and hung it on the rack by the front door. "But I was driving the van to have room to move boxes for you."

"Have a seat, then," Abner said, gesturing to the matching brown leather chair that sat a few feet away. "These two chairs used to sit on either side of a fireplace that I wish we had here right now. A fire would feel pretty good today." He took the book from his lap and stuck a business card in the pages and closed it. "Does this mean I can't hire you to move things for me any longer?"

"Not at all. I'd rather do that than haul passengers around." He looked over at the elderly man. "I quit that job some time back. I've been fetching and carrying strictly for you for a while now."

"I can't provide enough business to support you, you know. I have this place full for now. I have to sell some before adding anything else."

"I know. I don't expect you to. The job as a cab driver was just to have something to do, more than to make money."

"Independently wealthy, are you?"

Pernell laughed. "Not hardly, but I have enough."

Silence lay between them. Abner wanted to ask, but wouldn't. It wasn't his business, he supposed.

Finally, Pernell, sensing the old man's curiosity, sighed. "See, it's like this. Last year I got back to the States from Afghanistan. Did two tours of duty over there. Saw a lot of stuff I didn't want to remember but couldn't forget."

Again, silence filled the room.

"My best buddy over there, he was from New Orleans," Pernell finally said. "He didn't come back."

The feeling of grief, as if it were a living, breathing person, sat with them.

"He talked about this city all the time. The good. The bad." Pernell leaned forward and rested his elbow on his knees. "He wanted to see it again. To hear the music and smell the food. He wanted to dance and sing. See Mardi Gras one more time." He shook his head.

"And there was a girl. A woman he had met years before. He wanted to see if he could find her again." He leaned back into the soft plush leather as he ran his hand over his face. "He couldn't shake her memory. Any time he was in the States he'd come here and look for her, but he could never find her. He thought if he just looked hard enough . . ."

Both men sat unspeaking, contemplating the unfairness of war.

"So when I got patched up to where I could take care of myself," Pernell said, taking a deep breath, "I thought I'd come see if this city was all he had said it was. If he couldn't enjoy it, I'd enjoy it for him."

"And have you been?" Abner asked. "Enjoying it for him?"

"In a way, I guess I have. Not the way lots of folks enjoy New Orleans. I haven't been partying. Drinking. Carousing. Not that. But then, that's not the way he would have enjoyed it either." He sat staring into nothing. "But I have been looking and listening. Learning what makes the city so special. Enjoying in my own way, I guess."

Thunder rolled through the air, and the two men sat listening to the rain pattering against the glass. After a minute, Pernell started talking again. "I took the job driving a taxi. I could work when I wanted. Lay off when I didn't. See New Orleans from top to bottom. Learn my way around. It was an easy job. No thought required beyond how to get from here to there, and these days a GPS does that for you. And it gave me time. Time to think." He stared at a spot in the ceiling. "Time to write."

"Write?"

"Stories." Pernell said, and Abner thought he wasn't going to say any more, but finally he explained. "About the war. About what I had seen. And when I got all that out of my system, ridded myself of it, mostly, I started remembering all the stories my buddy had told me about New Orleans, so I started writing those. I couldn't think of another way to honor him, so I decided to preserve those memories he had shared with me. Put them down so they wouldn't die with him. Thomas might be gone, but his reminiscences would live on."

Pernell sighed. "He didn't leave any family, but he left that." He picked at the knee of his pants, as if picking off bits of lint from the clean surface. "As long as I can do that for him, it won't be like he died in vain. Maybe sometime, somewhere, someone will read them and he'll live on."

Abner wanted to ask Pernell if *he* had family somewhere, somebody who would read his stories and remember him when he was gone, but he hesitated. One never knew where ghosts were hiding, ready to jump out when least expected. But as if he intuited the old man's curiosity, the soldier began to talk again.

"My parents are gone, but I have sisters who want me to come to them. If I did, they'd wart me to death. 'Pernell, you're too thin. Pernell are you getting enough sleep? Pernell, why don't you do this, or that.' Worrying about me.

"Here, I can eat and sleep and work when I feel like it. And I'm getting better. Much better. I'm not as jumpy as I was when I first got out of the hospital. And I sleep most nights." He relaxed into the soft leather that cocooned him. "And I enjoy working for you." He looked at Abner.

"I enjoy looking at all the things you have collected from around the world. I like the stories you tell about what they are and where you found them. The magic they are supposed to have keeps my mind turning with 'what-ifs.' It makes me want to write about them as well— about the magic. And it makes me sad to think that these endless, stupid wars that men create for no sensible reason destroy priceless artifacts around the world. It's up to men like you to rescue and preserve these items else they will be gone, just like Thomas and his memories would be gone if I don't save them, all because men fight wars to prove what? That they are mightier than the next fellow?"

They sat in silence once more, the words that had been spoken bouncing around the room and echoing in their minds.

"These are treasures," Abner finally said, gesturing around the room. "My treasures." His eyes had a sheen of tears that had not formed enough moisture to roll down his cheeks yet. "It is my dearest hope that I can find new homes for them before my time in this incarnation is finished." He looked around. "There is somebody for each item in these rooms. There is something . . . magic or spirits . . . I don't know what . . . but something that led me to buy them, and now those spirits will put the proper buyer with the right item for them. And you have a part in it."

"Me?" Pernell's eyebrows raised. "How so? You are the one who saved them."

"Ah, but I was lost as well, you see. Locked into my prison of old age, just as my possessions were locked into the boxes that held them prisoner. I was unable to do anything but sit and dream, and even my dreams were dying in the jail of mediocrity. Without you—you and T. Wayne, I would not have been able to accomplish what I have done so far.

"My move here has set me free again. Oh, old age is still around me, knocking on my door, but with the help of my assistants, here I am. Free to see my dreams come to fruition. Each time someone buys one of my treasures I rejoice that it has broken from the prison of a box in a desolate storage room, unseen, unloved. That it has a new home with someone who will appreciate its specialness, its magic, if you will." He leaned his head against the back of the chair. "If you hadn't come along, perhaps I would not have been able to accomplish what I have done so far. The spirits sent you to me. I am sure of it."

"I am happy to have been of help," Pernell said. "and speaking of our young friend, I am concerned about T. Wayne. Do you know anything about him?"

"Nothing," Abner replied. "But I, too, am concerned. He's running from something, of that I am sure, but I'm afraid to push for information. He is liable to run again and be lost from me. At least now he has food to eat, and a safe place to stay."

"He is like the young boys I saw in Afghanistan. No home. No family. Living on the streets."

"He's sleeping here," Abner gestured toward the back of the building. "in one of the empty apartments. I told him I knew where he was spending his nights, but I don't want to press too hard. At least I can see that he is fed each day, and for now he is sleeping inside, protected from the weather."

"He's smart, I can see that. He learns quickly."

"Yes, he is. He absorbs everything I tell him and wants to know more."

"He would probably do well in school."

"I would like to know more about why he is alone, but I can't ask."

"He opened up to me just a little," Pernell said.

"Oh?"

"We were going to get a load for you. It was the time you sent the two of us."

"Yes, I remember."

"He said his grandmother had died and Children's Protective Services wanted to put him in a foster home."

"And he ran."

"I assume so." Pernell shook his head. "And if we press too hard, he'll run again."

"Yes, I think so.

"So what do we do?"

"Be easy. Be careful. Don't frighten him away. At least now he's safe and well-fed."

"I hope we can come up with something to save him before it's too late. Before some unscrupulous person takes advantage of him. Before he loses so much time living on the street that he can't catch up in school."

"Yes, yet I see the problem of trying to cage him," Abner said.

Again silence filled the room with its presence.

"Did you . . .?" Pernell began.

"Yes?"

"Did you say there was an empty apartment here?"

"There are two. Are you looking for a place?"

"Yes, I am. Where I am living now has become increasingly noisy. Too noisy for me to concentrate on my writing. Too noisy to sleep at night." He shifted in his chair. "The people in the next apartment fight day and night. Children run up and down the stairs. I can yell at the fighting couple to quieten it down, but I can't get on to children just for being children. It seems like this would be an ideal place to live."

"It is, that is, it is for me. I can't speak for you. Would you like to see?"

"Yes, I would. Do you have keys?"

"No," Abner replied as he struggled up from the cushy seat. "But I understand that they are similar to mine, and you can look across the courtyard at the outside of one, and upstairs over me at the other. If you are interested, I'm sure Addie would come show you."

"And it's quiet here, right?"

"Yes. Quiet and peaceful." He went to the door to the street and turned the sign over from Open to Closed. His gnarled hands clicked two sets of locks into place. "Come, we'll go see." He grasped his cane and led the way through the storeroom and into his kitchen.

"I haven't seen the inside of either of the apartments. I'm assuming they are similar to this." He opened the French doors leading to the courtyard. "The ground level unit just across the way," he pointed with the cane that steadied him when he walked, and the snake wrapped around it looked as if it readjusted itself, "it has a tenant now. A young

133

woman who works at Simon's Place. She's very quiet. You'd never know she's there.

"The apartment above her is empty. That's where T. Wayne has been hiding out. He sleeps there. I should make him leave, but I can't bring myself to do it.

"And above here," Abner pointed at the ceiling. "is another empty apartment. It's slightly larger than these other three. It extends above the shop, you see, and has two bedrooms and baths."

"I wouldn't need that just for me," Pernell said. "That upstairs unit across the courtyard looks perfect. Quiet," he said, looking around, "Peaceful. No yelling and screaming. I could probably sit and work out here on nice days."

"Indeed you could. I've been eating breakfast outside."

"And I'd be handy if you needed me for anything," Pernell said.

"Yes. Handy for both of us. It must be unlocked, since T. Wayne has been hiding in there for weeks. Go on and take a look—see what you think."

CHAPTER TWENTY-ONE

"Thanks for meeting me like this," Pernell said.

"I don't mind at all," Addie replied. "My husband will be off work soon, and we had planned to meet here for dinner anyway, so this was convenient for me. But I'm glad it stopped raining before I got out and about."

They were sitting at a table in Simon's Place, which was not as busy as usual, due to the inclement weather. The waitress set glasses in front of each. "Thanks, Estelle," Addie said. "I'll wait to order when Parker gets here." She turned back to Pernell. "So you want to rent an apartment in Broussard Court? Amazingly, I've rented almost all of them without even trying. People tell me that my great-aunt always said that the spirits would send her the person who needed to live there."

"I helped Abner Crowbridge move in," Pernell said, "so I got a look at the place then and thought that it looks like a peaceful place to live."

"It is. Mr. Crowbridge occupies a lot of it, what with the apartment to live in and two shops full of merchandise to sell."

"And he says he still has more to come after he sells a bit to make room."

"He seems to like it there, and I'm glad to have him, both in the apartment and in the shops."

"Everything fits him like a glove. He really likes it there."

"Now we have Lexi Hobart in the ground floor apartment across from Mr. Crowbridge. She works for Simon. They're going into an expansion of this business," she said as she gestured toward the rear of the room.

"Really?" Pernell said, then took a sip of his iced tea. "Expanding how?"

"Using the other room back there," she indicated with a nod of her head, "for parties and banquets and such. They've made up fliers and contacted people who might be interested. They have a customer already."

"That quick, huh?"

"Yes. A tour bus company had a cancellation. That is, the place they were taking the people on the tour had to cancel at the last minute due to a fire in the kitchen. The way I understand it, Lexi showed up handing out fliers just at the right time, so they have a room full of people back there—or will shortly."

"Someone's misfortune was Simon's gain."

"Exactly," Addie agreed. "So you want to rent an apartment. Which one did you chose?"

"The one bedroom. The other one is nice, I'm sure, but I don't need two bedrooms for just one person."

"I thought you'd pick that one. You said you wanted a quiet place to write?"

"Yes. The apartment I'm in now gets noisier by the day. I can't take it any longer."

"The woman who used to live there, Evie, she wrote too. She lived there for some time, a couple of years I think. Madame was still alive when she moved in, and she stayed until she got married and moved to his place."

"Do I need to fill out a contract?" Pernell asked.

"Yes. I have one here," Addie said and pulled it out of her oversized bag. Together, they read the terms and filled out some blanks with his name and phone number. He was about to sign when a man walked up.

"Good evening." He extended his hand toward Pernell. "I understand you're moving into Broussard Court. I'm Parker, Addie's husband. Welcome to the neighborhood."

Pernell stood and shook hands. "Pernell Roberts. Pleased to meet you."

"Pernell Roberts, huh, "Parker said. "I know that name. Are you kin to the actor?"

Pernell laughed. "No. My mother was a fan of the television show, *Bonanza*. Never missed an episode. The story goes that she went into labor with me and refused to go to the hospital until she watched the end of the episode. She had a little crush on Adam Cartwright, my father told me, and with our last name being Roberts, it was like it was ordained to name me Pernell. I'm just lucky she wasn't taken with Dan Blocker or I might have been called Hoss."

They all laughed. "Sit down, you two," Addie said. "Let's order. I'm starving."

"You're always starving," her husband said.

"I'm eating for two," Addie said, patting her rounded tummy. "I have to keep our baby fed." She looked around the room. "Estelle," she called to the waitress. "We're ready to order."

"You need a menu?" Estelle asked Pernell when she walked up.

"No, I think I know everything Simon serves.

When they all had ordered, Pernell looked toward the entry. "I hoped T. Wayne would show up. I'm going to hire him to help me move the few things I have. I try to have an excuse to keep an eye on him."

"Mr. Crowbridge said that he thinks T. Wayne is sleeping in the apartment you're renting."

"I know. He told me that as well," Pernell said. "I wish there was some way I could help T. Wayne without scaring him away. If he thinks he's going to get in trouble, he's liable to disappear."

"He seems like a good kid," Addie said. "A hard worker, and smart."

"He is," Pernell said. "But he's running from something."

"Or someone."

Just then the subject of their conversation walked up. "Ah, T. Wayne," Pernell said. "I was hoping you'd be by here this evening."

"Mr. Crowbridge told me you needed me," the boy said. "He told me to come over here." He looked at Addie and Parker suspiciously.

"I've just rented an apartment in Broussard Court," Pernell said. "Could you help me move my things from my place?"

"Sure thing!"

"Sit down and have something to eat with us while I finish my meal." The boy looked around at the group. "This is the lady who owns Broussard Court and her husband," Pernell explained. "I was filling out the rental contract."

"Pleased to meet you, T. Wayne," Parker said, and Addie murmured her agreement.

"Evenin,' T. Wayne," Estelle said as she walked up. "We got some good soup tonight. Vegetable beef. You want a bowl?"

The boy hesitated and Pernell spoke up. "Bring him a bowl, please. And a glass of milk to go with it. Put it on my ticket."

"Yessir. I'll sure do that."

A short while later the party finished eating and stood to leave. At the same time, a couple who had been seated several tables away also stood and started toward the door.

"Thomas!" the woman said, coming to a stop a few feet away. "I've been looking for you!"

T. Wayne flinched, a frightened look on his face. Pernell put his arm around the boy's shoulders, his hand firmly halting any possible motion toward escape. "And you are . . .?"

"Althea Simpson," the woman replied. "I'm a caseworker for Children's Protective Services. When Thomas's grandmother died I located a foster home that would take him, but when I returned to the apartment, where he was supposed to be waiting for me . . ." she glared at T. Wayne, "he was gone. The neighbors had no idea where he was. We've been looking for him ever since." She looked to T. Wayne

138

again. "That wasn't the right thing to do, Thomas. You need to come with me. With no family to care for you, you're in protective custody. "

T. Wayne tried to take a step back, but Pernell's strong grip held him.

"I think not," Pernell said.

"And who are you?"

Pernell took a deep breath. His instincts had served him well in the midst of war in a foreign country, and they kicked in now. "I'm his uncle," he said, and gave T. Wayne's shoulder a squeeze.

CHAPTER TWENTY-TWO

Althea Simpson looked back and forth between the man and boy. "Uncle? I don't believe you," she said.

"Why?" Pernell queried.

"For one thing, I never heard anything about an uncle. There is nothing in our records about him having an uncle. On top of that, Thomas is black and you are white."

"T. Wayne's mother is black. His father, my brother, was the same color I am."

She studied the two of them, as if she could intuit the truth. Finally she picked up on the word Pernell had used. "Was?"

"He died in Afghanistan," came the solemn answer.

"How come you weren't in Thomas's life before now?"

Think quickly, man! It's important. T. Wayne needs help! He needs me!

"I was in Afghanistan too. And I was injured there. The same incident that killed his father put me in the hospital for a long time. When I got out, I came to New Orleans because here's where my brother had been living. Looks like I came just in time."

"Yes. Well." Althea Simpson tried to think of something else to disprove the story he was telling. When she couldn't, she tried another tactic. "Do you have an acceptable place for Thomas to live? You'll have to be vetted before we can OK you to be his guardian. Do you have a job?"

"I work for Abner Crowbridge," Pernell said. *That's not much of a lie. I do work for him when he needs me.*

"Abner Crowbridge? The businessman? The philanthropist?"

"That's the one."

"He lives in a big house over in the Garden District."

"He used to," Pernell said, speaking with authority. "He lives at Broussard Court now, down the street. He has a shop where he sells antiques."

"I don't believe you. Why would a rich man like Abner Crowbridge be living here?"

"You'll have to ask him that," Pernell said.

"I own Broussard Court," Addie said, inserting herself into the conversation. "I inherited the apartments when my aunt, Madame Badeaux, died. Mr. Crowbridge most certainly does rent an apartment as well as space for a shop in Broussard Court. Mr. Roberts speaks the truth."

"And I've just rented an apartment there," Pernell said, nodding toward Addie, "so I can be handy when Mr. Crowbridge needs me. It has *two bedrooms and two bathrooms,*" he looked meaningfully at the landlady, daring her to contradict him. "It's very nice. Roomy. Furnished. Big courtyard. Plenty of room for both T. Wayne here and myself."

"That's right," Addie spoke up. "They'll have a comfortable place to live. I used to live there in Broussard Court myself."

"And you have Thomas in school?"

"I will," Pernell said. "I need to find the school for this area and register him as soon as possible." *I hope that won't be a problem.*

"I'll need to get your full name and your phone number, and the address where you and Thomas will be living. Next week I'll need to fill out some papers and have you sign them. We'll probably need to go to court and have a judge approve this arrangement." She glared at him. "And as I said, I or somebody will have to inspect the living arrangement to see that it is appropriate."

"Sure thing." He gave T. Wayne's shoulder another squeeze, but this time it was a 'good for us' squeeze instead of a 'keep your mouth shut' squeeze.

When the social worker left, everyone gave a sigh of relief. "I guess you got that," Pernell directed toward Addie, "we'll need the larger apartment." He turned to T. Wayne. "I guess I have a roommate, Bud. That OK with you?"

"You mean I'll be living with you?"

"Yes. Unless you want her to find you a different foster home?"

"No! I mean, yes! I mean . . ." T. Wayne shook his head. "Yes, I'd like to live with you."

Addie reached into her handbag and pulled out the fold of bills Pernell had given her for the first month's rent. She took one from the top and handed it back. "Here. You just got your rent reduced by a hundred a month. You'll need it to feed and clothe a teenager."

"Thanks," he said. "Let's go get my stuff from my old place," he said, putting his arm back around T. Wayne's shoulder. "And get moved into our new home."

CHAPTER TWENTY-THREE

As the group of chattering people gradually filled the bus, Trudy settled into a seat by the window. A tall, attractive man stopped in the aisle beside her. "May I take this seat?" he asked.

"Certainly, John," she replied.

"This has been a great trip," he said. "Too bad it's over."

"I agree. I wasn't ready to leave. There's so much more to see and enjoy."

"What do you want to do that you didn't get to?"

"Just browsing. Looking in all the fascinating shops that I didn't have a chance to visit." She didn't want to tell a new acquaintance that she wanted to visit the cemetery to look for her parents' graves. That was private information that she didn't want to explain.

"Same here. Too much to see and not enough time."

The bus driver walked down the aisle, counting under his breath, looking from passenger to passenger. When he reached the front of the bus he picked up the microphone. "Everybody's here and accounted for," he said. "Did everyone have a good time in New Orleans?" A resounding spattering of 'yes' and 'yay' filled the air. He took the driver's seat and clipped the speaker to the front of his shirt. "Onward to Saint Louis!" he said, and put the behemoth into gear, edging out into traffic.

"Before we arrived you said you wanted to see if anything was familiar to you. Did it?"

"No, not really. I guess I was too young when I left to have any distinct memories."

"How old were you?"

"About four or five, I think. Grandmother never told me exactly."

"No information about where you lived?"

"No. The only thing she told me was that my parents died and she came and got me and gave me a home. I've known that since I was little."

"And you couldn't ask her for more information?"

"No, I couldn't. From the few things she told me, my mother, her daughter, ran away with my father—before I was born—and they were out of touch until the accident. I guess the hospital got in touch with my grandmother and she came and got me."

"Too bad you couldn't find the answers you were looking for. Maybe you can come back someday when you have more time and look again."

"Yes. I plan to do just that when I am able. The whole town seemed familiar to me, but not enough to set any bells to ringing." Trudy sighed and shook her head. "I had been looking forward to this trip for so long. I guess I thought being in New Orleans again would open up doors in my brain and I would remember more than I had already, which wasn't much."

"I'd like to come back again myself," John said. "I'm like you, I'd have liked to explore more. This short trip was just enough to make me want to see more. Hear more music. Taste more." He grinned. "I loved the food." He became solemn again. "Too bad . . ." He stopped speaking and squeezed the space between his eyes with his thumb and forefinger.

"Too bad?" Trudy questioned.

"Too bad that my wife didn't get to come with me. For years she had looked forward to visiting New Orleans."

"I'm so sorry for your loss," Trudy said.

"And I for yours." They sat in silence as the bus made its way onto a major highway and took up more speed, barreling toward the north and home.

"I enjoyed your company," John finally said. "It was sort of a memorial to Doris to take this trip at all. She wanted to go so badly, I decided that I would go by myself and see it for her. But somewhere along the way I realized how very miserable and isolating it would be, seeing all the sights alone. I was grateful for your company, Trudy. Grateful to be able to have a conversation about what we were seeing and hearing, with someone else who hadn't seen the city before."

"I enjoyed your company as well. Like you, I was anticipating a solitary trip. Not that I wanted it that way, but there was nobody to travel with me. Grandmother died just last week, and although I thought about canceling my adventure, the travel company wouldn't return my money, and I'm too much of a cheapskate to throw away that much. The trip was better, though, for having you to discuss things with."

"Enjoy the food with," John said and grinned.

"Listen to the music with."

"Next time" began many sentences. "Next time I go I want to explore some of those interesting shops. There was one in the next block from where we ate that first night, but it was closed. It had the most ornate cabinet in the window I wanted to see and touch," Trudy said. "It absolutely fascinated me."

"Next time I want to sit and listen to the music longer. I didn't get enough."

"Next time I want to explore the cemetery. That was something on my list that I didn't get to do."

"Next time, I want to find out more about hoo-doo before I go, so I can ask questions."

When at last the bus pulled into the lot in Saint Louis, Trudy and John were still talking.

"I was wondering," John began and trailed off.

"Yes? About what?" Trudy asked.

"If you would give me your phone number. Maybe we could have lunch together sometime. Talk about the trip. Talk about other things." He seemed shy for a man in his fifties. "I . . . uh. . . haven't asked a girl for her phone number since high school." He looked away and grinned before looking back at Trudy. "I don't know how to do it anymore."

"You did just fine. I'm not used to being asked for my number. I'll be happy to give it to you."

They changed phones and put their number in the other person's directory.

"I imagine I'll be pretty busy, so don't think I'm just putting you off. I have to go see my grandmother's attorney, and when I get her business squared away I need to look for a job."

"I understand. We can work out something, I'm sure. I need to check on my stores. I left a son in charge of each of them, and I'm sure everything is running smoothly. They would have called me if it wasn't. But still, I need to check in."

As they made their good-byes, John grasped her hand as if to shake it, but at the last minute he raised it to his lips and brushed it with a kiss. "Until next time," he said.

CHAPTER TWENTY-FOUR

"I'm Gertrude Ann Miller, and obviously I'm not dead."

"I don't know what to say." The receptionist frantically looked at whatever was on her computer. "I had the appointment on the calendar, then we got word that she . . . er . . . you were dead and the appointment was canceled."

"Well, I'm not, and I need to see William Mulder. I made the appointment two weeks ago, and here I am."

The young woman, who was identified by a discrete sign on her desk as Naomi Pell, picked up her phone a punched in a couple of numbers. Turning her back to Trudy, she pushed away as far as the phone cord would allow and spoke quietly into the receiver.

"If you'll have a seat, Miss Miller, someone is coming that will clear this confusion," she said when she hung up the receiver. Trudy walked toward the chairs that waited against the wall across from the reception desk, but she didn't have time to sit down before a man entered the area from a corridor leading further into the depths of the law firm. He was frowning as he approached the receptionist. Their heads close together, they had a whispered conference before he straightened and approached Trudy.

"Miss . . . er . . . ah . . . Miller?"

"Yes. Gertrude Ann Miller," Trudy said. She offered her hand, which he accepted, shaking it briefly before releasing it.

"I'm sorry for the confusion," he said. "Please, let's go to my office and see how I can help you." His outstretched arm invited her to precede him along the hallway.

They passed several doors before entering a pleasant room, furnished with a large expensive looking desk, shelves full of books, and several comfortable looking chairs. It was a rich room, made to make a client feel important and welcome.

"My name is William Mulder," he said, and reached over and straightened a sign on the desk that reminded the visitor, in case they forgot, with whom they were speaking. "Please, have a seat." He motioned toward one of the plush chairs facing the desk.

"As unlikely as it may seem," he said, as he went behind the expanse of polished walnut and sat in the high-backed leather chair, "we evidently have two clients with the same name. I cannot think of any other reason this mix-up would occur." He smiled at Trudy. "You said that your name is Gertrude Ann Miller. Is that correct?" He turned to a computer screen to his right and typed. Frowning, he looked back at her. "Tell me why you are here."

"This firm, Mulder and Schmidt, is, or was, my grandmother's law firm," Trudy said. "She passed away, and I thought I'd better inform you of that and see what needed to be done as far as any business of hers is concerned."

"And what was your grandmother's name?" he asked.

"Ruby Miller."

More typing on the keyboard produced another frown. Mulder looked at the computer screen, then at Trudy, then back at the screen.

"Where did your grandmother live? What address?"

Trudy gave the number and street.

Mulder leaned back in his chair and stared at the screen. "Where do *you* live?" he asked, the words sliding out of the smooth tone he had been using into one that was slightly harsh.

"At the same address."

His piercing stare all but called her a liar. "How long have you resided with . . . er . . . your grandmother?"

"Thirty years. Since I was five years old." *Surely he has a record of all that on file.*

He leaned forward and rested his arms on the desk. "Why don't you tell me your story? Why are you here? What do you want?"

"That's what I've been trying to tell you," Trudy stated in a firm voice, "My grandmother, Ruby Miller, passed away. As her attorneys I thought you needed to know."

"How did you know that Mulder and Schmidt were her attorneys?"

"I went through her papers and found the firm's name on several of them."

He frowned as he picked up a pen and started twirling it on the desktop. "You didn't know until then?"

"No, I didn't. She was a very private person and kept all her personal business under lock and key. When she died I used the key she kept on a ribbon around her neck and unlocked her office. When I went through her papers I found the name of your firm."

"Who can vouch for you? Who can back up your story?"

"Back up . . ." Trudy's anger, which had been building throughout this nonsensical conversation, threatened to spill over. "Why in the world would I lie about something like my grandmother's death? If you don't need to know anything about it, or her, I'll just leave." She stood up.

"Please wait!" Mulder raised both hands. "It's just that . . ." He shook his head. "You have no idea how confusing this is."

"Why don't you tell me, then. I'm in the dark here, and I need to know. Are there others relatives I know nothing about? What happens to her house? Her possessions? Do I need to move out? She was so secretive about everything, I have no idea about her life or finances. If I have to move out of the house, I need time to find a place to live." Trudy said in a rush. "And a job," she added in a low voice.

William Mulder stared at her for a full minute before he spoke. Putting his hands on the desk, he stood. "What you are telling me fits, in a way, with what I see on the computer, but it makes no sense. No sense at all.

"It so happens that Augustus Schmidt is in the office today. He's one of the founding members of the firm, and as such he remembers people and cases that had their origins many years ago, like this one. He may be able to get to the bottom of this. I'll go fetch him." With that statement he exited the room.

Growing more nervous by the minute, Trudy tried to distract herself by admiring the furnishings and bits and pieces of the room. It was a serene chamber, meant, she was sure, to calm and reassure clients who came to the dignified law firm of Mulder and Schmidt, although it wasn't doing much to soothe *her*. The walls were a soft shade of blue, adorned with ornately framed landscapes. The embellishments that graced the tables and shelves, bits of pottery or metal, miniature paintings on small easels, added to the sense of wealth. Try as she might, the peaceful surroundings did nothing to sooth her frazzled nerves. But for one thing, she might have just left. Abandoned the whole mission.

There was a chance, a slight one perhaps but a chance, that in the records that Mulder and Schmidt had in their possession were the answers to all her questions. Who were her parents? Was her mother really Ruby's daughter? What was her name? Who was her father? Were her parents married? Where are they buried?

She walked around the room, admiring each painting and every carefully placed urn or or bowl that graced the tables. No matter how long she had to wait, no matter what she had to endure, she wasn't going to give up.

I can't leave. Not when there is the chance I can find out who I am. I am more than Ruby's granddaughter. This I do know. This is my chance, my one and only chance, to learn my history, and I can't blow it by losing my temper and walking out.

CHAPTER TWENTY-FIVE

When Trudy had waited until she thought she could wait no more, the door opened and an elderly gentleman entered the room. A small man, stooped and bent, he leaned heavily on a cane as he made his way to stand in front of Trudy.

"So you're the one who has the office in an uproar," he said.

"I . . . I didn't mean to," Trudy said, suddenly shy in front of this old man. "I came because I thought you needed to know about my grandmother . . . about Ruby's death and . . ."

"And?"

"And I thought I might find some answers to my questions."

"You might," he said, then sat down in a chair facing Trudy. "Then again, you might find even more questions." He frowned as he settled into a chair and folded his hands together over the brass handle of the cane that was propped between his knees.

Trudy noticed William Mulder still standing by the door. He looked as if he couldn't make up his mind whether to stay or go.

"William," the elderly man said, "this will take some time. Would you ask Naomi to see to some liquid refreshment, please? A pot of coffee to keep me going, William, and water. Plenty of water. I imagine I'll need it to wet my throat. I have quite a story to tell.

"Something for you, Miss Miller? Would you like coffee as well, or tea perhaps, to keep you refreshed as well? We have a fine selection of teas, both green and black."

"No, thank you." The old man sounded as if this was a party, not a serious discussion about life and death, and Trudy was having a hard time keeping hold of correctness and decorum, not to mention good manners.

William Mulder said nothing but gave a dip of his head and slipped out the door, pulling it shut behind him.

"Let me introduce myself," the old man said. "My name is Augustus Schmidt. Why don't we start with you telling me about yourself and your grandmother. What is your name, my dear?'

"My name is Gertrude Ann Miller."

"Do you have any official papers with your name on them? Something to prove you are who you say you are?"

What an odd question! "No. I just know that is my name. Oh . . . wait. Yes, Grandmother showed me my Social Security card one time, years ago, when I first went to work. It had my name on it. But I don't have it. She didn't give it to me. It's probably in the papers in her office, but I didn't see it when I was going through them."

"Your grandmother showed you a Social Security card with the name Gertrude Ann Miller on it?"

"Yes, that's right."

"But she kept it in her possession?"

"Yes."

"I see. Go on with your story. How did you come to be living with your grandmother?"

"My parents were killed in a car accident, and Grandmother was the only relative I had. She took me in."

"And you were how old?"

"About five years old."

"What do you remember of this time? Do you remember your parents?"

"No, not really. I have vague memories of them—of being in my mother's arms, of being loved and loving them in return, but that's about all."

"You weren't in the accident that killed you parents?"

"No. Grandmother said I was with a sitter at the time, so I wasn't with them."

"So she came to where you were, which was . . .?"

"I believe it was New Orleans. Sometimes it was hard to understand exactly what Grandmother was telling me, she rambled on so, but I'm pretty sure it was New Orleans. I have a few, vague memories of there. Some of them—those of the crowds of people at Mardi Gras—are frightening, but others seem interesting and fun. I try to remember more, but bits and pieces are all I remember. Things that make no sense."

"And your grandmother came there and . . ."

"She came and rescued me, so I wouldn't have to go to some orphanage to live."

"Ahhh. Yes, I see. She came to New Orleans and rescued you. And so you have lived with your grandmother ever since?"

"Yes, that's right."

"Tell me about your schooling."

"I went to a church school."

"Here in Saint Louis?"

"Yes. At the church Grandmother and I attended."

"And you matriculated?"

"Yes. After that, I got a job and later I attended some business courses."

"And that was here in Saint Louis also?"

"Yes."

"And you work where now?"

"Actually, I was working at Acme Digital Systems, but business was slow and I was laid off two weeks ago. I was going to start looking for another job as soon as I got all of this business concerning Grandmother taken care of."

The door opened and Naomi Pell entered baring a tray with cups and other settings. William Mulder followed with a pot in each hand. They placed their loads on the credenza sitting nearby.

"I'll take a cup of coffee, black, and a glass of water," Augustus Schmidt said. "Right here," he patted the small table beside his elbow. "I'll need it," he said under his breath.

"Ahh," he said after taking a sip of the dark brew. "William, you may as well stay and listen. I've been dealing with this business for a long time now, but I imagine you'll have to manage it in the days to come. Evidently there has been more going on than I was aware of." He took another sip and stared off into space as William took a seat where he could observe both Schmidt and Trudy.

"Many years ago Joseph Miller was a well-respected businessman in Saint Louis," the elderly man began. "He was the last of a line of entrepreneurs, men who could not fail. Their businesses, whatever they were, succeeded. Saint Louis was a booming town, and they boomed right along with it." His attention fixed on Trudy, observing her interest in what he was relating.

"But their luck changed," he said as he placed his cup and saucer on the table by him, "not in the business sense, but in personal safety. The Great War, the first one, took the men, one by one, and disease took the wives and daughters, until only one family member was left: Joseph.

"His brothers, his sisters, his cousins, all met with the grim reaper in one manner or another, and their descendants suffered the same fate. Some people said that it was Fate. That the Millers one and all gained what they owned by methods that were anything but honest and fair, but . . ." he shrugged. "I cannot vouch for that. Only that Joseph was left, and he was rich enough for all of them. Before you judge him to be lucky, however, you must know that Fate had other plans for him." He reached for the glass of water and drank.

"Joseph was married to a lovely lady. Ruby was her name."

Trudy took a deep breath. So her grandmother was widowed, and it sounded like Augustus Schmidt was saying that she was rich. Although they had never done without anything when Trudy was growing up, it certainly didn't seem like they were rich, either.

Schmidt smiled at Trudy. "I know what you are thinking," he said. "But all is not what it seems." He readjusted his position in the chair. "These old bones," he said, "are hard to get comfortable." When he got settled, he took another sip of coffee, then set the cup back on the table at his elbow.

"Now I am going to tell you some things that are going to be hard for you to understand. Hard for you to accept. But you must hear them, my dear, and you must believe them, as unbelievable as they may be." He grasped the arms of his chair and looked intently at Trudy.

"Joseph and Ruby had two children. The boy, Joe Junior, was wild and head-strong. He finally killed himself with his drunkenness and wild driving, and he took other people with him. The lawsuits over that mess took a large share of the family fortune.

"The daughter . . . ." he frowned, "she . . . had a difficult birth. The cord was wrapped around her neck. It deprived her of oxygen for critical minutes, but she survived." He sat, unspeaking, as he struggled to form his words. "I don't know . . . doctors didn't say . . . if that was what caused her . . . problems, but she wasn't right. She was . . . odd."

He looked intently at Trudy as he spoke. "Her name was Gertrude Ann."

"But . ." Trudy resisted the truth that was coming. "But I . . . I'm OK. Aren't I?"

"You are more than OK. Gertrude Ann was only a few years younger than me. I remember her well. We attended the same parties. Knew the same people. We were not friends in the truest meaning of the word, but acquaintances, most certainly."

"But . . ." she began once more, more confused than ever.

"Just listen, my dear. It will become clearer to you." He picked up the cup of now cold coffee and took another sip. When he scowled at the taste, he set the cup aside, twisting his mouth, and William Mulder hurriedly stood up and retrieved the coffee pot, pouring more steaming liquid into the cup.

"As Gertrude Ann grew up it became more obvious that she could not function as an adult and would be unable to do anything to support herself. Remember, we were of a similar age, so I could observe her problems. My father was her father's lawyer, and we were social equals, so we were more involved than most lawyers and clients were. In a sense, I grew up with Gertrude Ann.

"I observed her when she had spells when she wandered around, mumbling to herself, ignoring the world around her. There were days when she wouldn't accept what she didn't want to hear. For periods of time it seemed as if she lived in another world. In some areas she was an adult. In others she was still a small child."

"You are describing my grandmother. Are you telling me that she wasn't Ruby? That she was Gertrude Ann?"

"Yes, my dear, that is what I am telling you."

"She moved everybody into another generation," Trudy whispered. "Her mother was Ruby. She became the mother of me, so she was Ruby, and I became Gertrude Ann. I became her."

"There's more to the story," Schmidt said. "Much more you need to know."

Trudy sat back and looked at the old man delivering this bizarre tale. How could there be much more than had already been told?

"When she was a teen, Gertrude Ann became pregnant. By whom, nobody ever knew. Whether it was from love or rape was also unknown."

"I . . . I . . . ." Trudy stuttered. She felt the blood drain from her face. The vision of a loving mother and father was being assaulted by rude images she didn't want to face. Were they only creations of her imagination?

"No, my dear! Not with you!," Schmidt leaned forward to insist.

"She told me that her daughter was my mother," Trudy said. The tears that were forming threatened to spill over.

"No, not that either," he insisted. "There was a miscarriage, at least that's what they called it. Maybe it was, or maybe . . . ." He settled back into his chair, looking at the carpet, avoiding Trudy's gaze. "In any event, she lost the baby. There was no baby."

Trudy thought back to some of Ruby's meandering statements about babies lost and babies found and other claims that had been undecipherable. They were beginning to make sense in light of what Schmidt was telling her. Not really sense, exactly, but something more to grasp, to consider. Possibilities, if nothing more.

"In those days, doctors did things that would not be ethical today. They performed a tubal ligation on Gertrude Ann. There would be no more babies. That particular future disaster was averted."

"So she had no daughter," Trudy stated.

"No my dear. No daughter. Or son, either, for that matter." He leaned back, pressing his fingers together in a steeple as he observed Trudy dealing with this information.

"As her parents aged, they became aware that Gertrude Ann would never be able to fully deal with life. Oh, she could keep herself clean and well-dressed. She could managed to get through each day as it presented itself, even if that meant wandering throughout the house talking to herself. She could even do a minimum of food preparation for herself, if necessary. What she couldn't do, could never do, was have a job and make the money to support herself. They did not want to put their daughter in an institution, a place where she would be confined like a prisoner. But they had to plan for the future. Gertrude Ann's future. So what they did, you lived the results of it."

Trudy was beginning to understand. The story Augustus Schmidt was relating fit the woman she called her grandmother to a tee. "What did they do?" she asked, leaning forward in anticipation.

"Several things," he said. "First, they bought the house where you are now living. Had it painted and repaired and furnished with whatever

Gertrude picked. They told her it was her very own house, where she would live forever, and she was to make it as pretty as she wished."

"I imagine she was happy to do that," Trudy said. "She always seemed to be very pleased with where we lived. She would talk about the furnishings—admire them. I'd even see her run her hands over items and smile."

"Yes, I believe she was. My father, you see, was put in charge of her estate, and there are files, numerous files, that relate everything. There was money, you understand, plenty of money, even after the claims against her brother's behavior were settled. Maybe not a large amount in today's terms, but a large amount in those days. There were funds in an account for taxes, for repairs, for any unexpected expenses. Gertrude had a monthly stipend, and she could spend it however she liked." Schmidt took a sip of water before continuing.

"This law firm, Mulder and Schmidt, has always managed Gertrude Ann's business. After my father set it all up, Gertrude Ann moved into her house. She liked it far better than the mansion her parents occupied. From that time forward it has been the job of a junior partner to deal with the bills. They see that the taxes are paid, that repairs are made, that the janitorial firm sends a person once a month to clean the house and report back about how they find Gertrude Ann is doing."

"She argued with them, the cleaning ladies, that is."

"I imagine so." Schmidt chuckled. "She argued with everyone. About everything." He smiled at the memories. "Someone from this firm calls once a month to check on her. First it was my father. Then it was me. Later, that duty was passed along to a younger member." He looked toward William Mulder, who had been sitting quietly, taking it all in. "Lately it was you, wasn't it, William?"

"Yes sir. I call once a month, like clockwork. Have for years."

"Learn anything new?"

"From the phone call? No, sir. Not a thing. From this conversation? A lot."

"So how do I fit into this?" Trudy asked.

"That is the question, isn't it?" Schmidt frowned. "Perhaps we ought to have been more diligent. Asked more questions. Been suspicious. But we weren't. Didn't." He sighed. "When William came to my office today and told me about you, that you were here, claiming to be Gertrude's granddaughter, my first thought was that it was a scam."

"I'm not . . ." Trudy started, but Schmidt hushed her with a wave of the hand.

"I know, my dear. I know. For one thing, a scammer would have been better with the details. If you truly did think you could come into money, you wouldn't have claimed to be the person whose name the money was in. You wouldn't have claimed to be Gertrude Ann Miller. Anyone doing their homework would know who that name belonged to, and that we would know that fact. You can't run a scam with a half-baked story.

"So what is the answer? When William came to my office to tell me about you, I pulled the records—records that go back decades—and found mention by the housecleaners that a child lived in the home. That there were clothes and toys, school books, things a child would have use of. When asked about the items by either the housecleaner or me or William here," he nodded toward the man sitting enthralled by the story, "Gertrude would explain that a neighbor child spent time with her while the mother was at work. She was simply babysitting. I don't know why we were so ready to accept that explanation, but we did."

"So where did I come from?"

A serious expression settled on Augustus Schmidt's face. "I can't give you an answer, my dear. As near as I can surmise, she stole you. She saw you and wanted you, so she took you for her own. Or maybe somebody gave you to her."

"Gave me to her?"

"It's not impossible, my dear. Perhaps some poor woman, or even a couple, could not raise you. Perhaps there was illness, or poverty, or . . ." He shook his head at the mystery.

The question that burst from her lips was the one Trudy had been puzzling over for her entire life.

"Who am I?"

CHAPTER TWENTY-SIX

T. Wayne bounded up the outside steps, along the balcony, and through the door into the living room. He paused to notice the bandana tied on the door knob to the bedroom. Grinning, he quietly walked the opposite direction, toward the kitchen.

When they moved in together, they had worked out the signal that indicated Pernell was busy and not to be disturbed unless it was an emergency. He had explained that it was an old signal, well-known by men of the world. "And you are almost a man, T. Wayne, so you ought to know. When something is tied to the door knob, it means the guy is entertaining company. *Woman* company. Understand? He is not to be disturbed unless the house is on fire or something equally important."

T. Wayne had looked at the floor and nodded his head. He wasn't a baby. He knew what went on between a man and a woman.

"But . . ." Pernell had said, "that's not what it's going to mean in our apartment."

T. Wayne looked up, caught by his inclusion in the term 'our apartment,' but also by what the kerchief on the door knob could mean besides the obvious signal.

"In this apartment it's going to mean I'm busy writing and don't want to be disturbed. Understand?"

T. Wayne nodded once more. *No woman. Writing. Check. Got it.*

"Or it might mean that I wrote all night so I'm sleeping in the daytime."

T. Wayne hadn't ever thought about any writing that could be so important that a person would stay awake all night doing it, but OK. That was cool.

"If Mr. Crowbridge wants me, he usually just calls me directly, but if he should ever tell you to get me, you get me. Any time. Sleeping or not."

"I understand."

He didn't quite understand what Pernell wrote, but that wasn't his, T. Wayne's, business anyway. Maybe someday the older man would tell him, let him read some of it or something, but until then, he'd keep his nose out of other people's business. It enough to share space with the veteran, to have a dry, comfortable place to sleep where he wouldn't be run off by a business owner or attacked by another transient looking to steal whatever T. Wayne had. Not only that, but he had food to eat any time he wanted, something that hadn't happened since his grandmother died, or at least after the money his granny had secreted away was used up.

He went to the kitchen to look for something to eat. Seemed like he was always hungry these days, even when he had consumed a meal only a couple of hours before. Pernell said, and Simon too, that he was a growing boy, but T. Wayne thought he'd probably grown as much as he needed to.

Although he'd shot a few hoops, he wasn't really interested in being a basketball player, but when you were African-American and over six feet tall and still growing, that's what people thought you ought to do—play hoops. Lots of guys he knew in the old neighborhood said that either basketball or football was the way out for black youths, boys on their way to becoming young men with no future except by way of sports. T. Wayne didn't know whether to believe that or not. He didn't want to, because he really didn't care much for either sport. Not for playing, that is. Watching was OK, and playing a bit of one-on-one was fun, but nothing to base your life on. There were too many interesting things in the world to learn about without spending all your time with a ball of one kind or another in your hands.

Nothing in the refrigerator interested him, so he took an apple from the bowl on the kitchen table and went to his room. It was the best room ever. When Pernell had taken T. Wayne to the upstairs apartment for the first time, he had said, "I think it is best for me to have the rear bedroom. You take the one facing the street. I don't need to be disturbed by what's going on outside, and you don't need to be upstairs over Mr. Crowbridge's bedroom. You might thump around and disturb him."

That was fine with T. Wayne. He liked to watch the street scene outside his windows. People coming and going, shouting to others, laughing, talking. If Broussard Court had been in a busier section of the city it might have been different, but here where the businesses closed at night and the people who lived above or behind the shops were seldom wandering the streets past dinnertime, T. Wayne could sit at the window and do his homework or daydream or read a book, or even go to bed and fall asleep without being disturbed by tourists or nighttime revelers, much less the neighbors, like it had been in the old apartment.

He pulled his books from the new backpack that Pernell had bought him. The old one, the one he used when he first ran, was torn and dirty. Even the sight of it brought bad memories, and he and Pernell had decided that the bad parts of life were over. Over for both of them. The old pack was shoved under the bed, still holding his grandmother's Bible and all the memorabilia it enveloped. Even if he would never carry it again, neither would he get rid of it. Ever. It was all he had to remind him of her.

"It's up to you, T. Wayne, to figure out how to put the bad memories aside while keeping the good ones," Pernell said. "I write about mine. Put them into stories. At first, they were all the experiences I couldn't hide from, but gradually I began to get rid of the bad ones." He paused before continuing. He rested his elbows on his knees and looked at the floor. "War. Loss." He closed his eyes briefly. "Death."

He took a deep breath and sat back, purposefully ignoring the thoughts that were trying to push into his consciousness.

"Sometimes I still have to write about something I really don't want to remember, but once I've written it, it sinks a bit. It goes into hiding." He ran his hand over his eyes. "Sometimes I have to write it more than once, because I didn't get it all into the first story, or I didn't get it right. So I write it again. And again.

"And finally I get it all in there. The horror. The sadness. Admitting to being afraid." He sat staring into nothingness. "And when I finally own up to all of it, the memories fade. They don't ever go away entirely, but they don't bother me any longer. They stop keeping me awake at night. They stop coming upon me unexpectedly, making me freeze up, unable to work or think of anything except that memory."

Sometimes T. Wayne thought maybe he ought to write about what frightened him, like Pernell did. But he shoved the thoughts into the back of his mind and concentrated on the good things instead. Life went better when he could do that. Maybe that was sort of like what Pernell was telling about.

Like the new apartment that he and Pernell shared. It was the best place he had ever lived. Even when he was with his grandmother, the last place they lived was small and worn, as if it had held scores of people just like them. People with little money. People who just got by. People who were as worn down by life as the rooms where they ate and slept. Here in Broussard Court they lived in a place with big rooms overlooking a pleasant courtyard on one side and the businesses of the neighborhood on the front.

And even though his beloved grandmother was gone, T. Wayne no longer was alone, living on the streets, sleeping behind garbage cans or in doorways, holding his fear inside so nobody could see it. The idea that a man, and a white man at that, had claimed to be his uncle in order to save T. Wayne from being put into a foster home somewhere with a family who just wanted the money for taking care of a boy who had no home and no family of his own, had upset all his previously held beliefs. Six months ago he would have suspected evil intent from a strange white man who had befriended a poor black boy, but now all those thoughts had been overcome by Pernell's never-ending kindness. Not only to T. Wayne, but to the old man who lived in the apartment below theirs.

And Old Crow was kind as well. He took time to talk to T. Wayne, tell him about the strange and interesting countries and peoples he had encountered in his travels. Explained about the curios he had collected and the practices he had observed all over the world. He was never too busy to answer the questions the boy asked. He made T. Wayne think that he just might like to learn more about those countries. Abner Crowbridge was a teacher, but not in a classroom. T. Wayne wondered if maybe he could be a teacher someday. Maybe even a real one, in a school. For the first time in his life he was beginning to think of what his life could be like.

T. Wayne sat at the table in his bedroom and worked on the math problems he had brought home from school. He was still being 'evaluated,' the school counselor had called it, filling out forms and taking tests to determine what classes he ought to be in. The math test was one of several assessments he had to complete before his final schedule was set.

When he and Pernell had accidentally run into the social worker at Simon's Place, it had set them on a path. "We'd better get to the school before that Miss Simpson checks to see if you're enrolled," Pernell had said, but to T. Wayne's surprise they went shopping first, buying new jeans and shirts, and even a jacket and a raincoat and shoes. "You want to fit in," Pernell had said. "Dress and look like the other students. We may need to get you a school uniform. Just let me know."

When T. Wayne was dressed in a way Pernell deemed to be appropriate, he drove them to the high school located closest to where they lived.

"Good morning," Pernell had announced himself to the lady at the front desk in the room labeled "office". "We're new to the neighborhood, and I'd like to enroll my nephew in school."

From there it was forms and more forms, and finally they were sent, assisted by a map of the school, to the counselor's office at the end of the main corridor on the first floor. She was sort of youngish, not like the old lady teacher who was the counselor at his old school. She had asked about a jillion questions. "What grade were you in?" she asked when T. Wayne admitting that he hadn't started school this fall like he should have. To be truthful, he hadn't finished last year's classes either. Granny's death had put a stop to his studies.

"What classes did you like, T. Wayne?" Miss Bowen, the new counselor, had asked, using the name he preferred instead of calling him 'Thomas.' It seemed like she was actually listening to his answers. "What did you not like?"

Eventually they worked it out that he liked math and history, tolerated English, unless it was reading stories and telling about the meaning of the story, which he liked. Grammar, however, he didn't care for. Pernell just listened without commenting, although he told T. Wayne later that it sounded just like what Pernell would have said about himself.

The counselor asked about sports. "You don't play basketball?" she asked, just like everyone did after scanning T. Wayne's six foot frame.

"No, ma'am," he answered.

"Football?"

"No, ma'am."

So she put him in a Phys Ed class that mostly did running, near as he could tell. And a class called "keyboarding".

"That's the modern equivalent to typing," she said. "You'll take keyboarding for the rest of this semester, then basic computer the second semester. Do you have a computer at home?" she asked.

"Not yet," Pernell spoke up to answer the question. "But he will."

The answer surprised T. Wayne. Computers cost a lot of money, he knew. He hadn't even dreamed about one when Granny was alive. They barely had enough to pay the rent and buy food. There surely wasn't any left for something like a computer. He wondered if he would be expected to make enough money to pay for it.

"We'll play around with your schedule for a week or so," she said. "You can take these tests, and depending on how you do on them we'll adjust your classes to fit where you need to be."

"I'd think you would just send for his records from his previous school," Pernell said.

"Oh, I will, but if I were to wait until we got an answer we might be still waiting next spring." She leafed through some papers on her desk. "You can do some of this paperwork while you're here. I called them tests, but they aren't the kind of test you can pass or fail. They are just to determine how far along you are in different subjects."

Pernell paid some money for fees and a lunchroom ticket, and after asking T. Wayne if he could find his way home, he left.

Now, some three days later, T. Wayne tackled a math test that wasn't really a test. It was to determine how much he knew about different kinds of mathematics. "Just go as far as you can on each page," Miss Bowen had said. "When you can't work out another answer, go to the next page."

So he sat at the small table in his bedroom and worked problems: addition, subtraction, division, multiplication, fractions, geometry, algebra, and a few problems that T. Wayne didn't know what to call. 'Trigonometry' it said at the top of one page, and 'Calculus' at the top of another, but he had never heard those words before and didn't know how to pronounce them, nor did he know how to work the problems. They looked interesting, though, and he thought he might like to learn what they were about.

He was placed in a World History class, which was going to be exciting, he could tell. Maybe it wouldn't have been so thought-provoking a few months earlier, before he met Mr. Crowbridge and heard the stories about the old man's travels around the world, and if he hadn't seen the furniture and curios brought back from his travels. But now T. Wayne wanted to know more about the countries represented by the unique items that he and Pernell had brought from the storage places around New Orleans to the shop, where they helped unwrap the treasures. T. Wayne helped put many of them in the shop windows to catch the eye of the passers-by. Some, Crowbridge claimed, had magic powers. Those were the ones that fascinated T. Wayne the most. Magic? Really? He had always been a sceptic. Magic, his teachers said, was foolery, nothing real. But Mr. Crowbridge was a smart man. He was not someone easily tricked. If he said magic, then there was magic. Something unexplainable.

So T. Wayne was satisfied with school and he was looking forward to what was to come. He had homework to accomplish over the weekend. After one more day of classes he was to write a paper about what subjects he liked and why he liked them. It had to be at least three-hundred words long, but not more than five-hundred. He wondered why he had to tell that information yet again, but Pernell explained that probably the subject wasn't the important part at all. The teacher wanted to see how well he wrote. It was another test that wasn't a test. How did he use words? Did he know anything about paragraphs and indents and punctuation?

"Hold up on that another day," Pernell said. "I'll help you with it. Not do it for you, mind, but . . . " So T. Wayne hadn't begun yet, waiting on the go ahead from Pernell.

He was putting his papers into the back-pack, ready to carry to school the next day, when Pernell stuck his head in the door. "Hey, Bud, how was school today?"

"Fine, good. I just finished my math homework."

"Great! So that's out of the way. What say we go down to Simon's for dinner. I meant to go the grocery and get some steaks and potatoes for tonight, but I got busy with the story I was writing and didn't do it. Can you stand Cajun food one more time?"

"Sure." Simon's Place offered such a variety he'd never get tired of eating there, and after going hungry if he didn't find anything edible in the garbage cans behind cafes or restaurants, T. Wayne decided he would never be picky about what he ate ever again.

They descended the stairs into the courtyard at the same time the resident of the ground floor flat across from Mr. Crowbridge came out her door. She was juggling several boxes plus some plastic bags hanging from her arms.

"Here, let me help you," Pernell said, and quickly went to take some of her burden.

"Thanks," she said. "I think I overestimated how much I could carry."

"Where are we going with all this?"

"Well, I'm going down the block to Simon's Place, but I won't ask you to carry them that far."

"That's just where we're going," Pernell said. "It's no trouble at all."

"That would be wonderful. Else I'd leave some here on the table and come back to make a second trip."

"T. Wayne," Pernell said, "How about you go see if Mr. Crowbridge wants to come eat with us, or if we can bring back something for his supper."

"Yessir," T. Wayne said and scurried toward the other apartment.

Pernell opened the big iron gate that led onto the sidewalk and slipped the latch back into the bracket after they had passed through. It would take a key to open it from the outside.

"I don't think I could have made it in one load. Thanks for the help."

"You're welcome. I'm Pernell Roberts, by the way. The kid is my nephew. His name is T. Wayne."

"I'm Lexi, Lexi Hobart." She nodded her head in greeting. "Pleased to meet you."

"I've seen you at Simon's Place. You work there?"

"Yes, sort of."

"Sort of?" Pernell queried.

Lexi laughed. "I don't work in the restaurant. Simon hired me to come up with a business plan for using the meeting room. That's what all this is," she said, nodding her chin toward the box in her arms. "I work from home, sometimes, designing pamphlets and such. I have more room and it's quieter. I can think better at home when I'm trying to plan advertising or mail-outs. Then I take it to work."

"It's handy to live and work so close together."

"Yes, it is. I was lucky to find the apartment so close."

They were almost to the corner when T. Wayne came jogging up behind them.

"Mr. Crowbridge says thank you for asking, but he has plenty to eat at home. Maybe next time." He crossed the side street in front of them and rushed to hold the door to Simon's Place open.

"This all goes in the back office," Lexi said, and she led the way through the dining room to the closed double doors at the back. She directed them through the darkened dining room where another door led into a storage area, full of tables of various sizes, chairs, several podiums, and stacks of table linens. "Stay there and let me turn on the lights." She opened yet another door and used her elbow to punch the switch, turning on lights.

"You can bring that box in here," she called out,

When Pernell entered the small room, he saw large calendar sheets pinned to the wall. A bulletin board held pictures and swatches, and next to it was a large chalk board with writing covering it.

"This looks like you stay busy."

"I think we're going to be. We have a lot of interest. People need a place to have a party or a meeting, and Simon charges a lot less than the big hotels. We're just getting started, but I think Simon has a winner here."

They exited the office and started back through the storage room. When they reached the auxiliary dining room, Pernell stopped and looked around.

"As you probably can tell," Lexi said, "we're about all set up for a group tomorrow. It's a baby shower and brunch. I'll come in the morning and work with the hostesses on the decorations."

"You furnish the decorations as well as the place and the food?"

"Only a few for now. We'd like to build up a supply for all different kinds of celebrations. Then we could charge more if we do centerpieces and all. It would be cheaper if you just rent the room and do all the decorations yourself. A greater price range means more customers."

"Smart business, You've been doing this long?"

"Yes, I worked for a firm in west Texas for several years before I moved to New Orleans."

Pernell perceived a drop in her voice as she spoke about moving to NOLA. "Are you liking it here?" he asked.

"Yes," Lexi said. She smiled. "Yes, I am. Especially since I got this job and found such a great place to live."

Pernell started toward the main part of the restaurant. "It looks like they're filling up. We'd better get a table or we won't have any place to sit," he said to T. Wayne. "Would you join us for dinner?" he asked Lexi.

"I need to confer with Simon before it gets so busy he doesn't have time for me. Thank you for asking."

"You're welcome to sit at our table when you are finished with business."

"You staying to eat?" Estelle said as she passed with her hands full of menus and napkin rolled silverware.

"Yes, we are."

"Got a table over that side," she motioned with her head. "You better go claim it iffn you wants to sit."

As they maneuvered their way to the far side of the room, a man sitting at a table by their path pushed his chair back and stood. "Major?" he said. "Major Roberts?" He stood stiff and straight as if he were at inspection and saluted. "Major Roberts. Sir!"

CHAPTER TWENTY-SEVEN

A few minutes later Pernell made excuses and led T. Wayne to a table on the other side of the room. His jaw was clinched tightly, and frown lines furrowed his brow.

"Gosh, he really thinks you're a hero," T. Wayne said as they sat down. "You saved a bunch of people."

"That was my job." Pernell's voice was sharp.

"But—"

"I don't want to talk about it anymore."

T. Wayne shrunk against the chair back and closed his mouth tightly.

"Sorry for being so cross." Pernell reached over and gave the boy's arm a squeeze. "Sometimes I just can't talk about it. Maybe someday . . ."

They had already ordered when Lexi approached the table. "I'll join you at your table if the offer still stands. It's getting crowded and I don't want to take up another table."

"Of course," Pernell said, and she placed her glass of tea and a napkin rolled bundle of silverware on the table in front of an empty chair. "Do you need to order?" he asked, looking around for a waitress.

"No. I was in the kitchen talking to Simon and placed my order then." She unrolled the square of white cloth and placed the eating utensils in a row before her. "So," she said. "Are you a New Orleans native?"

"No, I'm not. I used to know someone from here, and he made it sound like an interesting place to live, so when I got back to the states . . ."

"Back to the states? From where?"

173

"Overseas. Afghanistan. Hospital in Germany." He took a sip of water. "Are you from here?"

"No. I was raised in west Texas. Moving here was the first time I've been out of my home state."

"That's a big change, then, from west Texas to New Orleans in one move. What drew you here?"

"I was . . ." Lexi's voice trailed off, then she gave a big sigh.

"You don't have to answer," Pernell said. "It's none of my business."

"No, that's OK. It's just something I have to face, and it's hard to talk about it, sometimes."

"It is. I was just presented with the same question, how I ended up in New Orleans, and I think I blew it. Answering, that is. I almost lost it with somebody I used to know, a soldier I served with." He looked over at T. Wayne. "And I snapped at somebody who meant no harm."

"My problem, I guess, is facing facts, admitting what I've done instead of trying to not think about it."

Pernell raised an eyebrow but said nothing as he looked at her.

"I ran away from home," Lexi said, a grimace on her face.

"If I'm any judge, you're old enough to leave home without it being described as running away."

"You wouldn't think so if you listened to my father."

"Daddy's little girl, huh?"

"Not from my side of things. From his viewpoint, though . . ." She shrugged. "I ought to be what he wants me to be. And I can't."

"I get it," Pernell said. "I have sisters, and they are independent women who make their own decisions."

"According to my father, he should make my decisions for me. He doesn't approve of me, of who I am."

"From what I see, you're doing pretty good with your decisions. You have what looks like an interesting job which you're doing well, and you've found a nice place to live."

"You're right on both counts, but I'm not at home where my father can judge everything else in my life and tell me what I should do and what I shouldn't. Who I should *be*."

The conversation paused as their meals were set in front of them. Both T. Wayne and Pernell had hamburgers, plump and juicy and layered with the usual accompaniments. It took a minute to add the preferred dressings and pour a puddle of catsup for the fries. Lexi ate a spoonful of the jambalaya from the bowl in front of her and closed her eyes in appreciation of the Cajun dish.

Pernell didn't know how to respond to what Lexi was saying, so he let the conversation rest as he bit into his burger.

Simon had been walking around the room, as was his custom every evening, stopping at each table to greet the diners. He observed her tears as he approached their table. "Lexi, *mon chère*, is the jambalaya so bad you cry? Or is it too hot for you?"

Lexi, wiping away the tears that rolled down her cheeks, offered a crooked smile. "It's delicious, Simon. I'm just not used to the spices yet. Give my taste buds time to acclimate."

"These Texans," Simon said. "They believe they are so strong, and then they cry over the jambalaya." He winked at Lexi as he moved to the next table.

But Pernell wasn't so sure the tears on Lexi's cheeks came from the heat of the meal.

"I'm so sorry," Lexi said when he moved out of earshot. "I shouldn't have laid that all on you. I just haven't had anybody to vent to since moving here, and I guess it all had to come out."

"Think nothing of it. I can be a sounding board anytime you need one. I have things too . . ." He came to a stop as he gazed off into space. "Things that need to come out. So I write. I put it all down in black and white. That helps."

"Thank you for the offer, but you're a stranger. Even if we do both live at Broussard Court, we've only just met, and to spill everything out

175

like that . . . ." She shook her head. "I'm usually a more private person. Back home I had my bosses I could talk to, but now." She scooped another spoonful of jambalaya and sat mournfully looking at it. "But now I'm all alone."

"I get why you left home, but how did you chose New Orleans as a destination?"

"I worked at a florist slash caterer slash event planner back home. The guys who owned it, Chad and Barry, had friends here in New Orleans. They made arrangements for me to stay with Jon and Carlton until I could get on my feet. I was beginning to get worried, afraid that I'd never find a job and then this presented itself."

"It looks to me like you landed in the right place."

"Yes, I think so too. I'm doing about the same thing here that I did back home, except Simon's Place is larger, and he is offering more services than Chad and Barry did, so here I'm making more decisions." She scraped the last of the rice from the bowl. "And I'm making more money."

CHAPTER TWENTY-EIGHT

Abner Crowbridge had settled into a routine. He rose at the break of day, dressed and went to the kitchen to prepare his breakfast. If the day was pleasant, he used the wheeled cart to carry his food outside. He said that he 'liked the feel of the day' when he was sitting in the fresh air watching his small part of the city awaken. Even when he was the only person stirring in Broussard Court, he didn't feel alone. *Spirits,* he thought, *the spirits of the former residents are here around me, or perhaps it is only one, the essence of Madame Badeaux.*

Sometimes, when he rose later or sat there longer, he saw and spoke to the other residents. T. Wayne would come down the steps, his arms full of books. "What are you studying today?" Abner would ask, always interested in the varied subjects that were being taught in the schools these days. Chances were that whatever country or people or time period T. Wayne mentioned, Abner could come up with something in the shop that would pertain. "If you're interested, T. Wayne, stop in after school and I'll show you what I picked up in Timbuctoo when I was there." The young man was always interested in the stories Abner had to tell of foreign countries and unusual customs.

The delightful Lexi usually stopped to visit with Abner before she went to work at Simon's Place. Abner enjoyed hearing about the ideas she was incorporating to build business at the eatery. He hadn't dreamed there could be so many different kinds of meetings or parties or festivities people celebrated which required the help of a professional to arrange.

"It sounds like you are enjoying your work," he told her that morning.

"I am, Mr. Crowbridge, And everyone is so nice here. The people who work at Simon's Place as well as the folks who come to the events I help plan."

"I have found," he said, "that in most instances, people are pleasant when you are that way first, and you are a most agreeable person to be around, in my opinion."

"Thank you," Lexi said, and dropped her eyes. "Most people are, I guess, except the ones who want to change you."

"Want to change your mind?"

"Well, that and . . ." she clamped her lips together.

Abner sat quietly, waiting for her to expand her thoughts. When she remained silent, he prodded gently. "Change you how?"

Lexi took a deep breath, and folded her arms around her middle—a classic avoidance gesture, Abner knew. "Change your very being . . . who you are. *What* you are."

"Ah, yes," Abner said. "And it is extremely difficult to do that. Especially when you don't want to change."

"Or can't."

"Or can't. Somebody in your life, I take it, wants to change you?"

"Yes. My parents. My father and my stepmother."

"Hmm. Parents. Yes, we parents are prone to wanting our children to be just what we want them to be." Abner's mind went back in time to when Robert was Lexi's age. Did he try to mold his son into his own image? "We want them to be safe and successful, and it's hard to keep out of their lives and let them go wherever their own path leads them."

"I'm safe, and I'm successful. But I was those things back home. It wasn't enough, and I had to leave before they took another step to . . ." She stopped speaking.

"Yes," Abner said, after a pause. "I'd say you are successful, and you seem to do your job well and enjoy it. You have safe places to live and work. I can't think of another thing a parent might wish for."

"They wish I wasn't gay," she said before she could stop herself.

178

"Oh?" Abner didn't know what to say to that unexpected statement. "I am what I am. I can't change it."

"No. I don't suppose you can." Abner didn't know what else to add.

"If they loved me," Lexi said as she rose from the chair, "If my father loved me, he'd love me the way I am. He doesn't." She took a few steps. "So I left. I found a place where people like me the way I am."

She stopped just as she opened the gate onto the sidewalk. "Thank you, Mr. Crowbridge, for listening."

How much better it is, Abner thought, *to have your daughter by your side, gay or not, than to never see her again.*

* * *

After washing his breakfast dishes, Abner went through the storeroom and into the shop, turning on lights along the way. It gave him a sense of satisfaction to walk among the items he was so intent on finding homes for. Many of them were like old friends, having adorned his home for decades. Gradually, one by one, they were leaving, and he was keenly aware that he would not see them again. *Perhaps when they are all gone to new homes, I will be lonely again, like I was at Robert's home, with no old friends around me.*

Strange that I am so sure that each piece that leaves the shop with a new owner is going where it needs to be. Why do I have the notion that inanimate items have a certain place they should be? Aren't dishes and candlesticks and tables just things? Why should it matter who buys them or where they end up? They are, after all, only wood or stone or clay. They are made of the earth, as am I, and will return to the earth at some point. We are all just things.

As that thought bloomed in his mind, he felt a movement in his hand, and glancing down he saw the wooden snake coiled around his walking stick had adjusted its head to look directly at Abner, its beady eyes staring and its tongue flicking in and out.

This was not the first time the snake had shown its displeasure at something Abner was thinking or doing. The intriguing thought that it was magic was the reason he bought it in the first place. He appreciated the fine workmanship the carved serpent displayed, but it was the tale the old man in the bazaar told Abner that persuaded him to pay the steep price to acquire the menacing object, and he had never regretted it.

At first he and Latreece had discussed the story. Was it true? Or was it only a sales gimmick? There were times they had spent money on an item that didn't live up to the claims the salesman had bestowed upon it, but never as much as the snake stick commanded. But they were rich—at least by some standards—and could afford to take a chance on an interesting story about magic or supernatural powers.

"Treasure the snake stick," the old man told them. "I only sell it because I have need of the money, and I have only a short time left in this life. Treat it well and it will guide you from bad decisions. It will show displeasure if you are even preparing to do something you should not. It will warn of dishonest people who are trying to cheat you. Keep it close at hand as a valuable companion."

Abner had found all this to be true. He had no need of assistance to walk when he first made the purchase, but he took to carrying the serpent stick as a pretention, the mark of an important man, and as he aged he found that it had become so much a part of him that he couldn't be without it. From the time he got out of bed in the morning to the hour he returned to it at night, the snake stick was close at hand.

Seldom did it warn him, as it had just done, that what he was thinking was in error, but it had often cautioned him about the person standing before him, or signaled the risk in a business deal. Indeed, Abner Crowbridge was known for his judgement and acumen, but none knew how much influence came from the object beneath his hand.

He ran his hand over the smooth wood of the serpent's head and returned to the desk that was his center of operations. It wasn't just the walking stick that held magic. Every day that passed, other proof presented itself to show just how magical a place this was. Abner ran his gaze over the objects on the glass shelves in the front windows. Trying to commit the items to memory, he knew it was a fruitless chore, since somehow, someway, the next time he looked, the articles would have rearranged themselves.

The first couple of times this had happened, he thought his mind was beginning to slip, that old age was eroding his observations, but eventually he somewhat reluctantly came to the conclusion it was some sort of magic manipulating the merchandise. He filled the window with what he thought were interesting items to catch the eye of the passersby. Perfectly normal tea cups or candy dishes or Victorian hair ornaments. Before long a customer would enter, excited over their find.

"There is a tea pot in your window. It matches some cups and saucers I have. I have been looking for that tea pot for years."

And *voila!* There was the tea pot, sitting where it hadn't been when Abler sat down. How did it get there? And whatever magic moved it there, how did it know the pattern the customer had at home? It was a regular occurrence, happening at least a couple of times a day. Abner had given up trying to arrange the items, since they seemed to do better at selling themselves than he did. No sooner than did Abner place an item on exhibit than a customer would enter, excited to see the very thing they collected, except Abner had placed it in the shelves on the back wall, but it had somehow transported itself to the front window.

He turned his attention from the small items to the furniture. The day before, Abner sent Pernell to the last storage unit to be emptied. He told the former taxi driver to bring back whatever would fit in his vehicle. He'd make room in the shop no matter what it was.

One of the last pieces to make it into the shop was now sitting in front of Abner. It was a chair. A beautiful, velvet-covered chair. It's legs and hand rests were ornately carved of polished rosewood. The golden hue of the fabric glowed in the light from the various lamps around the room. He walked all around the chair, then went behind his desk and sat down to think about it.

The chair was special, no doubt about it, but it presented a problem. He and Latreece had been shopping at an old marketplace in Marrakesh, browsing among the gee-gaws and oddities displayed to catch the tourists' eye and persuade them to part with their money, the more the better. They had turned to go, having not seen anything to interest them, when the shopkeeper stopped them, unwilling to let obviously wealthy Americans leave without buying.

"Wait! Wait! See? See" he said. "Ancient bowl. Come from fifth century," he said, holding up an obviously factory made pottery piece.

"No," Abner said. "You can buy those anywhere. I'm not interested."

"Then this," the old man said. "Fine rug. I make you excellent price." He thrust it at Latreece.

"No," she held up her palm to ward him off. "Not interested."

"What you look for?"

"Only special things," Abner had replied. "Something I have never seen before."

"Something with power," Latreece had added.

"Power?"

"Special power," she said.

"The power the spirits give," Abner said.

"Wait," the old man said, and disappeared into a back room.

Minutes later he reappeared. He held aside the heavy cloth covering that served as a door. Two young men carried a chair through the opening and set it down on the pile of carpets against the back wall.

It was obviously old. The ornate carving on the rosewood arms was dull and lifeless. The velvet covering the seat and back had the dust of the ages on it. It was likely that under the dust there were worn patches and moth-holes.

"What is this?" Abner asked.

182

"Is Truth Chair."

"Truth Chair?"

"Anyone who sits in Truth Chair cannot lie."

"Really?" Latreece had said, skepticism exhibited in her face and voice.

"Is true!" He sounded as if he were trying to sound truthful and innocent. "I make you very good bargain."

"Can you prove that?" Abner asked.

"You sit in chair. You try lie." He pushed the heavy chair forward a few inches. "You see I speak true."

Abner and Latreece looked at each other. The Truth Chair was the kind of unusual relic they liked to collect from their travels. The chair and its story were sure to garner interest among their circle of friends if they took it back to New Orleans. It would facilitate entertaining evenings following dinner parties.

Of course, the story couldn't be true.

"You sit," the old man insisted. "You see I tell true."

Abner sat down. When he placed his elbows along the arms, wrapping his fingers around the carvings on each, he thought he felt a tingle, like electricity making tentative advances to him. He looked at Latreece, standing in front of him, surprise reflected on his face.

"You ask," the old man said to Latreece. "You ask question." He turned to Abner. "You try to lie."

"Ask away," Abner said.

"What is your middle name?"

This must be a test question, to see how it works. So I can feel it when I am telling the truth.

"Lorenzo," he answered.

"What is your favorite color?"

"Blue."

"What color is our front door?"

"Black."

"What food do I cook that you don't like but you've never told me?"

"Sweet potato casserole."

With that answer, Latreece glared at him.

"Why haven't you ever told me?"

"I didn't want to hurt your feelings."

This went on for several more questions, until the merchant finally asked, "You see? You see you have to tell true?"

"Why didn't you lie?" Latreece asked.

"I . . . I don't know. I kept thinking that I would lie on the next question, but I never did."

"And you don't like my sweet potato casserole?"

"Uh . . . I'm sorry, but I don't."

"And if you hadn't been sitting in that chair, I'd never know. You'd never tell me."

"Well, I didn't want to hurt your feelings."

"I would just have cooked something different. I . . ."

"You see?" the merchant interrupted, "you could not lie."

Abner and Latreece looked at each other.

"I didn't want to lie to my wife," Abner said, knowing full well that wasn't the reason.

"You buy?"

"How much?" Abner asked.

It was expected to negotiate the price of anything for sale in the market, whether it was for pennies or thousands of dollars. They haggled back and forth for some time before they reached an agreement. Each side had to be satisfied with their position when they came to terms and money changed hands, but they would each complain about the price they agreed on. The seller would grumble that he had paid more than that when he bought the item—that he would go broke selling below cost like that. The buyer would complain that he was being taken advantage of, that the price far exceeded the value. When both the buyer and the seller had vented enough, they picked up the Truth Chair, Abner on one side and Latreece on the other, and walked back to where a taxi waited to take them back to their hotel.

"Did you *try* to lie?" Latreece asked later that evening.

"Yes, I did. I did try, and I couldn't believe what I heard coming out of my mouth."

Now Abner sat looking across his desk at the chair and reminiscing. From the time they had gotten it home and cleaned it up, it had dominated any space it occupied. The wood gleamed, and the velvet, far from being moth-eaten, was rich and dense.

It had been in their home in the Garden District for some time before Abner figured out the true magic of it, or maybe it was Latreece that had discovered the secret. When they did, they put it in an out-of-the-way place. It was not a piece to be displayed where anybody and everybody would sit in it, because whoever sat in it was compelled to tell the truth. Not only did what they said have to be true, but the chair seemed to pull from them whatever was meant to be kept secret. Abner and Latreece had agreed. It might be a handy thing to have in a lawyer's office, perhaps even a doctor's clinic, but not in a home. Who would want to visit them if everything that was spoken was absolute truth? What if the chair made a man tell his wife that he was having an affair? What if she told her husband that she only married him for his money? They laughed when they thought of varied secrets that might come to light, but they saw the truth in it as well. Their friends would never visit again. The Truth Chair was relegated to an out-of-the-way spot, and eventually Abner took it to a storage unit when he took the furnishings that had been pushed aside in lieu of the purchases from their last trip abroad.

Now here it was, a problem once more. Should he tell customers about the magic? Or should he not mention it and let them be surprised? That might be embarrassing. They might even become angry. There were places in the city where you could take items for auction. Maybe that's what he ought to do. While Abner pondered, the chair sat there, its beauty and uniqueness calling out. *Come sit in me. See if you don't feel like a king or a princess.*

He was still pondering the problem of the Truth Chair when customers started coming into the shop and as was his habit, he began talking to them—telling them the stories that came with the oddities he had for sale. He sold a gewgaw here, a bibelot there. He sold a Victorian cabinet to a couple from Tennessee and called the moving company down the block to come pick it up and ship it to their home in Memphis. A woman with long, luxurious hair bought an ivory comb reported to enhance her beauty. He didn't think more about the Truth Chair until hours later.

Two women had browsed for over an hour, looking at all the items in the shop and discussing them in detail. At long last a decision was made and as they stood at the desk, the one holding a delicate china figure placed it in front of Abner. "This is lovely. Please wrap it carefully. I'd hate for it to get broken on the way home."

The other woman had sunk into the nearest seating, removed one of her shoes and was massaging an aching foot. "Yes," she said. "Be sure to keep it safe until the first time you get mad at Dave. Then you'll throw it at him, like you do everything you can get your hands on when you fight, and it will be gone," The buyer flinched and looked startled, but no more startled than her companion occupying the Truth Chair. "I don't know why I said that," she said.

Abner knew. The statement had been wrested from her by the magic that had been sleeping for decades.

The gate was open, the chair primed. Next was a husband who sat in the chair while his wife shopped. He informed her that her collection of antique stemware that they never used was useless, but if it kept her from buying more expensive baubles it was worth the trouble. An hour later a wife sat in the chair while she hunted for her charge card in her purse. The husband was griping about the high cost of the antique necklace Abner was wrapping. "It isn't nearly as costly as the jewelry you buy that whore you're keeping," she told him. "And not nearly as expensive as a divorce is going to be when I've had enough."

And so it went. Minor secrets or opinions as well as important ones were told. There were startled looks and mouths were held tightly shut, but too late. Abner was tired and hungry by the time a shower chased shoppers from the sidewalks. Turning the sign on the door to 'closed,' he retreated to his kitchen for a light lunch of ham and cheese with Milton's crackers. An apple, sliced into wedges, finished the meal. The sun was chasing the clouds away by the time he finished, so he returned to the shop and flipped the sign back over. Perhaps there would be a few more customers before the day was over, but it seemed like everyone had given up shopping for curios and antiques. With no customers, Abner sat and thought about the Truth Chair. He had forgotten just how powerful it was and how it forced the truth from you, whether you cooperated or not. It was interesting to watch the responses of the people sat there, briefly, and blurted out unintended statements before jumping up and hurrying to leave. Perhaps it wasn't as unhappy a circumstance to have a stranger blurt out the truth as it was for a friends visiting your home to make a faux pas. Abner decided to leave it in the shop a few days before making a decision about the chair's future.

When he was about ready to lock the door once more and retreat to the sanctuary of his apartment a lone man came in. He looked nothing like a typical tourist, or even a local person browsing among the treasures that might be found in out-of-the-way shops. Muscular in stature, his brown hair tinged with gray at the temples, his physique suggested that he might have once been a boxer or wrestler. He paid little attention to the items for sale throughout the rooms comprising the sales area, but instead he seemed to be looking more at the building itself, eyeing each niche and alcove made by the arrangement of the merchandise. He even opened the doors that led into private areas, such as the rest rooms and the passages leading to the living quarters.

"Can I help you?" Abner asked. "Are you looking for anything in particular?" The odd behavior had him on edge, particularly since the snake on his walking stick had turned toward the shopper as if also watching the man, its tongue darting in and out.

The man did not answer, but continued to study the shop carefully. Finally, he walked back to where Abner sat behind his desk. "Nice shop," he said.

"Thank you."

"Are there living quarters connected?"

"Why do you ask? Are you looking for a place to live?" Abner was suspicious. Surely he wasn't going to be held up. Any robber who knew what he was doing would pick a better mark than a small antique shop in a middle class neighborhood. He gripped the snake stick tightly. The serpent changed its position, ready to strike if needed.

The man looked intently at Abner, then seemed to relax as he took a seat in the Truth Chair. "Uh, no. Nothing like that." He ran his hands over the carving on the ends of the arms, his fingers tracing the pattern of the wood, then said, "I'm looking for someone. She's supposed to live here."

"Here? Right here?"

"More or less. Somewhere around here."

"Why are you trying to find her?"

"Her parents are looking for her, and they sent me to find her."

Abner's heart fluttered as he heard the words that had described Latreece and himself so many years ago. They had never found their daughter. He hoped these parents succeeded in their mission. But this was an unusual way to search.

"And you traced her to this place?"

"Yes. She's been seen around here." He looked around the shop, but his eyes never lit on any one curio. "Not in this shop, but close by. I thought she might work here."

"Then it's not a child you are talking about?" The only way a child would have been seen around here would be in the company of an adult. Although there were times a family, including children, would come in his store, it was not often. He didn't sell the kind of things that usually interested a family with children. But if this stranger thought she might work here, he was speaking of an adult, not a child.

"No, a young woman. In her twenties."

"Ah," Abner said and relaxed. "Not a kidnapping then." He mentally chided himself for always drawing that conclusion.

"No, not a kidnapping. She left of her own free will, but the father wants her to come home. He hired our firm to find her and persuade her to come back."

Abner was puzzled. "Persuade? In what way? What would you tell her that would change her mind about leaving her home? Evidently without telling her parents where she was going."

There was a smirk on the man's face as he replied. "I have a team. We are prepared to rescue people from situations where the circumstances are not in their best interests."

The explanation did nothing to allay Abner's unease. "What do you mean? What kind of situations?" It sounded like something out of a thriller movie, and if the young woman had left home of her own free will, why did she need rescuing?

"The father says she is living an immoral life, caught up in debauchery. He is willing to do anything to save her."

"In other words, you and your team would kidnap her." Abner's temper was on a short fuse, ready to explode at this explanation. He had read about such antics. Teams of religious people who went into communes or communities and took the intended subject by force.

189

"I wouldn't put it that way. It would be in her best interests, and her father only wants the best for his daughter. He wants to remove her from a life that would harm her."

"Is the daughter of age?"

"If you are asking if she is over twenty-one, the answer is yes, she is. But just because she is legally of age, that doesn't mean she isn't in danger. If it were your child in danger, wouldn't you do anything—everything possible—to rescue her?"

Abner's heart tore at those words. If only he could have done so when Lily had disappeared. "Yes," he replied in a voice filled with emotion. "Yes, I would."

"So," the man said. "Are there living quarters here?"

"There is a small apartment upstairs," Abner pointed over head toward the far side. "But it's not occupied."

"I saw the iron gate next to this place, locked like a fortress. You have to have a key to get in. It looks like a courtyard back there, and living quarters. A perfect place to hide."

"Yes," Abner agreed. "I live behind this side of the shop, and above me there is a retired army man and his nephew."

"I see. No young woman, then?"

Abner would not lie, but he also would not admit that there was, indeed, a young woman who might very well fit the description of the person who had run away from home. He wasn't about to tell this stranger about Lexi. As far as he could see, she wasn't in any danger, nor was she living in sin and debauchery. She had a responsible job at Simon's Place, earned her own living in a reputable profession, and was healthy and happy. She had introduced herself one morning when Abner was sitting in the courtyard and she stopped to speak to him on her way to work. Ever since then had gone out of her way to speak to him and ask how he was doing. She seemed pleasant and happy, and from what Abner could tell, Simon was pleased with the job she was doing for him. The restauranteur had commented about the increased business he was having due to the meetings in the auxiliary room. There was no reason, he thought, no reason at all that he should pull Lexi into this. After all, he, Abner, wasn't the person sitting in the Truth Chair. Nothing, no spiritual force or anything else, was forcing him to tell secrets to a stranger.

"Can you tell me one reason why, if there was, I should tell you, a stranger to me? For all I know, you might be a kidnapper yourself, coming with this wild tale."

The stranger bounded to his feet. "I'll take that as a yes," he said. He went toward the front door, but stopped and turned back, his hand on the door knob. "Don't get in the way, old man, or you'll be sorry." He exited and slammed the door behind him.

Abner heard a hiss, and when he looked down, the snake was extended several inches from the protection of the wooden cane, its tongue darting in and out toward the now departed man.

He sat and pondered the situation, trying to make some sense of it, or what he thought it might be. Somebody, Lexi's parents no doubt, had sent the man to find their daughter and probably to get her back home no matter what it took. Abner had read about dubious 'rescue' organizations that would go in a pull a child out of a cult. Perhaps this was one of those groups or businesses, but how anyone could condone such an action against another adult he could not understand.

Sighing, Abner pulled himself to his feet and started the process of closing the shop for the day. He didn't think he could deal with any more customers. His mind was too full as it was. There was no room for recalling the histories of the curiosities he had for sale.

Going into the adjoining space, he went to the light switches on the wall next to the castle doors. He flipped one and the overheard lights went off. Lamps all over the room remained lit, casting islands of light that reflected rainbows of color throughout.

Abner thought he heard the jingle of the strand of bells that hung on the front door to announce the arrival of a customer.

"We're closing," he called out. "Come back tomorrow."

There was a pause, then he heard a familiar voice.

"Dad?"

CHAPTER TWENTY-NINE

"What say, Bud?" Pernell entered the kitchen, where T. Wayne had papers spread out over the kitchen table. "You about finished with your homework?"

"Yeah," the boy answered and started gathering the work, carefully putting it in order. "I'm all done."

"So how's it going? You having any problems I need to know about?"

"Nah. Everything's copacetic." He had picked up using the word he heard so often from Pernell.

"Grades OK?"

"Yep. Better than OK. Teacher's thinking about moving me into a higher math group."

"That sounds good. That cool with you?"

"Uh-huh. I'd like that." Putting everything into a folder, he put the folder into the back-pack that lay to the side of the table. "Who's that dude down in the courtyard talking to Mr. Crow . . . er . . . Crowbridge?"

"That's his son. I stopped and met him on the way in."

"Son? I didn't know he had a son. He never mentioned him." T. Wayne couldn't imagine not mentioning a son. There must be something bad out of whack.

"I think things were kind of rough between them for a while, but it sounds like they are working it out." Pernell walked to the French doors that opened onto the gallery overlooking the courtyard below. "You ready for something to eat? Simon said they're having chili tonight at his place. They had a lunch meeting today in the room—The Texas Club. Simon made plenty of chili to serve and has some left.

They'll probably run out before the evening is over, he said. If we want any, we need to be early."

"I've never had any," T. Wayne said. "What is it?"

"Meat and beans, or just meat no beans, in a sauce. Spicy. Might be hot."

"I like hot. I'm in."

They descended the steps at the end of the gallery. Two men were still sitting there in the lowering light. "Gentlemen, we are going to Simon's Place for dinner. The special of the day is Texas chili. Would you care to join us?"

"Thank you, Pernell, but my old stomach would not tolerate such spicy food. Another time, perhaps. Robert," the old man said, pronouncing the name in the French manner, "you met Pernell earlier, and this is his . . . nephew . . . T. Wayne, who also helped me move into my shop and apartment."

"Good evening, T. Wayne. Thank you for helping my father. I'm very pleased to find him in such good company as you and your uncle."

"He has been worried about my welfare," Crowbridge said.

"When you run away from home and don't tell anybody where you are, we have a right to worry," the younger man said.

T. Wayne wondered how an old man like Mr. Crowbridge could possibly run away from home. Couldn't adults go where they pleased without it being described as 'running away'?

"As you can see," the elder Crowbridge said, "I'm safe and happy."

"Indeed you are. And after talking with you, I understand why you did what you did."

"We'll leave you now," Pernell said. "We need to get to Simon's Place before they run out of chili."

After they left, Abner addressed his son. "I'm glad you understand, Robert. Your home was in no way lacking. It just wasn't *my* home. My spirit, it was suffering."

"And you are home here?"

"Yes, I am. Not only am I surrounded by my belongings when I am in the shop, it makes me content to see them going to new homes, to people who will appreciate and enjoy them, instead of being locked up in barren storage spaces, unloved, unappreciated."

"You always spoke of the spirits that inhabited the things in our home. I didn't understand it then, and I'm not sure I understand it now, but if you are happy . . ."

"I am," Abner said. "Happy and content."

"The apartment seems to suit you."

"It does."

"And the people here watch over you."

"They do."

"And you are safe, comfortable and well-fed."

"Almost too well-fed. I enjoy Simon's cooking far too much."

"I didn't appreciate the difference," Robert said, "between your world and mine."

"I was not at home in your world. This . . ." he motioned around him, "is where I am comfortable, among the spirits of the past. They keep me company until it is my turn to move into the next dimension. I am at home here."

CHAPTER THIRTY

"So, do you like our special for the evening?" Simon asked when he walked up to the table.

"Yes!" T. Wayne said. "I mean, yes, sir!"

"Good. Everyone is commenting about it tonight. I might just add it to the menu, maybe once a week or so."

"I think you'd gain some customers, Simon," Pernell said.

When Simon strolled on to the next table, Pernell pushed the empty bowl away from him. He was frowning when he crossed his arms and leaned on the table. "We need to talk about something," he said.

Suddenly, T. Wayne was apprehensive. He had never heard Pernell use that tone of voice before. Something was up.

"You know that I write. Stories about the war, mostly, and about life."

T. Wayne nodded. That's about all Pernell did any more, write stories. When they first met, Pernell was a taxi driver. Then he was a mover. But now he was a writer. Evidently other people knew this, because his stories were being published in a variety of magazines— places that T. Wayne had never heard of. There were copies around the apartment, and T. Wayne read them and puzzled over the meanings.

"I've been contacted by a college, a small college, in another state. They would like for me to come give a talk, a speech, there. About the war. About my experiences. About writing."

"Gosh!" T. Wayne was impressed.

"And . . ." he looked at T. Wayne for the first time since he started talking, "If they like what they hear, I might be offered a job teaching there at the college."

T. Wayne didn't know what to say. Did this mean Pernell was leaving? Just when he had a home again, it might disappear. What then? A foster home? No way!

"Yeah?" T. Wayne looked at the tablecloth and started tracing circles on it with his finger.

"It's tempting. I think I'd like that. When I first came back to the states, I couldn't have even thought about something like that. It's taken all this time to regain a sense of myself—what I can do and what I can't. I was . . . " he leaned back and looked around the room, "I was lost. I was looking for a place to be. A place that felt like home, whatever that feels like."

T. Wayne nodded. He wondered if he was going to cry. He never cried. Never. At least since he was a little kid. But he didn't know if he could take one more time of the world being yanked from under him. Just as he had a place to live and plenty to eat. Just when he was in a school that he enjoyed and was learning new things, making friends, and dared to feel safe again, it was about to all disappear.

"The problem is," Pernell went on, "what about you?"

T. Wayne wanted to get up and rush away. Run away like Old Crow had done. Like *he* had done before. Run away and hide so they couldn't find him and take him to juvy or a foster home.

"They won't let me take you out of state," Pernell said. "I know, and you know, that we aren't really related."

T. Wayne nodded his head.

"So the only solution I can think of," Pernell said, and T. Wayne stopped drawing invisible circles and steadied his hand, waiting to be told that he was going to have to find a new home, "is to adopt you. Make you my son for real."

T. Wayne stopped drawing circles and looked up. He studied Pernell's face. He wouldn't be kidding about something like that, would he?

"Would that be OK? If I adopted you?"

T. Wayne nodded. He didn't know if he could speak or not.

"It is? Because I wouldn't do something you wouldn't like."

"Y . . yes," T. Wayne sputtered. "Yes, sir," he said in a loud, clear voice. "That would be OK." He let the feeling wash over him—the feeling of being wanted. He hadn't had that feeling since Granny had died. "It would be more than OK." He grinned. "It would be great!"

"Good! I was afraid you wouldn't like the idea."

"I like the idea. I like it." He didn't want Pernell to think that he didn't want to be the man's son—didn't want him to get the wrong idea. "I like it," he said a little louder.

"So, it would be copasetic if we moved to another city? Another state? If you wouldn't want to do that, I'd tell them that I wasn't interested."

T. Wayne was already blown away by the idea that he was to be adopted, but even the merest suggestion that Pernell would turn down a job, and important job at that, if he, T. Wayne, said he didn't want to move, was beyond belief. Nobody in his whole life had ever made even the smallest of decisions on what he, T. Wayne, wanted. Granny had to base everything on money. Could they afford it or not? Now here was this white man who had given him a home, bought him the things he needed for school, saw to it that he had food and clothing and most of all—safety, asking him if he wanted to be adopted and giving him the choice, asking if he would move to another state or not.

"It sounds cool!" T. Wayne said.

"Good. I was hoping you would say that." Pernell looked around the room. "Let's get on back home. It looks like they could use our table. The place is filling up tonight." On the way to the door, he spoke to Simon. "That chili was great. I hope you make it again sometime."

"Tomorrow," Pernell said as he and T. Wayne walked along the sidewalk, "I'll call Ms. Simpson and get the ball rolling. She'll tell us what we need to do."

When they reached Broussard Court, Pernell took out his key and unlocked the iron gate that guarded access to the courtyard and surrounding apartments. Abner was still where they left him, but now alone.

"Your son leave?" Pernell asked, although the answer was obvious.

"Yes, he did. His visit was a surprise, but a pleasant one."

"Then you worked out your differences?"

"We did," Abner replied. "And he is satisfied that I am safe and happy. All is well."

"I wonder if I might ask you a question?"

"About my son?"

"No, about adopting one of my own." Pernell placed his hand on T. Wayne's shoulder.

"Oh?"

"I think it would be wise for me to have an attorney on my side as we begin the process. Could you recommend someone?"

"Good for you," Abner said. He was silent for a few moments. "I have someone in mind, but let me check first. He is semi-retired and only takes a few cases these days. I think he would like this one. I'll call him tomorrow."

"That sounds good," Pernell answered. "I'll check back with you."

* * *

The next day when T. Wayne came home from school, he found Pernell sitting in the courtyard. "Hey, Bud," he called out. "How was school today? Learn anything new?"

"It was good," T. Wayne said. "I went into a new math class today. It's going to be hard, I think, harder than the one I was in, but the counselor said she thought I could handle it. If I can't, I'll go to her and tell her and she'll move me back to an easier class."

It's nice, T. Wayne thought, *to have somebody care how your day went.* From the time he started to school, Granny had been the person who did that until she died. It was something he missed. *I'll bet*

Pernell's mother or father asked him that when he was a kid, so he knows to do it now.

"How was *your* day?" he asked, conscious of reviving a tradition.

"Fine, just fine," Pernell said. "I called Miss Simpson and told her what we talked about. She said she thought that the ball was in our court to begin with. We need a lawyer to start the paperwork. She said that she had gone through your file recently, but she'd do it again. Your grandmother was legally your guardian, she thinks, but your birth mother and your father may need to sign off before I can adopt you."

"Why?" T. Wayne asked. "They neither one care a thing about me." He felt bitter inside. "If they cared a thing about me all these years, they would have been in touch. Why should they have the right to foul up things now?"

"It's the way to do things right," Pernell said. "And we're going to do things right and legal. OK?"

T. Wayne nodded.

"Mr. Crowbridge gave me the name of an attorney, a friend of his, and I went to see him. He said it would be best for us to find the names and addresses of both your parents and contact them ourselves about releasing their rights. We can give him the names and addresses and he'll do that for us, so it will be legal."

T. Wayne snorted. As far as he was concerned, they had no rights. None at all. His mother did whatever she did and was in prison for it. He'd never heard from his father, so obviously he didn't want anything to do with his son.

"How are we going to do that?"

"I've been studying on that. "Didn't you say you had your grandmother's Bible with you? And that it's full of papers and pictures and stuff?"

"Yeah," T. Wayne said.

"Maybe there's something in it that would help an attorney find them. If they can't be found, there's bound to be something that can be filed with the court."

T. Wayne nodded his head. He hadn't looked at a single scrap of paper from Granny's Bible. Bound as it was, by rubber bands stretching this way and that, it seemed as if it would explode if he took even one of the stretchy bands off. "You can look at it, if you want. I don't know if we could get it back together, though, if we take it apart."

"Maybe we could put it all in a box," Pernell said. "Then we could look at everything and see if there is a clue."

"Clue?" T. Wayne hadn't thought of this as a mystery, but he guessed it was, in a way.

"Clue to who your father is. Clue to how your mother might feel about the matter."

"Oh." He sat there, silent.

"If you want to, that is," Pernell said, but T. Wayne still said nothing. "If you want to call this whole thing off, we can. It is really up to you. It's your life, after all."

"It's yours, too."

"It is. But mainly it's yours."

"I do want to be adopted. It would be nice to have family again." They sat quietly for a few minutes as each thought about what adoption and family meant. "I guess I'm a little scared," T. Wayne said finally.

"Scared? Of what?"

"I don't know. Of what I might find out if I start looking at Granny's stuff."

Pernell was puzzled. "Of what you might find? What could you find that would frighten you?"

"I don't know." T. Wayne put his head back and watched the clouds floating by overhead. "Maybe my mother said 'take him. I don't want him. He's nothing but a bother to me' when she gave me to Granny.

She always told me that I was with her because my mother was in prison. What if she isn't, but she just didn't want me?"

Pernell's heart ripped just a little at those words. "Well, Bud, that's just a chance we have to take, and we won't know 'til we know. That's hard to face, I know, but necessary."

T. Wayne nodded his head. There had been a lot of hard things to face here lately. This was just one more.

"I can't change the past, but I can do my best to see that you have a good life from now on."

T. Wayne nodded again. "Yes sir," he whispered.

"So let's get started on this." Pernell stood up. "The sun is fixin' to go down. Let's move upstairs to our apartment to see what all we have that will help the lawyer do what he needs to do."

They went up the stairway to the second floor galley and then into their apartment. "You go fetch the Bible," Pernell said, "while I clear off the table." He took a dish towel and wiped away any crumbs that might be remaining on the table from breakfast.

When T. Wayne returned with the big, black volume in the hands, carefully placing it on the wooden surface. He tried scooting the rubber bands from around the bundle of papers, cards, and memorabilia, but they wouldn't roll off without tearing the edges of the items extending past the boundaries of the book.

"Let's take a shape knife and cut them," Pernell suggested. "If we decide to put it all back together, we'll get new ones."

That done, they carefully lifted the bits and pieces one by one, placing them in stacks on the table, beginning to get some order in the collection. One stack was greeting cards from various holidays: Christmas, birthday, Easter. There were a few receipts for items long gone, and several church bulletins from years gone by. There were yellowed clippings from the newspaper, mostly obituaries of older people that had been friends.

Searching among the pages, they found photographs. There were several of T. Wayne at various ages from babyhood on up. Pernell held out a pic of a young black woman, smiling as she leaned against the fender of a car. "Is this your mother?" he asked.

T. Wayne glanced at it. "Yeah."

"Nice looking."

As far as T. Wayne was concerned, anybody who got thrown in prison lost the right to be called 'nice looking.' He had seen that picture before, and it hurt when he looked at it. It made him think of what he had lost. A mother. He had lost a mother because she thought more about doing whatever she did to get thrown in prison for than she thought about her son. Granny kept telling him that he should forgive, but that wasn't easy. Not when it affected his life as much as whatever his mother had done affected his. He kept on looking, page by page, through the thick volume, finding more pictures.

Pernell, rifling through a stack of newspaper clippings and cards, stopped suddenly and studied a photograph. His voice sounded odd when he asked, "Who is this?" holding up a picture of a man in uniform.

"My father."

"Your father." Pernell almost whispered as he studied the image in his hand.

"Yeah. I think my mother gave it to Granny to show me, so I'd know what he looked like. But he was supposed to come back, and he never did, so what does it matter what he looks like?" He continued placing newspaper clippings, receipts, scraps of paper with phone numbers or addresses, all into their respective piles. "But his name isn't on it, so I don't even know my own father's name. Not that it matters," he added. "Since he never came back."

"He couldn't," Pernell said in the same funny voice he had used when he asked who the photo was. "He died."

T. Wayne stopped what he was doing and looked at Pernell. How would he know that?

"You don't even know his name. Your mother didn't even tell you that much." Pernell's voice was barely able to be heard. It was like he was talking to himself, instead of to T. Wayne.

"I was real little when she went to prison. I barely remember her. She didn't tell me anything about him. What I know, Granny told me."

"What did she tell you?"

T. Wayne shrugged and sat back in his chair. "Not much. She told me his name was Thomas, and my mother named me after him. She kept waiting for him to come back, but he never did. And then I was born, and my mother kept getting into trouble and she ended up in prison. I was about four or five, so she's been there about ten years or more. I went to live with Granny, and then she died, and here I am."

"Thomas . . ."

"Yes. That's my name, Granny said my mother named me after him. But I didn't want to be named after somebody who wouldn't claim me. I wanted to be called by my middle name, Wayne, but there was another boy in my room and his name was Wayne, so the teacher called me Thomas Wayne, like my grandmother did. It stuck, but it got shortened. I've been T. Wayne ever since."

"Thomas was your father's name. Thomas Elijah Pendleton. He was a fine man."

T. Wayne was puzzled. "How do you know?"

"I served with him. I knew him. He was my best friend." Pernell said. He looked at the photo in his hand. "I almost died with him."

CHAPTER THIRTY

It was a revelation to T. Wayne, who had always thought of the shadowy person who was his father as a no-good low-life, to learn how wrong he had been. Pernell had quickly told him so. "Thomas was a good man. He was brave," he told the boy. "He saved my life more than once."

As the sun set, they turned on the lights and kept talking. When they got hungry, they rummaged in the refrigerator to find something to eat. They couldn't be bothered with cooking, or even walking down the block to Simon's Place for a hot, fresh meal.

T. Wayne asked all the questions that he had ever considered about his father. Especially the big one. "Why didn't he ever come back to see about me?"

"He didn't know about you," Pernell said. "He didn't know you existed."

T. Wayne had never thought about that. For all his fifteen years, or at least the portion of it from the time he realized he had a father somewhere out in the world, he agonized over the thought that his father didn't care about him. If he did care he'd come see him. See if he was OK. See if he needed anything. That's what fathers were supposed to do.

T. Wayne knew other kids who didn't have fathers. It didn't seem to matter to them. Or if it did, they didn't let it show. He thought they probably hid it inside, like he did. He couldn't imagine any kid who really didn't care about their father, even if they pretended it didn't matter. But it mattered to him. Mattered a lot.

"Back then, about the time you were conceived, Thomas had been on leave in the states. When we met up again, he was talking about the girl he had met. A special girl, he said. 'This is the one,' he told me. 'The one I want to marry.' But she never wrote him, and when he wrote her, he didn't get an answer. Nothing. Nada.

"The next time he got state-side leave, he went looking for her. Looked all over New Orleans, to hear him tell it. But he couldn't find her. Couldn't even find one person who knew her." Pernell studied the photo in his hands as he spoke. "He got sadder and sadder. But . . ." he put the picture back on the kitchen table, "when you're a soldier, you've got to keep your mind on what you're doing. It's dangerous if you don't."

He stood and went to look out the French door at the black night outside. "Every time he was in the States he came to New Orleans. Looked for her. Asked around about her. But he never found out anything. Not one scrap of information." He turned and looked at T. Wayne. "He'd have liked you. You're just the son he would have wanted. Strong and resilient, like he was. Tough enough to survive when the going gets rough. That's you." He paused. "And that was Thomas."

They talked during the long evening. T. Wayne asked questions, and Pernell answered as best he could. Finally they got to the big question. The one it was hard to ask. How did Thomas Elijah Pendleton die?

"We were in a convoy, just tooling on down the road. It was a hot day, dust blowing up around the Humvee. We weren't expecting anything. We should have had an easy time of it. For once, nobody was shooting at us, and we were joking and laughing—trying to keep it light, you know. That's when the world ended."

"What happened?" T. Wayne whispered, wanting to know and not wanting to hear it.

"It was a mine. One minute we were going down the road, the next minute we blew up. There were two other men with us. They both died in the explosion. Thomas was still alive when the medics got to us, but he was hurt badly. They patched us up and sent us first to the field hospital, then to Germany, to the hospital there.

"I had shrapnel in me that had to be dug out by a surgeon, and I had lost a lot of blood, but Thomas . . ." he shook his head and pinched his nose with his fingers to keep from crying. "Thomas was in bad shape."

Pernell stood and looked out at the dark courtyard once again. His voice was tight, held in check by willpower, but still the emotion showed through. When he was able to speak again, he said, "The nurse brought me a wheelchair. They knew he didn't have long, and he wanted to see me."

T. Wayne kept silent. He wanted to hear and he didn't want to hear.

"Thomas wanted to tell me . . . tell me thank you . . . for being his friend. For saving his life a couple of times when we were in tough spots. And I got to tell him thank you for saving mine." A minute passed before Pernell could speak again. He put his hand on T. Wayne's shoulder and squeezed it.

"I think . . ." he swallowed hard, "I think that somehow Thomas arranged all this. From the other side, I mean. He arranged our meeting. He worked it all out. Since he wouldn't get to be your father, I'd take his place."

CHAPTER THIRTY-ONE

Lexi juggled the stack of catalogues in her hands as she struggled to open half of the double doors that were the entrance to Simon's Place. "Here, let me help you," a young man said as he rushed to her side.

"Thanks, Raoul, but I've got it." She started toward the swinging doors that led into the kitchen. "Is Simon here yet?"

"I think so," he replied and went back to checking the condiments and other assorted items that were on each table. He wiped each bottle and shaker, and used the cloth in his hand to clean an already spotless table before going to the next. "I think I heard him back there."

Lexi used her hip to bump open the right hand metal door that led into the kitchen.

"Good morning," she called out to everybody busy working in the hub of the restaurant.

"Morning," came replies from all over the room.

"Has Simon made it in yet?"

"He's checking in the produce man," somebody called out.

A waitress approached Lexi, a glass of iced tea in her hand. "You want some breakfast?" she asked, offering the glass.

"Yes, but let me get a spot and put these down." She straightened the stack to better hold it in one hand so she could take the tea. Starting back toward the door she had just come through, she said, "Tell Simon I'm here and—"

"Tell me what?" Simon asked as he came from the rear of the kitchen.

"Oh! Hi! I have some catalogues that have some possibilities for the dinnerware we were discussing."

"Good deal! I have a few things to take care of first, then I'll sit down with you. I'm thinking we need another dishwasher as well."

"That sounds like a good idea. With the event business expanding like it is, another dishwasher would help a lot."

"I never dreamed when I hired you that business would expand so rapidly. Not only all the events we're booking, but the customers who attend an event in the back room are coming back to eat in the restaurant and bringing their friends. We've never been busier."

A waitress started through the swinging door from the eating area. "Lexi, I just seated a woman who wants to talk to you. She came in and asked if Lexi Hobart works here. She didn't say what she wanted."

"Probably wants to talk to you about scheduling an event," Simon said. "You're bringing in business right and left."

Pushing the door back into the dining room, Lexi placed the load in her hands on a table near the kitchen access. A woman sat on the far side. Her silhouette and hair style reminded . . . *Surely not!* Lexi thought. *She just resembles . . .* She started across the room.

The woman raised her head. "Lexi?"

Lexi stopped and stood as if turned to stone by an evil witch. "Mother?" *No, not that. Never again.* "Margo? What are you doing here?"

The woman stood. "Looking for you."

"Why?"

"Because . . . because we miss you."

Lexi wished she could say "I miss you too," but she couldn't . . . wouldn't. Not after what she went through. Not after the ugly words from her father and knowing they were echoed by her step-mother, in private even if not directly said to the step-child who had grown to love her.

"Well, you found me." she said. "What now?"

"I . . . I don't know." Margo sat down.

As she approached the table, Lexi noticed that her step-mother was trembling. "If you're here to tell me what a bad person I am, to tell me that I'm surely going to hell, don't bother. My father has already told me all that."

"No. No I'm not." Margo twistedher hands together.

"And if you truly believe like he does, you don't miss me, either. You're glad I'm not there, soiling your perfect home and life." *And infecting your own daughter, the one I love, the one I've always called my little sister.*

"Lexi . . .," her face contorted as if in pain, and tears came to her eyes. "I've been praying about all this . . ."

"Good!" was the only thing Lexi could say.

"And I've been meeting with a couple of other people—women who have been praying with me."

Lexi snorted. "You mean I have a whole group of church members trying to pray me straight?"

"No! No, not that. They've been trying to show me how we . . . I . . . have been wrong." She rummaged in the purse in her lap until she came up with a tissue. "And they aren't church members, either."

"You mean my sin is being discussed in the whole community?" Lexi's voice was full of sarcasm.

"Please, Lexi. Please let me tell you. Let me apologize."

Lexi looked around the room. A few people had come in for a late breakfast or an early lunch, and she didn't want to make a scene. She pulled out the chair across the table from her step-mother and sat down. "Go ahead," she said. "Say what you have to say." She kept her voice low.

Margo took a deep breath. "These women, they have children who are . . ."

"Gay? Homosexuals?"

Margo nodded. "Yes. And they made me understand how wrong I was. Even if I don't agree with your . . . lifestyle, I can still love the person." She looked at Lexi, sincerity showing from her face. "And I do, Lexi. I do love you." She extended her hand toward her step-daughter. "And your father loves you too."

"Yeah, right," Lexi said, ignoring the outstretched hand. "As long as I do what he wants, and agree that what he says is always the right thing to do." She looked down at the table top. "And you're afraid that if I'm close to Jenny, I'll talk her into being gay too."

"I was wrong, Lexi, and I admit it. It *was* what I thought, but my friends, the other mothers, showed me how wrong I was. I ought to be teaching my daughter to be kind and compassionate. Understanding of others even when I don't agree with everything they do or believe. Jenny misses you, she misses you a lot. She doesn't understand what's going on."

"I miss her too," Lexi said, and her voice cracked.

"She was so young when your father and I married, you have been her sister since she can remember. She can't fathom why you left."

"How did you find me?"

Howard heard about this group that find people, children mostly, who are in cults. You can hire them to go in an rescue someone who can't or won't leave the group."

"Kidnap them, you mean?"

"Well, probably," Margo answered. "But Howard didn't want that. He just wanted to know where you were, and that you were OK."

"As you can see, I'm perfectly fine."

"Yes, I see that." She looked around the room. "This looks like an . . ." she paused, "interesting place. What do you do here?"

"She brings in business," a deep voice said.

"Margo, I'd like you to meet my boss, Simon Bondurant, the owner of Simon's Place. Simon this is my step-mother, Margo Hobart."

"Pleased to meet you," Simon said, extending a hand. "I am very happy to have met your step-daughter when I did. She was dining here with some regular customers of mine, and when I found out about her expertise in dealing with special dining events I hired her on the spot."

Margo looked at Lexi, her eyes wide. "I . . . I . . .guess I didn't really understand what you did for a living."

"No, I guess you didn't."

"If I had to give her a title," Simon said, "it would be special events manager." He had just said that when a baby's cry pierced the air. "Uh-oh. I hear my baby daughter calling for her daddy," he said, looking around. "There's my wife. I'd better go see what she wants. Nice to meet you, Mrs. Hobart."

Margo looked across the room at the woman standing by the front entrance to Simon's Place, holding a wailing baby and talking with a waitress. "You're an events planner?" she asked, turning back to Lexi.

"Yes. There is another large room through those doors," Lexi said, motioning toward back wall. "We plan, decorate, do the food, everything needed except sending out the invitations. We host birthday parties, showers, retirement parties, most any kind of planned get together. That's what I did back home, you know, except I wasn't the one in charge. Barry and Chad ran the business and I just worked for them. But I had enough experience to start a new service here for Simon."

"I didn't realize. I didn't know . . ." Margo trailed off. "Do you have a nice place to live? I mean, is it safe, in a good neighborhood?"

"I live in the next block," Lexi said. "And yes, it's safe and comfortable. And handy. I can walk to work. I never have to move my car."

A waitress approached their table. "Lexi, you want some breakfast? Or lunch?"

"Thanks, Estelle. Yes, I guess I'd better eat. Whatever is handiest."

"We got a good special egg scramble this morning."

"OK . That's great."

Estelle left, and Lexi saw her pause and speak to Simon on her way to the kitchen. He nodded, said a few words, then went back to playing with the baby in his arms.

Lexi had one more question on her mind before her step-mother left. "How is Daddy?" she asked.

"Not good," Margo replied. "He's in our hotel room. He wants to see you, and he doesn't want to see you. It's hard to explain." She sighed. "He's had some trouble with his heart."

Lexi gasped, but she tried to hold it back. She didn't want to care, but she did. And since she did, she at least wanted to keep it hidden. It was a vulnerability that could be used against her.

Margo held up her hand. "It wasn't a heart attack, his doctor said. It's stress. But he needs to calm down. All this is worrying him."

"I'm sorry," Lexi said. "But I don't see anything that I can do. I'm not going to change who and what I am. And I'm not going to move back home, if that's what he's thinking."

"To tell you the truth, I believe that's exactly what he thinks. He thinks if he apologizes enough that you'll move back home."

"No way. I'm settled and happy. I have a good job where I'm appreciated for my talents. I have friends. I have a nice place to live. New Orleans is an interesting place, and before long I'm going to start exploring the town a bit. I'm not going back to Texas."

"Will you come see him?" Margo asked. "Talk to him? Let him see how you are doing?"

Just then a bus-boy arrived bearing a large tray, laden with food. He set a plate on the table in front of each woman: steaming eggs scrambled with what looked to be all sorts of vegetables. Onions, bell peppers, tomatoes, and mushrooms. He placed a small platter of thinly sliced ham, and a basket of golden brown biscuits in the middle of the table between the two women. Small jars of jam and jelly adorned the display. He set a glass of iced tea in front of Lexi. "What would you like to drink, ma'am?" he asked Margo.

"My goodness," Margo said. "Coffee, I suppose. I wasn't expecting a meal. Do you eat like this all the time?" she asked Lexi.

"Not hardly. I do get my meals free as part of my salary, but it's usually nothing like this. This is the kitchen is showing off, I imagine."

"Yes ma'am. We takes care of our own," the bus-boy said as he left. "Can't be any place better than this."

Both women laughed. "He's afraid you'll leave," Margo said.

"Uh-huh. He works more hours when we have events scheduled." She motioned toward the back room. "He doesn't have to worry about that," she said. "I enjoy what I'm doing too much to leave." She reached for a golden brown biscuit. "Now, about seeing Daddy. You said he's in your hotel room?"

"Yes, he thought it would be better if he didn't come here."

Lexi was silent as both women sampled the egg dish in front of them. Finally, Margo spoke. "Lexi, he wants to see you. He's missed you so much."

Lexi remained mute.

"Won't you please come to the hotel and see him? It would mean so much to both of us."

Lexi took a sip of tea. "No, I think not."

Margo stopped eating and folded her hands in her lap. "No? Lexi . . ." She shook her head. "He's your father, Lexi. Doesn't that mean anything to you?"

"Of course it does," Lexi said as she broke open the biscuit and spread butter on the flakey interior.

"Please come, Lexi, and make up this . . . spat."

"More than a spat, Margo. Much more than a spat."

"It needn't be." Margo picked up her fork. "We can get through this."

"You forget, I know my father very well." Lexi took a sip of tea. "And my father doesn't give in like this."

"What do you mean?"

214

"Just what I said. My father doesn't give in. He said some hateful things to me. Very hateful things." She picked up her fork. "And he doesn't change his mind about what he believes."

Margo didn't look at her step-daughter, She poked at a bit of bell pepper with her fork and remained silent.

"So I have to ask myself, what's going on?" Lexi studied her step-mother.

"What's going on is he wants to see his daughter again," Margo said. "He wants to be a family again, like we used to be."

Lexi leaned back, her hands grasping the table on either side of her plate. Studying the woman across the table from her, she said, "I wouldn't put him past pulling something really underhanded. If I came to your hotel to see him, there very well could be the team of so-called rescue people waiting to grab me and take me away." She studied the older woman. "Is that the plan?"

Margo said nothing, but her cheeks were bright red. She gave up trying to eat, but sat there with downcast eyes.

"I thought so," Lexi said. She pushed the remains of her breakfast away from her. "But I would like to see my father one more time."

Margo looked up. "He really does love you, Lexi."

"If he loved me, he would love me the way I am, not the way he wants me to be." She looked around at the people who were filling the dining room. "I'll tell you what. If he really want to see me, he can come here." She placed her napkin beside her plate. "Tonight. I'll see to it that we have a private table, so we can talk. All of us. You, Daddy, me, and Jenny. But I won't be alone. I'll have protection nearby. He won't have a chance to have me kidnapped. Understand?" She pushed her chair back and stood up.

CHAPTER THIRTY-TWO

"I can't get over you doing this for me," Trudy said. She drew the seatbelt around her and clicked the buckle as she adjusted herself for the trip.

"I know this is important for you," John Lankett said. "But I have to admit something. It's an adventure for me. When you told me the story, it was like something out of a book. I'm looking forward to helping you solve the mystery of who you are almost as much as you are."

He checked traffic and pulled out onto the highway. "I just hope we can find out what you need to know," he said when traffic had cleared enough that he could carry on a conversation.

"I can't believe it, and I lived it," Trudy said. "What I need to know most of all is who I am. Even my name is bogus." She shook her head. "Tomorrow we'll start looking. But I don't even know how to begin." She was quiet for a few minutes as John converged with the stream of cars headed south. "I was *so* frightened," she said. "When I determined that I had to go back to the beginning of the whole thing, I was scared—I don't know of what. I'm afraid of what I might find out, and I'm afraid that I might *not* find out anything. I'm so glad you are going to be with me. It makes me feel safer to not be all alone, but safe from what I have no idea."

"I'm happy to do it. You know that I enjoyed our time together on the trip, and I wanted to get to know you better. I just never dreamed it would involve spending time trying to find out who you are." He chuckled. "You're the perfect example of a mystery woman."

"I'm a mystery even to myself," Trudy said, smiling.

"I want to confess something right up front," he said, now serious.

"OK." She looked over at him.

"I did a little investigating myself."

"Oh?"

"My boys were all up in arms about me going off with a woman I had just met, much less a woman with a wild story about who she was and where she came from."

"I can understand that."

"They insisted I do a bit of investigation first."

"And did you?"

"Yes, I did. I spoke with my lawyer and had him call your attorneys, the ones you told me about, Mulder and Schmidt. Seems everyone is just as baffled as you are about the situation."

Trudy sighed.

"The likeliest thing they can come up with is that the old lady, the one you thought was your grandmother, kidnapped you. Simply saw you and took you. There was a story on one of those true crime TV shows recently about a woman who did that. She took two girls—not at the same time—and raised them as her granddaughters. It was years before they figured everything out."

"That's what she always said, that she wanted me and took me, but I just thought it was the meandering of an old lady's mind. When she sounded rational she told the story about my parents being killed in a car wreck and she, as my grandmother, took me in. I didn't know until after her death that she told the attorneys I was a neighbor child that she was babysitting since the mother worked long hours."

"But there's no chance of that being true, right?"

"Right. They didn't find any neighborhood child here in St. Louis that I could have been. My attorneys, or rather *her* attorneys, checked out the other story with the New Orleans police. There was no accident, car wreck or any other kind, that killed a couple and left a little girl without parents any time around when it would have occurred." Trudy watched the passing scenery. "Of course, it was

217

recently, after she died, when I went into their offices and started making waves, which was many years after when it would have occurred."

"To bad nobody noticed back when it happened that she suddenly had a small child. If they had started asking questions back then . . ." John trailed off, silent for a while. "But then she was sane enough—had presence of mind enough—to know that what she had done was wrong and she had to keep it hidden from her attorneys," he added.

"I never thought about it like that, but yes, that's right. She was sane enough to lie about it."

Throughout the long trip south, the conversation touched on many things. Books and music and interesting things they'd like to learn more about. Food preferences and TV shows and which comedians made them laugh.

"I haven't laughed like that since Doris died," John said as they discussed a movie they had both liked.

"How long has it been?"

"Almost two years," he answered. "I still miss her, but I'm beginning to look to other interests. Other than the ones she and I shared, that is."

"It must be hard."

"Yes." He paused. "But it's getting easier." After a minute of silence, he spoke again. "I thought I was doing the best thing, turning my two stores over to my sons. I was tired of going to work every day. Tired of the same problems, the same questions, everything the same except Doris wasn't there at home at the end of the day. So I said 'here—you run them. You're going to inherit them anyway—you might as well start now.' Which was just what they wanted—to run the businesses without input from the old man. I have enough investments to live on. The boys can sink or swim on their own."

Again he was quiet, and Trudy didn't speak. His businesses and family weren't her concern, and she wouldn't offer any observations, lest he think she was stepping where she didn't belong.

"So now," he finally continued, "I'm bored out of my mind. I spent my life running first one, then two stores. What's selling and what's not. What should I order for next year. But I no longer care about any of that. I have no hobbies. I don't play golf, like friends my age do, don't fish, don't do anything at all. That's one reason I took the trip to New Orleans. I wanted to go, and I didn't want to go by myself, so when I saw the advertisement, I signed up." He glanced toward Trudy. "And I'm glad I did." He smiled, and she smiled back. "I made a new friend. *and*," he emphasized, "found myself in the middle of a mystery that's not in the latest best-seller."

Trudy smiled. Somehow, having another person to share this perplexing story with made it a little easier to cope with.

CHAPTER THIRTY-THREE

The next morning they went for breakfast in the coffee shop of the hotel where they were staying. "I'm at your disposal," John said. "What do you want to do today?"

"I'm flying blind, as they say. There was nothing we did on the tour, nothing we saw, that triggered any specific memories for me, but I still believe that my early years were spend here in New Orleans. It just feels right, you know?"

"Like you've been here before?"

"Yes, exactly. Like I've been here before, even if I can't point to anything and say "I remember that". Her brow was furrowed as she spread jelly on her toast. "It sounds aimless, but maybe driving around to see if anything sparks a memory."

"That's all I could suggest," John said. "You mentioned going to the cemetery. We could do that."

"Yes, when we were on the tour, I had thought going to the cemetery and looking for my parents graves was something I wanted to do, but . . ."

"But?" John looked at her with raised eyebrows.

"That was when I still thought my name was Gertrude Ann Miller."

"Oh, yes. I see the problem. You wouldn't know what name or names to look for."

"Since there are no names to look for, and there are no parents that were killed in a car wreck, I think a visit to the cemetery would be useless." She gazed off into space. "Now that I'm here, I don't have a direction to follow."

"Perhaps just driving around town would be best," John said. "At least to begin with. And if anything looks familiar, we'll stop and look closer, maybe ask questions."

Two hours later found them driving through a residential area. Fine homes, obviously very old, lined the streets. "I like this area—these houses," Trudy said.

"What do you like about them" John asked.

"I like the colors. Pink ones, blue ones, and there—that yellow one— I love that." She had difficulty turning this way and that, trying not to miss seeing everything on both sides of the street. "And the balconies! Lovely."

"Do you see yourself in one of those?" John asked.

She thought about that question with eyes closed. "The floors were wooden. Wide planks of smooth, shiny wood. When I sat on the floor, it was so nice and cool on a hot day."

"That's good," John said. "You're remembering things."

"I sat on the floor and played with my dolls. And I had a tea set. Little cups and saucers, and I used to pretend I was feeding my dolls tea." She smiled as the memories played in her mind. "My favorite doll, she had a dress made of the same fabric as the one I wore. I liked to wear that dress. I wanted to wear it all the time. It had flowers on it—tiny blue flowers." She frowned. "Her name—what was her name?" She shook her head as she opened her eyes. "That's all I can remember."

"It's something that you didn't remember before," John said. "Maybe more will come to you later."

"Maybe." Her sigh was tremulous. *Maybe.*

CHAPTER THIRTY-FOUR

The morning took them in all sorts of neighborhoods as they explored New Orleans. Past the memory of playing dolls on the floor of a house, possibly in the Garden District, nothing else presented itself to Trudy's memories. They drove through all sorts of areas—rich and poor, residential and commercial, but nothing more stirred her until they were on a street where the shops were festooned with gaily colored beads, masks, and costumes.

"Stop!" she suddenly cried.

"You remember something?" John asked as he pulled to the side of the street.

"All this," she motioned around them.

"Mardi Gras costumes," John said.

"Mardi Gras."

"You remember Mardi Gras?"

"Sort of." She was quiet as she looked around. The shop they were in front of had masks hanging from the eaves, along with streamers of green, gold and purple fabric blowing in the breeze. "Parades, and music. Lots and lots of people."

"Yes, I imagine so."

From somewhere in the area, a trumpet sounded. "Music," Trudy repeated. "I liked the music." She watched the passers-by, laughing as they made their way along the sidewalk. "And the people—they were so funny. The costumes. I loved the costumes. And they threw things to the crowds. Trinkets and beads. I tried to catch them. I wanted . . . I wanted . . . something, I forget what."

Her face was glowing as memories started pushing their way into the present. "And some of the women, their dresses were so . . ." She put her hands to her chest. "Their breasts showed, and they had painted things on them, like flowers and ribbons. Funny things, too. One woman had eyes painted on hers. But my mommy wouldn't . . . she wouldn't do that. It's not . . ." Her voice became childlike as she related what surely must have been memories. "Daddy, he whispered something in her ear, and I wanted to know what he said that made Mommy blush. And she said stop . . . stop talking like that. And he said something else I couldn't hear, and they both laughed."

John remained silent as Trudy rambled. Obviously she was remembering what she had seen as a small child. Or was it so obvious? Or would some people say she was only telling about what she had seen on television or in magazines?

The expression on her face suddenly changed. "But . . . it's . . . it's scary," she said. "I'm frightened."

"What are you frightened of?"

"I don't know." She was quiet, her face blank. "I don't know." She looked this way and that, her eyes darting as if looking for something to jump out and frighten her.

A few minutes later, as they drove slowly along the street, they talked about what she had remembered.

"Were those true memories?" she asked. "Or am I fooling myself."

"We can't know for sure," John said. "But I'll bet they are true memories."

A couple of minutes passed as they mulled over what Trudy had revealed, what it possibly could be that frightened her all those years ago.

"I'll bet," he said, looking at her, "that Ruby, or whatever her name was, grabbed you away from your parents at a Mardi Gras parade."

* * *

"Look, John. There's the restaurant where we ate on the tour."

"Simon's Place. Yes, that was good food. Want to eat lunch there?"

223

"Yes, I do. I wanted to explore the neighborhood that day, but we had to get back to the bus."

"Bus tours are a good way to check out a place to see if you want to come back and spend more time there," John said. "But they don't allow enough time to explore."

It took a few minutes to find a parking place, then walk a couple of blocks back to the eating establishment they had spotted. Seated in the midst of the lunch customers, they ordered something titled 'sampler for two' from the menu. The waitress assured them it would be plenty for both of them to taste several of the dishes for which New Orleans was known. "It's a good way to learn the difference between gumbo, jambalaya, and etouffe," she said. "And it comes with samples of several deserts as well," she told them. "Bread pudding, flan, pecan pie, and whatever cobbler the chef is serving today. It's big. Plenty enough for two unless you're really hungry."

"We'll take that," John said.

As they sat waiting for their meal, nearby the big double doors into another dining room were opened several times as a server went back and forth. It appeared that only one family was being served in the privacy the separate room afforded. Four people were seated in the large room. A couple, a young woman, and a young girl were having a lively conversation. A conversation that might even be called an argument. The older woman seemed to be on the verge of tears. She kept dabbing her eyes with her napkin. The man was red-faced and at first appeared to be angry, his voice raised loud enough to be heard in the main dining room. The child looked sad.

"I'm not the only person with drama taking place in their life," Trudy said, nodding toward the other room. "That family has something going on as well."

"It sure looks like it. I hope they get it worked out." He glanced that way as the doors opened once more. "I'm sure glad that my sons and I get along. I'd hate to be in some kind of a brouhaha with family members."

"Yes, I would too." She thought a moment before adding, "but I'd like to have the family, just without the arguments."

"You're right about that," John said. "With what you've remembered today about New Orleans and possibly your life here, maybe you're on track to find your real family. Or at least some clues."

"I hope so. This is the first time I've ever remembered a thing about myself at that age."

"It's promising." He placed his hand on top of hers where it lay on the table. "I think you've begun to break open the mystery of your past." He squeezed her hand.

Just then a man sitting at a table nearby stood. Holding a water glass in his hand, he tapped on the side of it with a spoon. Conversations stopped all over the room and all eyes turned toward him. "I'd like to make an announcement," he said.

"It's been a couple of years since I came to New Orleans. I had just been released from a military hospital where I had been recovering from injuries I had sustained in the war in the mid-east. I was in bad shape, mentally and physically, and I chose this city in which to recuperate because my best friend, who died in the same explosion that I experienced, was from NOLA, and I wanted to see the places he had been telling me about.

"It was here that I got well again—mentally and physically—and I gained many friends." He gestured around the room and clapping broke out, along with a few whistles. "I also gained a couple of things I didn't expect to find here in the Big Easy. A sense of home and a son." He put his hand on the shoulder of the young black man sitting beside him at the table.

"They say that if you pay attention, fate puts you to where you ought to be."

"Dat be right." "Sure 'nough." "You know it." Voices around the room agreed.

"So fate put me here, but now fate is telling me that it's time for my son and me to move on." The room was suddenly quiet. "I have been offered a job teaching a couple of classes at a small college in Missouri. This allows me time to continue my writing. I start at the beginning of the next semester. Thomas Wayne and I have visited there, and we are moving in the next few days, so this is a goodbye to all the fine people of this neighborhood. I . . .we . . . will never forget you." With that, he sat down to applause, and everyone broke into conversations, primarily about the announcement.

"Nice," John said. "It seems like a real neighborhood, where people are interested in each other."

"Yes. Wherever I settle, I hope I find a place like this. A home."

"If you believe what he said, fate will move you to where you ought to be and you'll find the home you're meant to find."

Trudy sighed. "I hope so."

"Perhaps it was fate that let you remember things from your past today. Things you didn't remember until you got back to New Orleans."

She didn't answer. The things she remembered, if indeed they were memories, rather than answering questions, caused more.

When they finished their meal, John said, "Would you like to walk around this neighborhood a bit before we go to the car?"

"Yes, I would. I think I remember seeing a shop in the next block when we were here with the bus tour. It had all sorts of interesting things in the windows."

"I remember seeing that. Let's go explore."

A short walk brought them to the shop in question. "There it is," John said as they approached. "Just past those iron gates."

When they reached the ornate ironwork gates, they stopped and looked through the loops and twists into a serene courtyard. "Wouldn't it be nice to have a place like this to sit and dream?" Trudy said.

"I'd like that. A good book, a comfortable chair, and I'd be set for an afternoon of reading and daydreaming."

Next along the sidewalk was the shop in question. The large windows on either side of the entrance were filled with merchandise meant to catch the eye of anyone walking along the way. Pieces of china, boxes made of parquetted wood, odd figurines, all that and more lay side by side with items of questionable purpose. Strings of beads mixed with carved wooden objects were meant to draw questions which could only be answered by the shop owner. The passers-by could see farther back into the room, where furniture of all sorts filled the space and lured them inside to browse.

A bright blue bench in front of the window drew shoppers to sit and rest. A big Siamese cat sat watching, and when Trudy came near, it meowed at her. "Hello there, kitty," she said, and extended her hand. It immediately began to purr and rubbed its nose against the sleeve of her shirt. "Aren't you the pretty one?" When she spoke, the cat stood and raised its front paws up to her chest, begging to be picked up.

"I've never seen a cat be so friendly with a stranger," John said.

"I like cats. I guess it knows it." She frowned, looking off into the distance as she stroked the cream colored fur. "I think I must have had a cat before. One like this."

"At your so-called grandmother's house, you mean?"

"No. Before that. Back in the time I can't remember. Ruby wouldn't let me have a cat. She didn't like them."

"Notice the signs," John said, pointing to squares of white poster board propped in the front window. 'Apartment for rent' one said, and 'Help wanted' the other. He looked pointedly at Trudy. "Aren't those the two things you said you needed to move to New Orleans?"

"I did. Maybe it's an omen."

They entered the quaint shop and were immediately surrounded by all sorts of ephemerae from around the world. The items everywhere about her immediately wrapped Trudy in a magic-like atmosphere. "Oh my," she said as she went from one item to another. She reached out one finger and touched the rim of a magnificent bowl, and it seemed to glow more brightly in the subdued light. "Oh!"

From one display to another, she went and could not resist touching, even though she knew she shouldn't. Every time she hesitantly reached out with a gentle touch, her finger activated some invisible adjustment that made the colors explode into glorious abandon, and an aura surrounded the item, changing it into something magical.

Standing a couple of feet back from the large front window was a wonderful cabinet. Tall and broad, it was covered with intricately carved figures, the swirls and petals so complicatedly weaving in and around that one could not tell where one image stopped and another began. People and trees, rivers and bridges, pagodas and flowers. All in glorious profusion.

"It's called a Story Cabinet," a voice from behind her said. "And it is magic. It will tell the story of the person touching it." The old man moved up to stand beside her. "If you do not want your story told, do not touch the cabinet."

"I want my story told," Trudy said. "I need to know who I am," she said as she placed both hands on the side of the cabinet closest to her. "I *need* my story told. Will it tell me who I truly am? Can the Story Cabinet tell me that?" The wood under her fingertips glowed even more as it morphed into images that had not been there when she first touched it. Leaves and stems and slender blossoms sprouted and grew. One at first, then more, and suddenly a profusion of blooms burst into wooden existence, growing up the side and around to the front more rapidly than the eye could follow.

"Lilies," she said. "They're lilies!"

"Yes," Abner said, "they are." Suddenly weak, he had to hold onto the back of the chair standing next to where he stood.

"I . . . it's my name! It's . . . it's Lily! I know. I remember!" She kept both hands firmly on the cabinet, and the carving exuberantly developed vines and tendrils that pushed aside the figures and symbols that had adorned the cabinet for decades, joyfully replacing everything there with more and more lilies.

"I know," she said. "I know my name!" Excited, she placed her cheek against the smooth wooden flowers. "It's Lily! My name is Lily." Immediately, her head swirled and she felt unsteady on her feet. She put a hand out, reaching for support as she stumbled backwards.

John reached toward her, and putting his arm around her waist for support he urged her toward the ornately carved chair that sat in front of a nearby desk. He eased her into it before he noticed that the shop owner looked as unsteady as John's companion. His face was ashen, and he used both hands to cling tightly to his cane.

"Here," John said, offering his hand. "You'd better sit down as well." He assisted the frail old man to the chair behind the desk. "You don't look well, either."

"I . . . " Abner stammered. "I can't believe it . . ." He kept his sight on the young woman sitting in the Truth Chair, her black curls shining against the gold velvet of the chair, her vivid blue eyes watching the lilies grow and change all over the rosewood—lilies replacing lilies, over and over again in wild profusion.

CHAPTER THIRTY-FOUR

Like water dripping slowly until it forms a small stream, then rushing forward, tumbling willy-nilly in its journey toward becoming a river, her memories slowed only briefly to gather themselves into semi-cohesion, then broke into wild abandon.

"My name isn't Gertrude Ann. She just named me that—the woman who said she was my grandmother. That was her name—Gertrude Ann. The attorney told me that. She called me by her own name. All those years, she did that. Told me my name was Gertrude Ann. And I hated it! Hated it!" She looked toward the cabinet standing a few feet away from her, lilies still expanding and spreading all over the wooden surface. "I had a name, a beautiful name. Lily. I loved that name. And I remember . . ." She stopped talking and just watched the cabinet. "I remember I like to watch the Story Cabinet. I'd put my hands on it, and wherever they touched, it would change to lilies. I liked doing that." She sighed. "I tried to remember the cabinet after she took me. I tried, but it got harder and harder. I still remembered, back then, that my name was Lily, but she said no. She said that I was wrong, that it wasn't my name. Said my name was Gertrude Ann." She wiped the moisture from her cheeks with trembling hands. "Why didn't I remember? I just forgot. Forgot my name. Lily. I forgot that my name was Lily. How could I do that? How in the world could I forget my own name?"

She looked at her hands, twisted her fingers around each other. "And when I forgot, there was no more Lily. Lily was gone."

"No. There was still a Lily in our hearts. In mine and in your mother's. We never forgot," Abner said softly. He didn't know if she heard him or not. It was like talking to himself. "Lily was still alive."

Tears ran down her face. "This last week or so, I had no name. None. I wasn't Gertrude Ann. I still answered to Trudy, as if that were really my name, but it wasn't. I knew it wasn't! I had no name." She drew in a shuddering breath as she closed her eyes for a moment.

Agitated, full of nervous energy, she ran her fingers over the curved wood that formed the arms of the chair. She didn't know until much later that the chair known as the Truth Chair was bringing forth all that had been dammed up inside for the last thirty years. All she knew was that the memories were returning to her more quickly than she could process them, and they spilled out of her mouth like water gushed from a gargoyle fountain. It would have been impossible to keep them inside, as impossible as it would have been to keep the Story Cabinet from forming lilies on every surface, replacing the ones it made minutes ago with new ones. Everything in her head was a jumble of pictures and feelings, falling in on each other until she could barely keep them straight.

Abner sat in silence as his own tears flowed. Everything he had dreamed of for over three decades was coming to pass. Given up for dead, his beloved child had been returned to him. A miracle had occurred, and she was there, in front of him, not as the precious child that had been stolen from him, but as an adult. He had missed all the intervening years—the important growing up years. Somebody—whoever this Gertrude Ann was—had been there, stealing the memories that ought to have been his. His and Latreece's. They ought to have been the ones to share Lily's life, not a stranger. He had no doubt, none at all, that this was his child sitting before him, with the truth pouring out of her, thanks to The Chair.

John pulled up another chair and sat in stunned silence as the story unfolded.

"I had wanted to take my dolly with me that day," the memory trickled from her, "the day I stopped being Lily. And Mommy wouldn't let me. She said she might get lost and then I'd cry, because my doll

231

would be lost forever. So I was angry. I wanted to do what I wanted. I wanted my doll." Her voice was strident as she recalled that day so long ago. "So when Mommy insisted I hold her hand, I didn't want to." She shook her head and clasped her hands to her chest. "No! And then . . ." she looked up at the ceiling all around the room, as if she could see things the other people in the room could not, "and then a float came by, and they were throwing beads, bright green and purple and gold, and there were silver ones as well—that's what I wanted—some of those silver beads."

She closed her eyes and her head dropped. The gaiety of the celebration disappeared in a flash. "There were some there on the ground. And I wanted them." The young woman sitting in the chair reached out, as if the silver beads were right there in the room with her. "I pulled my hand out of Mommy's grasp so I could reach for them. And the crowd moved around me, reaching for the beads from the float that the jesters were throwing. Someone grabbed my arm. I thought it was Mommy at first. She pulled me away, picked me up. And she hurried—hurried fast—away from where we had been standing." She shook her head and opened her eyes. "I knew . . ."

"Knew what?" John asked after a minute.

"I knew that I was lost forever because I hadn't minded my mother. Mommy knew," she paused, swallowed, "That's why she wanted me to hold her hand. She knew I would be lost forever." She sat back in the chair. "And I was."

The three adults sat in silence, pondering what had just taken place. The bell over the front door jingled as a group of women started to enter, laughing and talking. John rose quickly and took a couple of steps toward them. "We're just closing," he told them. "Come back another time, please." They looked startled, but turned back. He turned the knob on the brass lock and flipped the sign around so that 'closed' was presented to the world, then returned to his chair.

"Our world ended that day," Abner said. "Nothing mattered anymore, and didn't for a long, long time."

Trudy leaned forward and stared at the old man behind the desk. "D. . . Daddy?" she hesitatingly asked.

Abner stood, and holding on to the edge of the smooth wood, made his way until he was in front of the Truth Chair. Leaning over, he grasped her hands in his. "We never forgot you," he said. "You were always in our hearts and minds. On your birthday, we would say 'Lily is ten years old today' or 'somewhere Lily is celebrating her sixteenth birthday.' And we always prayed that you were happy."

John cleared his throat. This was a family matter, if ever there was one, but questions bounced around in his mind, demanding to be answered. "Did you never think she might be dead?"

"No. Never. Never."

Lily stood and put her arms around the old man in front of her. Their tears mingled as their cheeks touched, and their quiet sobs filled the air. The lilies on the Story Cabinet quit appearing except for a new one popping up here and there every few minutes, but the objects that Lily had touched around the room still glowed as if lit by a some source deep within.

EPILOGUE

Six weeks later: Thanksgiving

Simon elected to keep Simon's Place closed for the holiday. "This is a time for families," he said. "Anybody who doesn't want to cook can buy our special Thanksgiving dinner ahead of time and warm it up at home."

He was at the typical place for Simon on special occasions, standing at the head of a large table. A golden brown turkey set in front of him, awaiting his touch. Every dish imaginable found a place along either side of the flower bedecked runner that adorned the center of the snow white table cloth.

Before he touched the impressive bird with the carving knife laying at the ready, Simon said, "So many things have come to pass in this neighborhood since the last time some of us joined together in the spirit of the season. This is the day of all days to give thanks for all we have received. Mr. Hobart, will you lead us in prayer?"

Lexi's father looked startled, but with only a few seconds pause, he stood. "Dear Heavenly Father," he began. Those who knew the problem between this pious man and his daughter held their breath, but the words he uttered were both appropriate and non-accusatory, and when he spoke the final 'amen,' they let out the breath they had been holding. Lexi smiled at him, and his wife reached over and patted his arm.

"For those who have not shared our Thanksgiving table before," Simon said as he began to carve. "This is the time to go around the table and tell what you have to be thankful for this year." He placed slices of moist turkey on a plate to the side, piling it high before sending

234

it around and starting to fill another one. The other dishes were being passed as well: mashed potatoes, gravy, sweet potato casserole, green beans, broccoli, cranberry sauce, marinated mushrooms, yeasty rolls, their scent wafting around the room. Casserole upon casserole made a path around the table.

"I'll start," he said. He stopped carving for a minute. "I'm thankful again this year for my wife, Dani." He looked at the pretty woman at his side and smiled. "I'm especially grateful for my new daughter, Ramona." He glanced at the highchair where a plump baby was trying to get a green bean into her mouth. "And always grateful for my son, Morgan, and the joy he brings to us." He looked around the table. "And I'm thankful for all my friends, those who share this Thanksgiving table with us, and those who are not present."

He paused carving and looked toward the man sitting on his right. "Mister Crowbridge, as the senior member of this group, why don't you go next?"

Abner stayed seated as he spoke. "Truly, there are so many things I am grateful for this holiday I could speak all evening and not cover everything."

"Try!" Simon said, and everyone laughed. "But don't take all evening, please." Everyone laughed again.

"They say that if you trust, God, or Fate, will guide you where you ought to go. I am living proof of that. At the time, it seemed like finding the empty shop was only a happy accident, but I am convinced it was God, or perhaps the spirit of the one you call Madame, that guided me there."

Around the table people were shaking their heads in agreement. "He saw her cat there that day," Addie said. "and it doesn't appear to just anyone."

"A cat?" Lily said. "Was it a Siamese cat?"

"Yes," Addie answered. "It's a spirit cat, and it only appears to certain people. Have you seen it?"

"The first day I came here it was on the blue bench by the front door," Lily replied. "It was real pushy, wanting petted."

"That's the one," Simon said.

"So I rented the place," Abner continued. "And I hired help to move things from the storage places where they had been, many of them for a long, long time. Others that had lived in my home until my wife's passing and were filled with all sorts of magic and memories. And that is how I met Pernell and Thomas Wayne." He reached into his pocket and pulled out a folded paper. "I have a letter from Pernell and another from Thomas Wayne, who is now officially Pernell's son. I'll lay them here on the table for you to read at your convenience. Basically, they are happy where they moved to in Missouri. Pernell has spoken before several groups, and shortly he will begin teaching at the college. T. Wayne is doing well in school there

"But the big thing, the miracle in my life, is that my daughter, Lily, who was kidnapped when she was five years old, has found her way back to me." His voice choked, and he picked up his napkin and wiped his eyes. "God guided her back home, even when home is in a different location than it was when she left us." He turned to the pretty young woman sitting next to him, and they grasped hands. Cheers and clapping came from around the room.

Lexi looked at her father as he placed his hand on her arm. "I prayed God would send you back to me," he whispered. "I prayed that prayer every day, and He has answered my prayers, just as He answered that father."

"Don't push your luck," she said. "I'm not coming back to Texas. Be happy that you know where I am and can come visit. Be thankful I have a good job, a nice place to live, and friends like these."

"Yes. Yes, I am that," he said, and turned his attention back to the speaker.

"And I am happy to have found this wonderful group of friends and neighbors. Fate surely guided me here," Abner concluded.

Both Addie and Parker were thankful for the group of friends gathered together, and for the baby that would arrive in a few weeks.

Lexi was grateful that she and her father had come to enough of an understanding that they could get along without arguing, and that he had made a solemn promise to not have her kidnapped. "And I'm grateful that my father and step-mother are going to allow me to communicate with my step-sister," she said. She turned and put her arm around Jenny, who hugged her big sister.

Finally, the only people who had not offered thanks aloud were Lily and her friend John. He realized that it was going to be difficult for the woman he once called Trudy to speak anything of her life and how she ended up in New Orleans.

"I'll go first," John said. "I'm thankful for so many things it would be impossible to name them all. For my sons and their families back in St. Louis, and for this new group of friends here in New Orleans." He looked around the table. " I have the feeling I'm going to be visiting here often," he smiled at Lily, sitting by his side, "now that I have a reason for coming."

All around the table, everyone chuckled.

Lily looked up at him. "I'm so very, very grateful," she said, "for finding out who I am, and for finding my father." She looked at Abner, sitting on her left, "and for my friend, John, who helped me make my way here and search for the truth of who I really am." She suddenly became serious. "For a while, I was angry. Very, very angry, at the woman who stole me away from my beloved parents so long ago. But I couldn't stay that way. The more I thought about that poor woman who wanted a child so badly that she stole me, I couldn't stay mad. She wasn't in her right mind—far from it. She lived in a fantasy world, where I was her beloved granddaughter, and she provided for me the best she knew how. Anger would only eat into my happy future with my father, and I don't want that. The past is now over and gone, and I am thankful for my future here with all of you."

Cheers and applause sounded around the table.

Hours later, as the attendees left, hugs and kisses were passed from person to person, and the spirits that were said to inhabit Broussard Court and the neighborhood around it could be felt in the slight breeze that touched each person there that evening, spreading happiness and good cheer. The slight pink of the sunset paled, stars began to twinkle, and stories that were yet untold began to develop in the rooms and courtyards of New Orleans, waiting patiently to come to fruition before breaking into the lives of the inhabitants.

Rest. Sleep. Tomorrow is another day.